Falling

THE SOUL COLLECTORS SERIES

TARA BENHAM

ISBN-13: 978-1530873807
ISBN-10: 1530873800
Cover Design: Starla Huchton
Interior Design: Marisa-Rose Shor
Formatting: Athena Interior Book Design
Editing: Jessica Valliere

This book is dedicated to: My sister and my niece. For all the laughs you two provide. I love you!

Acknowledgements

Special shout out to Kristen G for the motivation.

To my tribe Amy, Meg, Paulette, Jenn and Kristen B., thank you all for the assistance and comical relief while finishing this story "BongBong".

Amy, thank you. More than words can say, Thank you!

Kimberly—loud shout out…You know why!!!

To Jessica V. and Peggy N. for the amount of effort you applied to edit this book because we all know sometimes the words and grammar can be hard for me.

To Hollywood Undead, Breaking Benjamin, Abandon All Ships, X Ambassadors, Adele, Starset, Five Hundredth Year, Chris Stapleton and Imagine Dragons. You are the soundtrack to this story.

And finally to those reading this now, thank you the most. I can write all day, but without you reading it wouldn't do much good, so thank you from the bottom of my heart.

Please enjoy! God Bless!

CHAPTER one

It is better to conquer yourself than to win a thousand battles. Then the victory is yours. It cannot be taken from you, not by angels or by demons, heaven or hell.
~Buddha

Throughout history there have been events that have shaped the way humans learn and grow. I have been a part of almost every major catastrophic event that has occurred on Earth, since the times of Noah. My first assignment was during the destruction of Pompeii. Since then I have seen the collapse of the Roman government, the ending of the dark ages, even the sinking of the Titanic. My assignments are never the same. Sometimes I am there to ensure that everything goes as planned in order for events to line up correctly and things stay on course. Sometimes I'm there to save the life or lives of those who are meant to play a major part in the evolution of history. And then sometimes I'm just there to be the first face seen by those who do not survive. I'm the only Soul Collector Angel, and with years of experience, I have learned to be excellent. To date, I have a perfect record for successful completion of missions. Recently, I had a break, which was nice because sometimes these assignments can be taxing, both emotionally and mentally. However, as of yesterday I was given a new assignment notification. The letter stated I was to be given the details for my new assignment later today and needed to meet with the Head Council for instructions. The letter was more formal than the normal call of duty letters I receive. I assumed the formality meant that the assignment would be a special one. The Head Council was made up of the Elders, who were the elite leaders of all angels. The Elders made sure things were just so, and if I was going to have to meet with them I needed to look more professional than usual. I was trying to decide what outfit to wear when my roommate, Aniston, came crashing into my room, landing on my bed.

We weren't allowed to choose who our roommates were while we were single and active in duty positions. If we were, I can assure you that I would never have picked Aniston. She was a Delivery Angel for the newborn humans going to Earth. She was a constant loop of unnatural happiness. I think the Elders thought her happiness would help balance out the effects of my job; however, I usually just found her to be annoying. The Elders were always concerned about the macabre aspects of my job. They feared I would start to get depressed or have a warped sense in regards to human lives. I, on the other hand, think it helped me stay connected to humanity yet also remain detached from the human subjects…seeing that they will all die at some point in time. When you have to make decisions like the ones required in my line of work, you cannot get attached to any of them. It would lead to heartbreak and possible errors when completing a mission. Aniston always says that makes me sound distant, I feel like it makes me sound prepared. She could afford to be attached though, her assignments were the beginnings, they were the snuggly little human babies just preparing for life, mine dealt with the endings of life.

"So, Bayla what's the word on the new assignment?" She made herself quite at home on my bed, propping her feet against the wall.

"I haven't heard anything yet because I haven't had the meeting. Speaking of which, should I wear one of the white, formal dresses? Or just a basic suit?" I chose to ignore the fact that she knew about my meeting, even though I hadn't told anyone. She must have read the letter, which could get her suspended from her duties if I let it slip that she was snooping on secret business.

"Definitely the formal dress," replied Aniston, still unfazed that I was giving her death glares for her continued presence. "You must be super excited. All my assignments are the same, take a baby and deliver it safely to it's new guardians. The most exciting job I had was two weeks ago when I had to have extra security to deliver that little boy to a family on Earth in a place called Kentucky. I had four of the Blue Angels tag along for that delivery."

While she was speaking about the antics of the Blue Angels, I was figuring the math in my head..., two weeks for us was about nineteen years for the humans on Earth. What would it be like to constantly live in a place where time was so different? I suppose it would feel the same to them, as our time feels to us. Hearing rustling of my sheets, I came back to attention. I realized she had moved to a seated position on my bed and was staring at me as if she was waiting for me for to answer some unheard question.

"What? I was tuned out again, I'm sorry." Tuning out people was a skill which I had perfected while on missions. Humans could be very mundane in their conversational skills.

She sighed, "I said, you'd better get dressed, you have fifteen minutes before you're late for your meeting."

I was still slipping my shoes on as I was rushing out the door. I am normally very punctual but something about being around Aniston causes me to be late. I am sure she could find a positive with that too, but I just found it to be an unwanted side effect to having her as a roommate. The meeting house was only a few blocks away and the closer I got, the more nervous I became. It was a formidable building from the outside. It had tall wooden doors, with handles that were taller than me. It was the place where the Elders held meetings, gave counsel when necessary, and where I was about to be given an assignment that I was certain would be more complex or important than all of my previous ones had been. I decided I needed to give myself a pep talk before entering so that I could present as confident in front of the Elders. Just as I stopped outside the door, taking a deep breath in preparation to enter, when Father Paul opened it and gave me a quick greeting.

"Good to see you Bayla. This is truly a matter of importance. We must get started at once. Let's head towards the main meeting room. They're waiting for us." He was ushering me through the hallways, walking as he spoke to me.

In Heaven, there were very few jobs that required more than one angel to be in the same position. Aniston was one of many Delivery Angels because of the amount of babies the Earth families were having daily. The Blue Angels were a group of elite angels who were trained for battle and provided security. And there were several Father Angels who served the rest of the angels. Father Paul was my favorite when it came to receiving assignments. He always looked as though he had some secret he was in on, but couldn't share. He provided one of the few outlets of joy in my job, and I appreciated him for keeping me grounded. Other angels my age speculated that he was always so happy because he was excited to be in the Angel Commission, or AC as we called it, even though he was of human birth many years ago. I didn't care what the reason was; I just knew my nervousness immediately melted when I saw his face trying to hide a grin as we headed towards the meeting room.

"Father Paul, do you know what my assignment is this time?" I knew asking him would prove futile, as he wouldn't break any commands given, to withhold information.

"I do, my child. But it is best if the Elders tell you." He winked, trying to reassure me.

FALLING

In hopes of settling my nerves, I tried to relax my hands at my sides, mimicking what Father Paul was doing. He had calmness radiating off of him, which I was trying to soak up. As we were rounding the corner to the meeting room, I heard the chatter of more than a few angels. In the hallway in front of me, there was a group of Blues waiting outside of the meeting room. The group included Aniston's crush, Hadraniel, a Blue-In-Training. Seeing that many Blues at once was frightening, to say the least; they were built bigger than the average angel, and had an air of power about them. My steps faltered some, but Father Paul kindly placed his hand on my shoulder and continued to lead me towards the meeting hall.

"Hey Bayla!" Hadraniel called out as I passed, which gained him a few glares from the Elder Blues. Had was in the same age group as Aniston and myself. He was handsome enough, I suppose. All of the Blues were handsome, with strong jaws and masculine features, but Hadraniel still had some softness to his face compared to the rest of them. He had nice blue eyes which was the sign of a Blue Angel, but he had lighter brown hair than the rest. He was very tall and strong, just as one would expect from a Blue. Even being a "Baby Blue", as the Elders called them, he knew better than to have spoken to me. I gave a quick wave, and a smirk as I passed. I noticed he looked sheepish at my response, but all thoughts were gone once the doors opened. Even some of the Elder Blues gasped at the sight that was behind the doors. It wasn't just the Elders in the room but the head angel, Elder Michael, was present as well. There was absolute silence as we all stood outside of the doors awaiting invitation to enter the room. Elder Michael only appeared for top level occasions. He was intimidating, to the say the least.

"Please come in and take your seat." His voice seemed to boom. He was standing at the center of the head table, surrounded by the other Elders, all of whom were standing as well.

Father Paul had to push me a little to get me to move. I think my brain had forgotten how to tell my feet to move. The table that was meant for Father Paul and me was at the front of the room with the Blue Angels scattered behind us randomly in chairs. We were all still completely silent as we took our seats except for the occasional scraping of chair legs against the floor. Michael continued to stand and take survey of us all, stopping to nod his head at someone behind me. The silence was broken somewhat, as whoever he nodded to closed the meeting rooms doors.

"Bayla" His voiced boomed once again. "You have proven yourself time and again to be proficient at your job which is why the Elders have decided that you are the best angel for this highly classified mission. In four human weeks there will be a cataclysmic earthquake in the land the humans call Kentucky. We have to send you there to ensure that Gray Ellison makes it out alive and safe. This earthquake is set to cause massive damage to the layout of the land, so you will need to get far away with Gray. At present moment, we cannot tell you the reason why Mr. Ellison is of such importance. All you need to know is that he must remain alive and safe for the mission to be successful."

Elder Michael kept constant eye contact with me for the full announcement of the assignment. I could only hear him, everything else seemed to disappear. I felt like my heart was in my throat, but I made sure to maintain eye contact and nod at appropriate times so as not to have my internal fear show outwardly. I have dealt with all kinds of events that were of importance. I have saved humans before, but something about this assignment felt ominous to me. Never had Elder Michael, or any other Elder's for that matter, specifically assigned me a mission that required that only one human survived. I was focusing on his words and maintaining a steady breathing pattern. When he had finished speaking, he excused himself to speak in private with the Elder Blue. I turned towards Father Paul, who to his credit managed to give me a smile, even though he looked nervous for me too.

"I was told to have you stay after the meeting to meet with the Elder Blue." Hadraniel said, coming up behind me as I was walking towards the exit with Father Paul. "I was asked to wait around as well, but I don't know why. Are you nervous, Bay?"

"Bayla," I corrected, "And yes, I'm nervous, but I'll be fine once the mission starts. I have a perfect record, so I'll be okay. I've had to save humans in other missions before, so I'm not too concerned. I just need the handout and materials so I can prepare."

"Bayla, I'm Zeke, the Elder Blue Angel. Elder Michael informed me that due to the nature of the mission, we will need to send a Blue with you. Before you say anything, as he told me you would try to protest, I'm to let you know you have no choice. This is his strict command. After reviewing the needs, it was decided that for mission purposes, Hadraniel will accompany you. He fits the appropriate look and age needed to make this go as smoothly as possible."

I slid my eyes over towards Hadraniel who seemed to be as shocked as I was at his assignment. I looked back at Zeke who had a slight smirk that disappeared as quickly as it appeared. He nodded his goodbye as I continued to stand there trying to process that I would have to work with someone. I had never been on a mission with anyone. Even on my first mission four years ago, for the destruction of Pompeii, I worked alone. Hadraniel had enough sense, as well as the courtesy, to not say anything to me while I worked through how I would make do with this news. I took a calming breath, said a quick prayer, and then placed a smile on my face before turning to face Had.

"Well, let's go pick up our mission folders so we can start planning. We have to head out soon." He nodded, indicating for me to lead the way.

The files were kept at the Blue's headquarters, which was a short walk from where we were. Hadraniel tried to make small talk for a while, but I was tuning out. I needed to figure out how I could keep him out of my way while completing the mission, but not get into trouble for not utilizing him in the way I'm sure Elder Michael was expecting. Working alone was one of the best parts of this job assignment, so why would they give me the assignment of a lifetime, then change the way I was going to have to try to complete it?

CHAPTER *two*

Growth is never by mere chance; it is the result of forces working together.
~James Cash Penney

Hadraniel and I made plans to meet at the center of the park, two hours after getting our mission files. This would allow us time to review all the information before we discussed what we each felt should be our first steps. I had decided on the public meeting area for two reasons: one being that members of the opposite sex were not allowed in private living spaces with each other unless so assigned; and two, I would never have heard the end of it from Aniston. I already knew it was going to be bad once she found out that I would be spending such a large amount of time with him one-on-one, even if it was for a mission and not by choice. Aniston has had the biggest crush on Hadraniel for as long as I have known her. I felt like I knew him already with as much as she has talked about him while living with me.

I was sitting down with my notes when I saw the shadow of Hadraniel's form creep over me. I shielded my eyes slightly to look up at him standing there, and he was grinning ear to ear. With the sun playing behind him, I could see why Aniston was crushing on him. He seemed to be glowing, which was funny seeing as we were angels.

"You ready to have a great meeting of the minds?" He bowed before taking the seat across from me. He was super silly, which was making it hard for me to begrudge his presence.

"I am if you are. I thought since I was more prepared for these things that I would review my notes with you first, and if you have any suggestions we can talk about them afterwards."

He simply nodded in agreement.

Looking at his files, I noticed he had made some fairly extensive notes. I wasn't sure if I was more impressed or nervous at the idea of having to share this mission with someone else. However, it seemed he might be somewhat of an asset. Since I started this job four years ago at fifteen, I have never worked with anyone. There was another angel that could do the job because my predecessor, Dabria, was still capable. Dabria had worked with her predecessor Karis, an Elder. Karis was killed during one of their missions, leading the other Elders to make the decision that Soul Collectors would be a solitary job. After the death of Karis, and then having to see the destruction of Earth during Noah's time, Dabria asked to step down. I asked her once why, and she told me she could still hear the screaming of all the people who perished from the Earth flooding. The job came with so much tragedy, but it wasn't all bad all the time. She had fun stories too. She told me about getting to judge which of the dinosaurs would survive, such as the animal now called an alligator. And of course the sea mammal the humans call the Loch Ness monster. She giggled about that choice when she talked about it. She said that the Elders weren't very pleased with her for that but because the animal stays mostly hidden, they decided to let it stay around. She was never tasked to train me or give me any trade secrets. On the day of my fifteenth birthday, I was called forth and sent to Pompeii with my mission folder only. I had to learn quickly, but once I figured out my style I was ready. It was an adrenaline rush to do these missions. The Elders were concerned that I would get depressed like the prior angel, but in all honesty, I loved it.

"I figured we could go as brother and sister, starting college away from our parents who are traveling missionaries." Hadraniel said, apparently not caring that I wanted to take the lead on this mission. "I don't know what you had in mind, but in reviewing where we were going, and the type of families that lived in Kentucky, I figured that that would be the best cover story. That or that we are newlyweds. However if we're to help this Gray guy survive, you may have to get him to fall for you…and that wouldn't work if we were married." He winked. My facial reaction to the wink and his suggestion must have been comical because he chuckled.

"I had written a similar scenario about being brother and sister as well, so I'm good with that decision. However, because of the nature of the event and how much our training and skills may be seen, I thought we might go with that our parents are dual military both on foreign assignments." He just nodded, so I continued. "I don't really have much of a game plan for how to get Gray to follow us out of town for when the event occurs yet. What I usually do is go to Earth with my cover story, observe the human or humans I have to save if there are any, and then wing it according to their needs and personalities."

"You're the expert, so we can go with that if you choose. However, missionaries may be more believable than dual military seeing as we would have to explain why their jobs would have had any effect on our training. As missionaries, we would be placed in precarious locations, possibly teaching us survival skills. Also, do we use our real names or do we have to have Earth names?"

"Point taken, we'll go with the missionaries' story. As for names, I've always used my name mainly because I have little interaction…but if you wanted a different name we could give you one."

"Just call me Had as I think it'll go over better than Hadraniel."

"That sounds good to me."

We finished reviewing our notes, and we actually incorporated quite a few of Had's ideas into our plans by the time we had finished. He'd brought out a map and showed me where the earthquake was going to occur, where Gray lived in reference to the fault lines, and the top three escape routes that we would need to take to get far enough away to ensure the safety of this human. The files didn't include why Gray Ellison was of such great importance. They did, however, indicate that he must remain unharmed and unaware that he was of importance, so as not to taint any future greatness he was to achieve. Normally I could not care less why a human was of importance, but Mr. Ellison did have my interest peaked because of the care that was being taken to keep his importance a secret.

"He's the baby the four Blues helped Aniston deliver two weeks ago." Hadraniel broke my train of thought with that statement, leaving me in complete shock. Mainly because the time differences between here and Earth had slipped my mind, but also because I'm pretty sure there was only ever one other baby that had been delivered by an angel with the protection of Blue Angels. I couldn't believe that this human was anywhere close to the same importance as the other baby, the one we call Jesus.

"Where'd you hear that?" I asked, still skeptical that this human, or any human, could be that important. I looked at the picture of him in the file. He looked like a normal human teenaged boy, buzzed dark blonde hair, blue eyes with green speckles, freckles across his nose, athletic body and tall even for angel standards. I wasn't impressed…but then it was hard to be impressed when you're surrounded by angels on a regular basis. I must have snickered at this thought because when I looked up, Had had his head tilted to the side looking at me like I might have something wrong with me. I didn't think he would understand why my thoughts were funny, so I just winked like it was a secret. "Spill it, Haddy." He grimaced at this new nickname I'd given him, but he didn't correct me.

"I accidentally overheard one of the Elder Blues discussing the boy with Father Paul in the meeting room earlier."

"Hmmm, I wonder why this 'boy'," I used air quotes, "is so important. Care to speculate?"

"I don't really have an opinion. I just want to complete the mission so that your record stays perfect, and maybe I'll get promoted." He stopped when he realized he had spoken out loud what I would guess to be very secret internal thoughts normally. When he noticed, I just smiled, and the wrinkles and concern on his face dissipated.

"That alone is an opinion." I was collecting my files to pack up and head home when I heard my name across the park. I looked up to find Aniston making her way towards our table. If I wasn't mistaken, I also heard Had make a groaning noise, but to his credit, he turned and smiled as she approached.

"Bayla, I thought you might be here when I didn't find you at home. Hadraniel, what are you doing here?" She kept looking between us, half expecting us to reveal some sordid secret love affair.

"I was assigned to help Bayla with her new mission. Unfortunately that is all either of us are allowed to say. Elder Michael commanded total silence on the matter." He spoke kindly.

At the mention of Elder Michael, Aniston's eyebrows shot up, and she seemed to step backwards in shock. She looked to me for confirmation, and I simply nodded. She stood in silence for a while before speaking again.

"Wow. Wow! You met the Elder Michael today, and he assigned you to a special mission? My Grace, Bayla, I hope you'll be okay." She truly looked concerned for me which made me feel bad for all the things I'd been thinking about her all day. Maybe she wasn't really all that awful to have around.

"Thank you Aniston. I'm sure everything will be okay. And yes, we have to leave very soon. We will be gone for four Earth weeks. So we really shouldn't be gone but a few hours for you." I was trying to make it all sound very professional so she knew that I had no interest in being near Had for that long.

"Is this your first mission, Had?" Her attention and interest were no longer on me, now that she knew I wouldn't really get much time alone with him. I needed to get back to our living space, so while they chatted, I seized the opportunity to leave. I gave a quick wave and excused myself. Even though we had planned out as much as we feasibly could, I still wanted to read through all the files again to make sure that I hadn't missed something that would be important later.

CHAPTER
three

A journey of a thousand miles must begin with a single step.
~Lao-Tsu

"Bayla, try to put in a good word for me. Please." Aniston had been following me around all morning as I was preparing to leave. I had to meet Hadraniel in an hour and wasn't close to being done because every time I turned around she was in my way. She had mentioned all of her positive attributes in case I didn't already know them, just so that I would have them handy for when I spent so much time with Had enduring the Earth hours. I was fairly certain I would not have time to talk about her, but I didn't say that, so I just nodded and threw in the occasional "Okay" when needed.

I was just finishing up putting the last of my things in a bag when there was a knock at the door. I quickly stood, looking at Aniston, who seemed just as surprised as I was that someone was here. She went to answer the door while I finished. I heard a gasp causing me to rush towards the door. Hadraniel stood at the door, looking somewhat sheepish dressed in human clothing. I had to admit he was kind of hot in human clothes, but I didn't understand why he was here.

"Hey! One of the Elders sent me to tell you we needed to leave now. I was given permission to come to your door only." He made a point to stand just right outside of the doorframe. He had a playful grin and was almost bouncing with excitement waiting for me.

"I was just finishing up. Let me grab my files, and we can be on our way." Traveling to Earth was not at all complicated for us. We went to our mission gate, typed in our destination, and we appeared. It wasn't fun and exciting like the humans assumed. While we could fly and could present ourselves with wings when necessary, usually we just transported to our destinations. It was rare to show our wings, even in Heaven. Not because of modesty or anything...more so because it would take a lot of space to have them out and spread while walking around. I gave Aniston a hug, more for her sake in front of Had than because I was sad to leave her. She took a second to react before she hugged me goodbye and sent me away with good wishes.

"I'm pumped! Aren't you?" Had seemed to be extra excited today, and it was kind of cute. He was doing circles around me, while carrying both of our bags, at his insistence. I could barely keep up with him as we made our way to the gates. I had to remind him continuously that I had to lead the way since I was the only one who knew where my transport gate was located.

"I'm having fun watching you have fun, but this is a normal day for me, Haddy."

"Must you call me that?" He didn't really sound upset, more amused.

"Well, since you're my brother now, I must have a nickname for you, right?" Apparently from the face he made, the thought of being my brother was repulsive to him. I wasn't sure if I should be offended or find it funny.

"Okay, yeah that makes sense. I'll call you Bay then." He stuck his tongue out at me as I made an equally repulsed face in response. I detested the shortened version of my name, but his point was made.

"This way." I pointed behind the meeting house. "My transport room is behind the main chapel. Father Paul will meet us there to help us on our way."

"I've never transported."

"It's not bad. There's no pain, it's just a little disorienting. You recover pretty quickly though."

"Sounds like an adventure."

"My children, are you ready?" Father Paul walked out like he knew ahead of time that we would be there at that exact moment. He was grinning like always, which was contagious. Even more so now with Hadraniel around.

"Yes," we answered at the same time, making Had smile and me smirk.

"Glad to see you adjusted to having Hadraniel along you with so quickly Bayla."

"Ah, he's not so bad. Especially when he carries my bag for me." I winked at Father Paul who let out a hearty laugh. "So do you have the coordinates, Father, or do I need to give them to you?"

"I have them ready. All you two need to do is step through the gate, and you'll be in Kentucky. Once there, another file will appear inside your bag with information on where you will be staying, and on an additional task that needs to be completed."

Father Paul didn't leave any time for me to ask questions. I had never been given additional tasks once through the portal. I know he saw my confusion, but he just gave a quick shrug, and pushed us towards the gate. Hadraniel didn't seem to notice my confusion or Father Paul's insistence. I opened the door, still pondering that exchange, and was getting ready to step through the gate when I felt a hand pull me backwards. I thought maybe Father Paul was going to answer me after all, but when I turned around, Had was standing at the portal looking slightly ill. Without saying anything to him, I smiled, took his hand, and we walked through the gate at the same time.

As I remembered how different Earth was to home, I looked around to reacquaint myself. After making my normal, quick surveillance of the area, I turned and noticed that Hadraniel was just standing there, mouth open and in awe. It had slipped my mind that he'd never seen the wonders of Earth before. As beautiful as our home was, Earth had its own beauty as well. Especially this place called Kentucky. In every direction I looked, there were trees, hills, grass, flowers and wildlife. Listening carefully, I heard the rushing of water as well.

"Wow, I never thought Earth would be pretty from all the stories you hear." Had was still taking in the sights while I pulled out the file to look up the new tasks and where we were to go.

"Yeah, it has its good points. I must say this is one of the prettier places I've been to lately. Too bad it's about to be destroyed. According this new information, we are currently standing at the epicenter of the earthquake, and all of this will be gone afterwards. It's really a shame. The new tasks haven't arrived yet, but I do have where we need to head next. There is a cottage in the woods, to which we have the coordinates, so we had better be on our way before it gets dark." I turned to make sure that Hadraniel was prepared to follow when I noticed his frown.

"I'd read that there was more gravitational pull here on Earth compared to home, but it's not the same as feeling it. Man, these bags are heavy, particularly yours! What in all of the Heavens could you have packed and needed that makes your bag this heavy?" The look on his face was so funny, I couldn't help myself. I started laughing.

"Oh Haddy, you'll adjust quickly, I promise. Here, let me take my bag and carry it." We walked in comfortable silence for a good distance, but then I decided to start pointing out things about our surroundings that I was familiar with that Hadraniel had probably never heard of or only had read about in books. We passed several deer, rabbits, squirrels, but also some snakes and skunks were in the path as well. I educated him on how the humans used the trees and plants for medicine sometimes, and how people would come stay out in the woods for fun sometimes, calling it camping. He was very interested, and would ask questions about things that caught his attention. We made it to the cottage in good time. Once inside, we took a quick tour and started putting our things away, trying to make it look believable that two teenage twins would be living there without their parents.

"Hey, Bayla." I heard Hadraniel calling for me from his bedroom as I was putting away my clothing for the trip. "I have the new tasks in my file."

I quickly made my way to his room to check out the new tasks. There were only two. One was to ensure that Gray's family did not know he was special, and that if a demon were to come around, we were to allow him some access to Gray but not enough to hurt Gray. That was a very confusing task. I'd never had to interact with a demon before. Usually there was just one who came around the same time I did. His name was Mephistopheles, and his job was the equivalent of mine, just for Hell. He came to collect the souls that I wasn't, but we never intermingled or even came in contact with each other. I was unsure, now that I was being commanded to not only interact with one, but to allow him access to my target for the mission.

"Why do we have to mess with a demon? Do you know which demon will be coming?" Had seemed more curious than scared, but there was some shaking to his voice.

"I would assume Meph is coming but who knows. He's the one who has worked opposite of me on each of my missions. Meph is the only one I know personally. However, with the way this mission is going, who knows who will be sent. I'm sure whoever comes will be clever. They'll want someone who is charming enough to weasel his way into Gray's good side."

"That's true. So, what's the plan for tomorrow?" Haddy mumbled, looking close to needing sleep.

"I think we should keep a low profile for the next day or so. Explore the town, allow those living here to see us some, because even dressed in human attire, you're going to draw a lot of attention."

He blushed, but recovered quickly. "I'm fairly sure I won't be the only one garnering the attention of the locals." He yawned and excused himself to his room. As he was shutting the door, I could hear a faint "good night."

"Good night."

CHAPTER
four

The oldest and strongest emotion of mankind is fear, and the oldest and strongest kind of fear is fear of the unknown.

~H.P. Lovecraft

I was up and cooking breakfast by the time Had finally made it to the kitchen. His hair was messy, his eyes were dark, and he was still yawning. Sleeping on Earth was completely different than in Heaven. You slept heavier here, partly because of the gravity difference and partly because of the time difference. I'd learned to adapt years ago, but poor Hadraniel was having to learn to adjust for the first time. He shuffled his feet towards the table and dropped into the chair with a groan. I had already decided that I was going to make a "normal" human breakfast for Had this morning. Humans knew how to make good food; plus this would allow his reactions to the food to be here, in private, instead of when we were surrounded by humans later. I was making eggs, bacon and biscuits with jelly. Food here was one of my favorite things about my missions. No matter which human century or country I was in, I always found the food to be delicious.

"What is this?" Had asked between yawning and stretching.

"A few select items from the local cuisine. You'd better learn to like it quickly, since there is a lot of socializing done here while eating." I wasn't concerned about him liking the food. It was almost a given, but I didn't want him to know that. With trepidation, he took a bite. As he was chewing, he appeared to wake up and realize that I wasn't going to be poisoning or punishing him.

"Oh My Grace! This may be the best thing I have ever eaten." He scarfed down the rest of the food in no time, making me chuckle. I haven't been around a lot of males, human or angel, but I'm quite sure they are all basically the same when it comes to food. Once he had polished off his breakfast he drank his juice and waited for me to finish, as I had learned to eat more slowly and savor the food. "What's the plan for today, Bay?"

Holding in my groan, I swallowed my last bite before answering. "We are going to be tourists to our new town. Since we just moved here we need to learn the area, and at the same time, snoop on Gray to see if we can figure out his regular hangouts and routines. Our notes said he works at a coffee shop in town in the evenings so that will be one of our last stops."

Hadraniel sat there taking in all I was saying, nodding. So far, it had been quite easy having him around. I was beginning to think that having to hang out with him might not be such a difficult thing to do. As I was considering all of this, he got up and immediately ran into the wall. In a fit of giggles, I tried to ask if he was okay.

"Apparently gravity also causes your limbs to tingle if you sit too long?"

"It's called 'falling asleep'. An example would be 'my foot fell asleep'." His eyebrows furrowed at my explanation. Teaching Had human things and sayings was indeed going to be fun.

"If you say so."

"Let's get ready and head out. We have a nice walk ahead of us to town, and we want to get there with time to check out our surroundings."

Hadraniel must have gotten guidance from Father Paul on human clothing, because when he returned from his room, he had on nice fitting blue jeans, a t-shirt with some human band on it and sneakers. His hair was still slightly unkempt, but it worked well for him. I had chosen to wear a mint green sundress and flip-flops. It was a nice warm day today, and I didn't want to be bogged down wearing something that would make it too hot for me. Plus I wasn't sure what the local girls would be wearing, but it seemed that a dress usually worked no matter the decade.

"Wow, you look great."

"Thank you. You're not looking too bad yourself, sir." I smirked but he took the jabs in stride.

The walk to town was rather quiet, but it was nice. The area we were staying in was beautiful. On our way into town, we found the waterfall that I had heard at our arrival yesterday. The town was quaint but active. There were old buildings up and down either side of the street, a fountain and statue of some important human dividing the street in the middle of the town, and plenty of people bustling around. We found a nice bookstore to stop in first. I found that old bookstores had a lovely smell, and as a bonus, usually an older lady worked in the area that you could chat with and find out useful tidbits of information. As we entered, we heard a male's voice from the back shout out a welcome. As we browsed around, the gentleman made his way forward. He was older with kind eyes and silver hair.

"Are you looking for anything in particular?" he asked with a slight difference in his speech than I had heard before, but it was soothing.

"Actually, do you have any books on the caving systems in this area?" Hadraniel spoke up before I had the chance. I wasn't mad though, because it was a great question; not just to get information about our area, but it was a good opener into for further questions.

"Yes, I think we do. Are you all new in town? I can't say I've seen you all around before."

"We just moved here. Our parents are missionaries, and we've traveled a lot. We heard this was a good college town, so they moved us here to get to know some people our age before school starts this fall." The story came easy to me. We'd rehearsed on the way into town.

"Well, I think you all will find a great group of kids your age here, as well as fun things to do, such as the caves." He handed Hadraniel two different books. One was on the caving systems, and one was the history of the town. "I think these are the best two books to start with so you can learn about our town here."

"Thank you so much. How much do we owe you?"

"I don't get many customers your age in here, so the first two are on the house." He winked as he disappeared to the back of the store to help another customer.

"Well he was very friendly. He seemed so familiar too." I wasn't really speaking to Hadraniel so much as at him. "Let's head down this side of the street to check out the different stores around here."

We spent the rest of the day checking out antique shops, which completely fascinated Had. We saw clothing stores, a hardware shop, a cute little photography studio, and a café where we decided to eat lunch. It was full of locals who were all interested in looking at us, but no one had really spoken to us except the waitress; she was an older lady whose lipstick bled into the lines around her lips, and her hair was in a wild bun with several pencils stuck into it. When she did speak, she made sure she asked questions loud enough for the whole place to hear. We decided to hang out in the café for a little while before heading towards the coffee shop. From listening to the people around the café, we learned that the shop was the place to be in the evenings.

The shop was chic and fairly up to date with the gadgets and technology we had to study before coming down here. Father Paul did deny us the use of cell phones, saying if we grew up in rural areas with missionary parents, we wouldn't have had the need for phones. Neither Hadraniel nor I had complaints about not having to carry a cell phone. However, looking around, I decided we would definitely be looked at strangely when we told people we didn't have phones. I made note that I may need to ask Had if he thinks we should purchase some while we were here. We found a table in the corner that had close access to the door but also put us in view of the other patrons of the coffee shop.

A pretty young waitress made her way to the table eyeing Hadraniel up and down like he was her prey. I was looking forward to seeing how this was going to unfold, as Had had very little experience with humans in general, let alone one who looked like she was on a mission. I scanned the menu lamenting the fact that black coffee didn't appear to be available. Since Hadraniel looked completely lost viewing the menu, I was pointing out possible choices for him when the waitress arrived.

"Hello, welcome to MyKale's Coffee Shop, I'm Hannah, your waitress. What can I get for you this evening?" She was almost purring, and Hadraniel looked completely mesmerized and frightened at the same time. I was kind of liking this girl right now.

"Do you have plain coffee?" I asked, causing her to scrunch up her nose at my order, but nodded that they did.

"What about you, handsome?" Hadraniel's face turned crimson, and he started to stutter before a word even made it out of his mouth.

"My brother will have the same." I giggled. He looked at me, his eyes showing how thankful he was to me for saving him.

"Two plain black coffees coming this way."

"She was deathly frightening." Had's eyes were still wide, making me laugh even harder.

"Oh, Haddy, don't be afraid of a little human girl. She was just trying to flirt. You should try to talk to her when she comes back."

"Oh yes, Haddy. Please do." I didn't know who the voice belonged to, but I could feel the closeness of his breath on my neck. Turning, I saw one of the most beautiful men, human or angel, I had ever laid eyes on. Instantly I knew he had to be the demon. He was dressed in distressed tight black jeans, a heather grey v-neck t-shirt and a leather jacket. His dark hair was pulled up in a loose bun with the underneath shaved, and his face looked as if he hadn't shaved in a few days. I was now the one staring. He was almost too beautiful to be real. His eyes were hidden by the shadows, but even without seeing them, I knew they were going to be grey. I could just tell. "Hi, I'm Declan. And if I were a betting man, which I am, I would say you two are the angels on this mission. Am I right?" His arrogance instantly took away any of the awe I was in just moments before.

"That's right. I'm Hadraniel, not Haddy, and this Bayla."

"The infamous Bayla. So nice to meet you finally. I've heard so much about you." He smirked, and leaned against the table between myself and Hadraniel. His eyes were gray as I expected, but they were lined with a dark blue circle. I feigned little interest in him when I responded.

"Shame. I haven't heard anything about you before...Declan, was it?"

He chuckled at my remark.

"No, you wouldn't have. This is my first assignment. Who's the hottie?" Declan was eyeing Hannah as she made her way back with our drinks. She sort of tripped and then regained her balance after seeing Declan watching her.

"Girl, I really need to be friends with you." she somewhat whispered in my direction as she placed our cups on the table. "Hi, I'm Hannah, can I get you something?"

"Please. I'll take a caramel macchiato." His voice was smooth like honey as he ordered. Hannah stood there with her mouth open. I

31

am pretty sure she forgot to breathe. I cleared my throat in hopes of helping her out somewhat.

"Yes. Yes I'll get that right to you." I turned her shoulders and nudged towards the kitchen shaking my head. Looking between the two men at my table, I could see how a human girl would be overwhelmed.

"So have you met the target yet?" Declan said nonchalantly.

"We haven't, but we just got here a little while ago. Have you?" Had answered before I had a chance to respond.

"No. I saw him earlier clocking in, but haven't had a chance to meet him."

Hadraniel and Declan started discussing possible ways to meet Gray, when I saw him talking to Hannah, who was behind the counter. He was taller and leaner in person, than he was presented in the pictures from my files. He was wearing dark wash jeans, a tight fitting white t shirt and some combat boots. I watched them interact and judging from their body language, I could tell they were closer than just coworkers. I watched as they casually touched each other, whispered to each other and laughed at what the other one said. He noticed I was watching, and we ended up making eye contact before I could look away.

"Guys, I think I just got his attention by accident."

"Bay, you're blushing. What's wrong?" Had looked very concerned. It was endearing.

"I stared a little longer than I should have, and we made eye contact." I groaned, and then buried my face in my arms.

"He's coming this way."

"Great." I mumbled from my hiding place. The boys just chuckled. Declan was definitely not like the other demons I had worked with.

"Are y'all new here?" Gray's voice was deep and raspy.

"Yes. I'm Had and this is my sister Bayla. We just moved here. Our parents are missionaries, and thought we needed to find a stable place to live and go to college. This is Declan."

"Hi. I'm new here too, but mainly because I travel to new places until I'm bored and then move on to the next." Declan said with an engaging smile.

"Nice to meet you all. Stick around for a while. The band's about to start. Y'all will enjoy the show I'm sure." He smiled warmly and made his way back to the front counter where Hannah was getting Declan's drink to bring over.

"He seemed nice." Declan sounded almost disappointed.

"Of course he's nice. Why else would we be sent here to save him if he wasn't nice?"

Declan and I exchanged looks, but neither of us responded to Hadraniel's innocent statement. Declan must have been savvy enough to know that not everyone saved from these events are necessarily good. They just have to be important. They still had free will, even if they were targets for events such as the one we were awaiting. I wasn't too excited about having to work with Declan, but so far he seemed to be a thousand times better to work with than Mephistopheles.

Gray and his band took to the stage of the coffee shop. They all looked pretty similar. Blonde hair, tall and lean. As they started to play though, the words were so entrancing I was no longer aware of their looks. The words were stirring, talking about filling empty spaces, and the music felt like it was meant to feed the soul. I was so caught up that I didn't realize that Hannah had joined the group at our table.

"Gray said y'all just moved here for college? Where will you all be going?" Hannah asked while never taking her eyes off the band.

"We are starting at the university here for the fall semester." I didn't really want to get into too much detail, so I paused wondering how to ask the next question. "Can I ask you something personal? Earlier you were clearly flirting with my brother, but I noticed something between you and Gray."

She smiled and nodded sweetly.

"Gray and I have been together since we were fourteen. I flirt with customers for tips. Besides, have you looked at the two men at your table? I'm pretty sure a nun would flirt with them." She giggled.

I couldn't help but grin. She seemed very nice and innocent. She had lovely soft blond curls and light brown eyes that were full of mischief.

"I suppose they're nice to look at, I hadn't really noticed." That lie came easy. Declan was anything but unnoticeable. Even now as he just stood by chatting with Hadraniel and watching the band, he looked like he belonged on one of the magazine covers humans obsessed over. He was breathtaking.

"What do you think about the band? Gray's been thinking about skipping college and taking them out on tour at small venues." Hannah seemed unsure about this decision.

"I'm not too up-to-date on music having lived in a third world country mostly, but I am loving it so far."

"Do you all live here alone?" There was concern riddled in her voice. Humans at nineteen tend to still live at home and rely on their parents so Had and I being on our own seemed a little bit of a foreign concept to her.

"They are renting us a cottage out in the woods and have plans to visit a few times a year to check up on us. Since their missions keep them fairly busy, we are used to being alone." I smiled hoping that she bought my story.

"Too cool. Is it safe to assume you all haven't really explored or met anyone yet?"

"Yes. Today's actually the first day we've had a chance to get out of the house and explore." I didn't feel the need to explain that we just arrived yesterday.

"Well there's a bunch of us going to the local quarry to swim tomorrow if you three want to join." She eyed the guys too, who by this time were listening to our conversation.

"Cool. Count me in."

I literally had to control the visceral reaction to roll my eyes at Declan's readiness at the chance to join. This was going to be a challenge, working with him. He shouldn't be affecting me at all.

"Us too, for sure." Hadraniel looked at me as he answered, and I just nodded.

I couldn't really refuse any opportunity to get to know Gray. I hadn't failed at any of my missions before, and I didn't plan on failing this time either.

"Unfortunately, I must return to work." Hannah grinned. "Make sure you get with me before you leave so you can get all the details."

"We will. Thank you." I must admit this was not the worst mission I've been on, but then I heard Declan speaking and almost had to retract that statement. Working with him might make this the worst after all.

"What are your plans to save dear, sweet Gray?" Declan had mischievous eyes but there didn't seem to be much evil to him, which took me aback. Mephistopheles oozed evil from every inch of him while Declan just reminded me of a bored little boy.

"Oh no, mister. I may have to play nice with you, but I don't have to share my game plan."

"Mister?" There was amusement in his eyes when he responded. "That's a first."

"It didn't seem appropriate to call you devil or demon. I don't like working with you, but I don't have to be rude about it." My matter of fact statement made Had cough into his coffee.

"Feisty. I like it." Declan's grey eyes danced with enjoyment as he sipped his macchiato.

Gray's band finished their set and were greeted by a hearty round of applause from the audience. Looking around, I noticed most of the patrons seemed to be a younger crowd and possibly regulars to the coffee shop. So far this town seemed to be very laid back and accepting, which would certainly help this mission. Hopefully we would have very little questioning of our actions and sudden appearance.

"What'd ya think?" Gray came up to the table with an expectant look.

"It was great. You all are awesome. I really loved the first song." He had a goofy lopsided grin. I still wasn't sure what was so special about him that he needed saving, but it wasn't my place to judge.

"Thanks. Hannah told me that she asked you to join us tomorrow. It's gonna be epic for sure! If you'll excuse me, I need to get ready for the next set."

CHAPTER
five

Satisfaction lies in the effort, not in the attainment. Full effort is full victory.
~Gandhi

"Hadraniel! Hurry up. We need to be meeting the group at the coffee shop in thirty minutes." I hollered up as I was making breakfast.

"I found swimming trunks, but do I need anything else?"

"A towel for sure, a shirt is up to you. I have a dress that goes over my swimsuit." I loved the clothes of this era. However the swimsuits are a lot more revealing than I'm used to. I had a two piece packed too but wasn't brave enough to wear it. I went with a deep purple suit that had a silver buckle on the neck and the sides cut out. I hadn't been swimming in a quarry before but I was guessing it would be similar to that of a lake or pond. Hadraniel came down carrying towels for both of us.

"I'm ready if you are, I'll just grab some toast to eat on the way."

"Sounds good to me." I replied. Having someone constantly around wasn't as annoying as I had expected. He proved to be good with following the timeline that I wanted, as opposed to pushing one of his own.

The walk into town was quiet. It was still rather early in the day. Last night, I'd spent time studying the map provided for us that showed where the damage would occur. I was saddened to know this beautiful area would be gone in no time. The area was lush and green. The smell of earth was clean and refreshing. Soon it would be destroyed and replaced with water. These parts of my jobs left me feeling blessed but sad at the same time. I would be the last to really appreciate the beauty of nature in this place, knowing no one would see it again.

Each of my missions have been special for different reasons but I did have my favorites. This mission currently was creeping into my top five. My number one to date was Pompeii. Although it was one of the most destructive missions it was still special because it was my first.

"You're very quiet this morning."

Hadraniel's statement brought me back to the reality that I was not going to be the only one to enjoy the last of this beautiful location this time around.

"Sorry. I was just thinking how sad it will be that in a few weeks this place will not be here."

"That is sad. I figured you were used to that though. You've always seemed so level about your job." It wasn't a false statement but it stung a little.

"My job does require some distancing. That does not mean that I don't feel *something*. I appreciate the feelings that others have about these missions as well. To survive though and be able to keep myself sane, I have to remain detached. This mission is completely different than my others. I normally don't interact with my target until almost the very end and never with help or mandatory involvement of a demon."

Had seemed pensive as he listened to me talk. He was very attentive to whomever he was conversing with, even when home.

Aniston had good taste when it came to crushes. He was kind and sweet. I hoped he reciprocated her feelings. They would make a good couple when the time came.

"Has working with me been so awful for you?"

"Nah, you're not so bad." I smirked at his scowl. "For real Had, it's been different, but not bad. I enjoy your company and you have had some wonderful ideas. Plus your good looks may have helped us with the in-crowd." Pink shot across his face with my compliment.

"Well, Bay I hate to tell ya, but you're not that hard to look at either." My first reaction was to stick my tongue out at him, only increasing his smug grin.

I suppose for human standards I was pretty. I had long wavy brown hair, ice blue eyes and was short. When most humans are asked to explain the image of an angel they say things like "blonde", "beautiful" and "tall". I didn't fit that description as much as Aniston did. Aniston was beautiful and tall and funny. Even if I found her annoying because she's so chipper, she wasn't as bad as I made her to be. I figured this might be a good time as any to mention her to Hadraniel.

"So, Haddy. Do you have a crush on anyone?" Crimson flooded his face, and he squinted his eyes pretending to be blinded by the sun, that was barely squeaking through the leaves in the forest. He pursed his lips, and cleared his throat.

"You're really nice Bayla, but…"

At first I was shocked, but when I realized he thought I meant me, I burst out laughing.

"Well, I'm not that funny of a person to like am I?" He seemed almost indignant.

"No, Haddy, not at all. It's just I didn't realize how that would sound. You are a great catch, I just don't see you, or anyone for that matter, in that way. I was speaking about Aniston." The flush appeared in his cheeks again.

"Oh. Yes. Aniston." He cleared his throat. "She is pretty. Why? Did she say something about me?"

"Maybe." Oh I haven't had this much fun in forever. I could be a matchmaker. Well, here on Earth. At home we actually had matchmakers to ensure that those who chose to date would have their matches approved.

"Good. Tell her I asked about her too then." The red was fading from his cheeks, but there seemed to be a little more pep to his step.

We went back to our comfortable, companionable silence as we finished our trek out of the woods and into town. It was quiet this time of morning, especially since it was the weekend. Even on missions, Angels tend to go to church, so I was glad they invited us today instead of tomorrow. As we neared the coffee shop, we could hear the chattering of a group of people. We rounded the corner and there had to be about fifteen people hanging outside the shop. I had never had to talk to that many people at once. My steps faltered slightly. Hadraniel, acting very brotherly, wrapped his arms around my shoulder, gave a quick supportive squeeze and then pulled me towards the group.

"Had! Bayla!" Gray hollered at us in greeting. I was thinking maybe we would get a chance to hang out with Gray and Hannah without Declan, until we got closer and noticed he was in the middle of a group of girls. He smirked when he noticed me watching. "Guys, this is Had and Bayla. They're new here. Their parents are missionaries, so they'll be going to college here while their parents travel. Guys, this is the group."

We gave a quick wave, before being escorted to vehicles we'd be riding in, to take us to the quarry. I was placed in a car with Hannah, Declan, Gray and a girl whose name I didn't catch, but she didn't seem to mind. She was more concerned with Declan than with me. Hannah and I chatted about the quarry, my parents, her parents, and what classes we planned on taking. I really liked Hannah, and had started formulating a plan that would probably require that she was with us when we saved Gray. I wasn't technically prohibited from her saving her, like in some situations, but I knew it would be frowned upon.

"Did you know Declan before last night? He keeps watching you." Hannah whispered.

"What?" I went to turn in order to see what she was talking about but she grabbed me to keep from turning.

She giggled at my response. "He's so handsome. It almost hurts to look at him." I only nodded in response. Why would he be staring at me? Miss Big Boobs, Blonde Hair was completely enthralled and using her best tricks to keep his attention. I didn't need to look at them to know this. I could hear them.

"He's okay, I suppose." I could feel heat spreading across my face, causing her to laugh again. "We haven't ever met face to face before, but we knew of each other before last night." That wasn't a complete lie. I knew there was a demon coming, and most demons knew me because of my job and status. I was expecting Meph, so getting Declan was a definite plus.

"Well, you're a lucky girl either way."

"Tell me about the quarry. I've never been to one before, especially to swim." Changing the subject seemed to be the best way to avoid furthering the conversation about me and Declan.

"We should be there soon. It used to be a limestone mine, but after they stripped it, it filled with water and it's been the local swimming hole ever since. It's a beautiful area. Most of the local teenagers and college student hang out here during the warmer months. When it gets colder, we have bon fires. I can't wait for you all to get to join us then. It is one of my favorite times of year."

Her enthusiasm was contagious, but unfortunately for her, the quarry would not be there come this fall. I'm not sure what has gotten into me this mission, but all of these new feelings and emotions were present. I didn't like this change. I could not get attached to these humans, or this place. I blame Hadraniel and all of his wonder of this place. I smirked at the thought of his being at fault.

"What's on your mind over there Bay?" Declan asked

Smirk gone. Frown now present.

"Bayla, please." My voice was a sugary sweet tone. "I was simply thinking about the quarry in the fall."

I had decided that the best way to deal with him was not to feed into his goading. He was so different, but he was still a demon. The less I revealed to him the better. I shot a blinding smile at him, and with much amusement received a pouty glare from Blondie beside him.

"Yes, what a pity we won't get to see it then, huh?" He was not planning on making this easy for me. I didn't get his game though, he needed them to go with whatever plan he made, and not mine. Scaring them was a good plan I suppose, but not one usually used by a demon. They much preferred tricking others into following them, as if it was their idea the whole time.

"Why won't you all get to see it?" The dense one spoke.

"Well, because…" Declan started

"Because we will be out camping most weekends of the fall doing research on the flora and fauna of the local area, and Declan agreed to help us out." I shot him a warning glare. Different teams or not, I was still the superior on this mission.

"Yes, that." Declan winked.

He. Winked. At. Me.

What was this dude's motive? I knew little about male Angels, less about male humans, and even less than that about male Demons. I get that they are charming to get their way, but not towards angels. There was an unspoken agreement. They were fallen angels, or the descendants of those who had fallen. They were everything we stood against. I had never met another demon like Declan. Ever. Not that I had met a lot, but still he was just so unlike the others. I wonder if this is why Father Paul asked me to allow him to work with us some. I was still dwelling on all of this when I felt the vehicle stop.

"This place is gorgeous." I gasped.

We were parked in a gravel lot, but you could see most of the quarry in front of us. There were cliffs with trees, a beach, and still dark blue water. The place was quiet; I assumed because we had gotten there so early. The group from the other car had already exited and were hauling things towards the beach. I hopped out behind Hannah, taking my bag as well as the beach blanket she handed to me.

"If we stay all day and night like we usually do, you'll be amazed at the night sky. There's little light out here other than the fires people build, so the stars are clearly visible. It's a beautiful sight."

"This place is amazing isn't it, Bay?" I turned to fuss at Declan, when I realized it was Hadraniel, not Declan, who had spoken.

"Absolutely, Had. I can't wait to go for a swim. How about you?" It wasn't nice to tease him. Swimming on Earth was going to be another new experience for Had. He took the ribbing in stride and just smiled.

"Let's go dive off one of the cliffs, Had." Gray suggested.

Declan was standing behind him though so it was safe to assume he was the one who made the original suggestion. I silently held my breath, hoping Hadraniel wouldn't allow himself to be goaded into doing something he wasn't ready for yet.

"Nah, I'm good man, thanks. Maybe later. I think I'm going to swim out to the platform and chill for a while."

I sighed a breath of relief. No one seemed to notice, thank Grace. It wasn't that I didn't think Hadraniel couldn't make the jump, he was a Blue-in-Training for Grace's sake. But he needed to learn to maneuver in the water first before jumping into it. I don't know why I continued to be surprised by his good decisions. He has done nothing but show me how smart he is with most of his decisions and suggestions.

"Wait up, Haddy. I think I'm going to join you." I spoke up before he got too far away.

"Cool."

For the rest of the day, we lounged, swam, jumped, ate, laughed and just hung out with our new group of friends. After his initial threat of spilling the beans, Declan was well-behaved the rest of the time. I'm sure it had more to do with the fact that we were all having fun, and not dwelling on what our futures were going to be. And soon. Earlier on the platform, after discussing in length with Hadraniel my plans for including Declan, he agreed. We would be giving Declan a brief outline of our plan with as little details as possible. That way I could say I included him some, without giving away any help to his plan.

The night sky was starting to creep in and overtake the daylight. The oranges, purples and pinks were radiant out here, reflecting on the smooth surface of the quarry water. Orange was such a soothing color, I loved how it looked next to the darkness that was winning.

"This is my favorite part." Declan was standing close by me, with awe on his face. "It's quiet out where I am staying. Just me and the animals out there, so I spend a lot of my nights watching the darkness take over, and the stars come out." He sounded almost lonely. I had to tell myself not to pity this man. He was not good. He was demon, to the core.

"Earth can have some of the most spectacular night skies. I agree. I think my favorite view was from the Titanic. The water was still, and there was absolute darkness. The air was crisp and you could see the stars everywhere in all directions. It was quite a sight. Your fellow demon was on that mission, but I doubt that he once looked at the night skies."

"Mephistopheles and I are not the same perso....err demon. I was never like him. I guess that's why I wasn't given any missions until now. And even that's only because my 'look' fits more appropriately than his ever could, or I wouldn't be here. Hadraniel said you two wanted to talk to me." Quick change of subject, smooth.

"Not here, not now. Let's just enjoy the sky and the company. You can come to our cottage after church tomorrow and we will discuss it then."

"Sounds good to me."

We headed back to the group. He went and sat by Alissa, as I discovered was Blondie's name. I laid down beside Hannah, and gazed at all the stars that were out. All was silent for a while and I was beginning to drift off, when someone suggested we load up and head home. I was not ready to leave this area, but I knew I had church early in the morning. I'd gotten the directions from Hannah for the church Father Paul suggested we attend. The trip home was quick and quiet as most people in the car were asleep other than Gray, who was driving, and Declan. Declan and Gray chatted, while I pretended to sleep.

"Thanks for the invite today. I had fun." Declan said.

"You're welcome, dude. Alissa really seems to like you."

"She seems like a nice girl. I'm not really interested in her though."

"Oh yeah? Got your eyes on someone else?" Gray chuckled. "Maybe Bayla?"

"Bayla? Nah, I mean she is absolutely one of the most breathtaking girls I have ever seen, but our backgrounds are so different it would never work. She's pure goodness, man. I, on the other hand, have a bit of a wild streak."

"Right on." Gray high fived Declan, who just smirked a little.

Hearing Declan say I was breathtaking, made my stomach knot. I was not this girl. I was not going to be this girl. I was Bayla, angel, Collector of Souls. I was strong, disconnected, and perfect at my job. This was the kick I needed to get refocused. I could not allow this demon to affect my decisions. These humans were nice, but I had a mission. One I would not fail, even if I didn't know why Gray was so special. I would save him, complete the mission, and return to my home in Heaven to await my next mission. I turned and really went to sleep this time.

CHAPTER
six

Be alert and of sober mind. Your enemy the devil prowls around like a roaring lion looking for someone to devour.
~1 Peter 8 (NIV)

We left early for church to ensure that we had time to get there and still look presentable. When we got into town, the bookstore owner who had introduced himself as Mr. Whitstock, asked to join us on our walk. He was a nice gentleman, and seemed very kind. We walked along in silence a while before Mr. Whitstock turned to speak to me.

"I noticed you seem quieter today. Is something on your mind?"

Funny how this man who barely knew me could read me that easily. What was stranger was that I wanted to talk to him about my problems. I knew I would have to choose my words carefully, but I really thought he could provide some good insight.

"Well, I feel like I am missing something important, like in a puzzle. I can't really give you any details, but I feel a little more lost than normal. I am good at what I do, and usually I'm able to stay on task. For some reason, there seems to be something different this time."

"I'm betting you already know the answer. I would even dare to say you've figured out all the clues needed to understand what you should be doing, even if you don't understand the purpose behind it. Sometimes help comes even when it shouldn't be given. I say you wouldn't be thinking so much about these issues, if you weren't sure of your path." With that he sped up to walk with Hadraniel but not before giving me a wink and pat on the back.

There was something about Mr. Whitstock. I couldn't seem to figure it out, but I would add it to the mystery that has become my mission. No wonder Elder Michael put such an emphasis that I must not fail. Something big was going to happen, and I feared it wasn't just the earthquake.

The interior of the church was beautiful. There were cedar benches, pristine white walls, and stained glass windows depicting the stories of different great men in the Bible. Hannah was sitting beside the story window of Noah and his ark. She smiled and motioned for me and Hadraniel to join her. We sat down just as the choir began to sing. I loved hearing hymns. Music fed my soul, and the choir was very good. It allowed me time to re-center myself and my thoughts back to the mission at hand. I would save Gray, hopefully Hannah, and if my suspicions were true, like Mr. Whitstock somewhat eluded too, I'd be saving Declan too.

The preacher stood up to begin his sermon for the day, but I got lost in my prayers and thoughts. I asked for guidance on how to handle this situation and to detach myself and my feelings from the situation. I couldn't allow emotions to cloud my decision. All of my choices on past missions were based on the best way to accomplish them with little thought as to how it affected the humans. I needed to continue with these practices. The Elders entrusted me, alone, to figure out this mission and to complete it. I didn't need to know the why, just the how. As I continued to pray, I came back to the conclusion that I had to learn to trust and let go. I had to stick to being just a collector of souls, not a redeemer. Redemption seemed to be the message of the day. The pastor was reading from Romans 3 when I came back around.

"For all have sinned, and come short of the glory of God; Being justified freely by his grace through the redemption that is in Christ Jesus; Whom God hath set forth to be a propitiation through faith in his blood, to declare his righteousness for the remission of sins that are past, through the forbearance of God."

When he finished, we ended with a prayer. I felt renewed and ready to face the meeting with Declan. I stood up to leave. Turning to Hannah to thank her for the invite, something caught my eye. I turned towards the back where I saw Declan sitting, dressed very nicely. I was stunned. Demons, or fallen angels as they were called in Heaven, could come to church, but most chose not to for obvious reasons. He appeared to have tears running down his face. I watched for a while until he noticed. He then wiped his tears, and his looks of sadness changed to one that was more closed off. I was beginning to wonder if this was not just an act. He gave a nod, and left out the back door. Hadraniel was looking just as taken aback as I was about Declan's appearance. Hannah mentioned that she had invited him last night, but I wasn't paying a lot of attention to her at the moment.

"Bayla?"

"I'm sorry, what did you say? I was in la-la land."

"I asked if you like to join Gray and me for lunch today." She responded with a smile.

"That's very nice, however, we already told Declan we would meet with him for lunch today at our cottage. He hasn't had a home-cooked meal in a while." I tried to present a smile that didn't show any emotion other than content.

"Oh, how very kind of you." She drew out the very and waggled her eyebrows at me.

I gave her a playful nudge and giggled. We said goodbye to her and Gray. Mr. Whitstock stopped us at the door and told us to stop by tomorrow as he had found a book for us that he thought would be of interest. I smiled and thanked him. Even Hadraniel seemed to be confused as to how Mr. Whitstock appeared to know things without knowing anything.

"Does he seem really familiar to you? Like he knows something?" Had asked on our walk back to the cottage.

"He does, but he seems harmless. We can use any help we can get, so I definitely think we should go to the store tomorrow to see what he has for us." Had nodded in agreement.

"Tell me more about Aniston?" He was looking to his feet, but I could tell he was embarrassed.

I snickered but spent the remainder of our walk discussing Aniston with him, telling him about her likes, dislikes, silly quirks and all the comments she had made about him. He asked about her age, her job, and how I liked living with her. He found it particularly funny when I explained my suspicions that she was assigned to be my room because she was so perky.

"You do seem more approachable and friendly now."

I winced. "I'm letting myself get too involved. You'll hear my plans when we meet with Declan. I haven't deviated much from what we originally planned before getting here, but I am going to detach myself from the group. I cannot let the humans cloud any hard choices I may have to make when the time comes."

"Whatever you think is best Bayla...you're the expert. However, I think the way you are doing things now is more beneficial. You have to realize that knowing these people and allowing yourself to live and feel can be beneficial, it doesn't all have to be a hindrance. Life is going to happen either way, you might as well enjoy it while you can. You know better than anyone knows how quick it can be altered."

I was stunned into silence. Somewhere Father Paul was mentally high fiving Hadraniel. Father Paul always tells me I'm too dark and uninvolved. I knew Hadraniel had a point, but I didn't know how to do that. He seemed so natural at mingling with the humans. Maybe having witnessed all that I have, I knew how this was going to end. I knew saving Gray wouldn't keep him safe from feeling all the things that were going to come with the aftermath of the earthquake. I knew that whether I allowed myself to open up, or if I stayed away, I would still pity him for those emotions.

"Took you long enough." Declan's voice broke my train of thought. He was sitting on the steps of the cottage. Gosh, he really knew what clothes accentuated his body. He still had his church clothes on - khakis, a sky blue button-down with the sleeves rolled up and boots. He knew he looked good too. He was staring at me as I took him in. I shook my head, remembering the promise I made myself last night.

"Sorry, we were stopped by the bookstore owner."

"Ah, yes, Mr. Whitstock, he's very helpful. So, what's for lunch?"

"Bayla made some kind of soup and taught me how to mix a salad. We figured we could eat first before discussing our plans."

"Sounds good to me." Declan rubbed his belly and licked his lips.

I didn't think I could ever get used to this demon. Lunch proceeded without any further sarcasm or real issues. We discussed the sermon, and the area where Declan lived, and how he was liking his first mission location. He was definitely very charming. I had to remind myself throughout lunch that it was his job to be charming and not to fall for this act.

"Shall we move out to the garden area to have our business meeting?" I asked. Sitting outside would allow me to have a visual reminder of the devastation that would be occurring soon.

The boys simply nodded, grabbed their lemonade and followed me out back. The view from our garden area was a meadow full of flowers and surrounding trees. It was quiet, peaceful, and private. Privacy was very important for this conversation. I hadn't lied to Hadraniel when I said we would be sticking to the original plan for what to share with Declan, but I would be adding him into the getaway plan. I needed to know where he was going to be during the quake.

"Do you want to go first, or would you prefer we start?"

"You can start." Declan raised his glass in my direction.

"Our plan is to continue to gain the trust of the group by joining in on get-togethers as much as possible in hopes of being able to invite them somewhere the weekend of the quake to ensure their safety."

"I must say, I'm kind of let down, Bay. I really was expecting some large elaborate plan. You are the Great Bayla, Angel Collector of Souls! I came here expecting to be blown away. It's a nice plan, I suppose. And If I wasn't in the picture," he was making grand gestures with his hands as he spoke, "I'm betting it would work great too. Your goal is to save him from the quake, but MY goal is that he doesn't survive. Which really sucks because he's a pretty cool dude. I don't have a plan...yet. Well, other than to make sure your plan doesn't work." There was an air of arrogance to him that betrayed any and all previous displays of being a semi-decent guy. "Thanks for the info, though, because now I know I just have to keep him from going with you for that weekend and stay here where the quake is going to hit. I may even use that pretty Hannah as bait." He winked, finished his lemonade and stood to go.

Hadraniel was scowling. I could feel his anger building up, but I placed my hand on his shoulder before he had a chance to stand. I didn't need him to mess up this plan. While Declan had been harsher than I'd anticipated, he did do exactly as I had expected. He would use our plans to build his and work against us. I knew his type, demon or human. He would accept the challenge that went with the deal I was about to present to him.

"If you're so sure it'll be that easy then how about a wager? You can use whatever plan you decided upon just now, BUT you have to make it work while on the campout I have planned for that weekend. You have to get them to leave the area and follow you to wherever you plan on letting them die. Because that is what they are going to have to do for you to win. They will all have to die. I'm game though, if you are." Hadraniel was staring at me in shock, almost disgusted with what I was saying to Declan.

Declan's smirk shifted into a full blown ear-to-ear grin. "Sounds good to me. Not only do I win, but I beat Bayla the Great AND I get to choose my winnings from the wager to be determined at a later date, of course." He put his hand out in front of him, waiting for me to shake on it.

I reached towards his hands when I felt Hadraniel jerk me away.

"Just give us a minute please." He pulled me to the far corner of the garden. "Have you never heard the old saying to never make a deal with the Devil? He is his representative after all. What exactly are you doing?"

I hadn't told Hadraniel my suspicion about Declan and our mission. I wasn't going to either. The less he knew, the better off he would be. I figured this was going to happen so I knew I had to have a reason to give him without giving away too much or flat-out lying.

"Father Paul told us to include him, remember? This was the only way I could think of that would get him to agree. Besides, I don't plan on losing Had so I'm okay with making the wager. However, you do not have to make the wager with him. It can be on me." I reassured him with my authoritative and confident tone that I was sure I knew what I was doing. He just nodded, and my gut clenched with sudden doubt. I turned to head back to where Declan had perched himself on the back of the chair, leaning his elbows on his knees. When he noticed us approaching, he looked up, and his hair fell into his eyes. I stumbled a little at the look he gave me causing the doubt to grow into fearful uncertainty… maybe I didn't know what I was doing. I shook my head to clear my thoughts. Why was I letting this man - scratch that - this *demon* get to me as much as I was?

"So is it a deal?" He stuck his hand back out towards me, smirk on his face.

"Deal." I shook his hand.

The ground shook, not hard, but enough that I feared maybe I had made a mistake. Seeing the grim frown on Had's face, I realized he was thinking the same thing. Declan on the other hand seemed unfazed by the movement that had just occurred. An angel and demon had never made a deal before that I was aware of, and I'm sure that this was going to cause a huge problem with Elder Michael even if I did succeed.

"Nice working with you guys. See you in town tomorrow. I have to head back to my place." The arrogance that had just been present, seemed to fall away like a curtain and the vulnerability that had been there last night returned. He left and headed in the opposite direction from our cottage.

He was so mercurial that I was unsure of anything other than I had literally just made a deal with the Devil. And I had only a small inkling of what I thought may or may not be a secret mission within the mission. I decided right then and there I would definitely be seeking out Mr. Whitstock tomorrow for the book he wanted to show us, but also to figure out how much information he had about our situation. First, however, was to use the internet to research what the tremor was related to and if I needed to move my plans up.

CHAPTER
seven

When you cease to strive to understand, then you will know without understanding.

~Chinese proverb

After all the research we had done last night, we found that tremors such as the one that occurred concurrently with my handshake with Declan were normal precursors to large earthquakes. From what we could find, there would be a few more before the final catastrophic one. Unfortunately, based on the research we completed, it seemed as if no one in the news or seismology departments in the local area seemed to be tracking or predicting the one that was quickly approaching. We ate in silence before heading to town to meet Mr. Whitstock. The walk into town was silent. Hadraniel still wasn't very happy with me or the decision I'd made last night. He felt that I hadn't carefully considered everything before making the wager, and that his opinions had not been heard. I tried to explain to him that I had a plan, and I would give him more details later, but that wasn't good enough for him. He threw it in my face that I thought I was better than him, to which I readily agreed. Upon further reflection, this may not have been a tactful admission, but I had only meant better in the sense that I had more experience with missions than him.

The bookstore was quiet when we entered. The bell above the door tinkled, alerting Mr. Whitstock of our arrival. He didn't look surprised at all to see us; he simply smiled, motioned for us to follow him as he took off towards the back of the bookstore. This area was set up with tables for people to sit and review books, enjoy a cup of coffee and chitchat. We were the only ones in the whole store. He had several books laid out, pages marked, and four steaming cups of coffee already sitting on the table awaiting us. I noticed the fourth cup just as Declan came from over from another aisle.

"You two are later than I expected, but the coffee's still hot. I found a few more books I thought you might find of interest. Sit, and enjoy! I doubt there will be much traffic today so we can do as much research as you need."

Mr. Whitstock sat, glasses sliding down his nose, in front of book labeled "Limestone Caves." The book in front of me was labeled "Kentucky Fault Lines." Declan was reading about campsites in the area, and the remaining book where Had sat was labeled, "Angels and Demonology." I stared at Mr. Whitstock. This man definitely was not as he appeared to be. He caught me staring, wiggled his nose and pointed to my book indicating I needed to get to reading. He left little room to allow me to question how he knew as much as he did. Then it hit me! The wiggle, the wink, the familiar grin...Mr. Whitstock was Father Paul. The realization made me gasp aloud. Both boys glanced up at me. Mr. Whitstock simply shook his head slightly warning me to not mention this discovery at all. I had never been given help before on any case, and now I had a Blue-in-Training, Father Paul and a demon. This mission's level of importance just increased greatly, meaning that my deal yesterday just became even more of an issue. I pretended that the coffee I had sipped was hot, and the boys went back to reading their books. I decided I needed to read too, since "Mr. Whitstock" took the time to personally select these books for us to review.

Hours passed, as we each finished our books and traded with each other. We took breaks to stretch, to eat, and to discuss any new discoveries that we made. Declan was pleasant today, and seemed to be very honest in sharing his findings. Pure mystery, this one. Mr. Whitstock, as I decided to continue to call him to avoid exposing him, only occasionally provided his input. He allowed us to discuss our opinions freely with each other. He had to have invited Declan, and with the conversation we had yesterday, I now knew my suspicions were true. I had another mission to save Declan as well...though why I still couldn't figure out. I had never known the whys behind any of the missions that were deemed rescues versus soul retrievals. I just completed the mission and returned home. However, I couldn't seem to let this go. During this break, the guys decided they needed more food. They volunteered to walk to the café to procure food for all of us. I was glad, because this gave me time to address Father Paul.

"Why are you here? I've gone from working alone to needing three people with me for this mission. What gives, Father Paul?" I didn't give him much time; I was questioning him right as the door closed behind the guys.

"Bayla, I cannot help you more than simple guidance. Elder Michael sent me here because he knew you would figure out the need for Declan. He knew you would have questions. He is only permitting me to agree if you are correct. I cannot independently or freely give you information. You must come to me first. I had hoped you wouldn't figure out it was me so early. I don't want you to think that any of us are doubting your abilities...quite the opposite actually. We have never been surer of the decision to send you on the mission. Hadraniel was just for extra support and hopefully to help teach you a few things. You must not let him know about Declan."

"Can you tell me why? Why Gray? Why Declan?"

He shook his head and walked back to the table. He handed me the "Angels and Demonology" book and went back to reading his campsites guide. I'd known it was a long shot that he would answer, but I had to try. I had already read most of the book in front of me and was just merely skimming when a section titled "Falling" caught my eye. I began reading about when Lucifer defied God and was sent to Hell. I read about the other fallen angels, and the story of how the demons were created. The section talked about how many of the Fallen were thought to have tried to rise again, with little success. Some realized their mistake a little too late. Others who were the children of the fallen felt they had the right to try to be redeemed as it hadn't been their choice that made them a Fallen. I became oblivious to my surroundings as I became immersed in the story of the children of the Fallen; their legends and myths, how they tried to help angels, and humans throughout history, yet were overlooked for various reasons. Reading this was just causing more frustration for me. Why have me try to help Declan if it was impossible? The guys walked in just as I had decided I needed a break. I moved to another table that had open space so I could eat and not see a book. Thoughts kept racing as I ate my burger.

"Why the frown, Bay?" Declan asked, almost sincerely.

"I didn't realize I was this hungry, I suppose."

He chuckled. I honestly didn't know if he knew about this part of my mission. My Grace, I didn't know if he even wanted to be redeemed! I couldn't outwardly ask him, either. I could feel my eyebrows furrowing again. I needed to finish eating and get back to the book. I needed answers. This was beginning to get more complicated than I had originally thought. If the Fallen couldn't be redeemed, why was he even a part of the mission? Why would they give me a mission at which I could not succeed? How could I continue to have Hadraniel help me without telling him this new information? I was wracking my brain. I finished my burger and took my soda back to the table with me so I could finish the book. Both Had and Declan had already looked at this book, and hadn't shared this information, either because they didn't find it beneficial, or because they hadn't even read this part.

I was scanning the remaining few pages with little to no help of finding answers. Close to the end was a story that told of a chance of a rising for the fallen angels. The story explained that if a Fallen gives his life while saving an angel they have the opportunity to be redeemed. It told of different Fallen that had never been truly able to give their lives selflessly. I knew that Declan would never willingly give his life in exchange for mine or Hadraniel's. This mission would be my first failure even if I saved Gray. I hung my head, taking deep breaths. I felt an encouraging hand on my shoulder before Father Paul spoke.

"For He knows all things, O ye of little faith."

I looked up as he made his way to his seat. My eyes caught Had's and noticed a glimmer of recognition in them. If he had figured out who Mr. Whitstock really was, he was smart enough not to say anything. He looked at me for some answer, but I went back to saying a prayer for guidance and breathing through this new feeling. My body and mind felt like they were spiraling. Everything started closing in on me, and felt like I couldn't breathe. It was beginning to be too much. I jumped up and ran towards the door. I needed air. I heard Hadraniel somewhere behind me yell my name and Father Paul telling him to let me have a moment. Nineteen years...I had been alive nineteen years and had never felt this way before. I had read about this feeling when studying humans. It was classified as stress or anxiety. I was pretty sure I was close to a panic attack. I cannot fail, I cannot succeed. Elder Michael had to have made a mistake. Maybe, he knew I would fail and was trying to teach me a lesson in humanity. I didn't know, but I felt completely lost.

Sitting outside seemed to help some. The breeze was nice in the shade, as it was a little too warm out today. I had just leaned back against a tree on the sidewalk with my eyes closed, when I heard footsteps approaching. I looked up just as Gray was stooping down to be level with me. He was dressed in casual clothes so I assumed he was not heading to work.

"Hey. You okay?" His voice was steeped with concern.

"Yeah, just got a little overwhelmed with the study session going on, so I came out to rest my eyes and brain."

"Studying already? Classes haven't even started yet." His eyebrows creased in concern at the possibility of how nerdy Hadraniel and I might be. It made me giggle.

"Not for school, things for our parents. What are you doing? No work?"

"Actually I was heading somewhere alone, but would you like to join me? It'll give us a chance to talk, give you a break and I can show someone new my love of this place." He was grinning a boyish grin now.

"How could I not join you after that mysterious invite?"

With that he stood, and as he rose, he grabbed my hands and helped me off the ground. He suggested that I may want to let them know I was leaving, but I waved it off. I needed the time away from that whole situation, and this gave me a great opportunity to learn about Gray. I needed to know what made him so special that I needed to risk all these things to save him.

"So, where are we going?" I asked. He kept a decent pace that let me walk comfortably. He was so tall that I would have had to run to catch him if he walked any faster.

"That's a secret."

"Ok, why are we going there?"

"Another secret." He was enjoying this, keeping me in the dark. His eyes danced with amusement.

"Fine. Can you tell me about what you're planning on studying in school then?"

"I'm going to double major in art and teaching."

"Art? What kind of art?" I had assumed music because of his band and his talent.

"Drawing, mainly, but I love to paint, sculpt, all things artistic. The teaching degree is so I can provide a living for Hannah when we get married."

Hannah had mentioned that she and Gray had been together for a long time, I just didn't realize it was that serious. From my understanding, average ages for humans to marry changed from century to century. I'm pretty sure the current society would agree that nineteen was pretty young to get married. He seemed to be a normal human male. Normal goals, normal talents, normal, normal, normal. Why then was he needing to survive this catastrophic event? In our mission files, it was stated in no uncertain tones that collecting his soul was not an option, he must survive the event. We chatted some more about him and Hannah as we headed to his secret spot, but the talking stopped completely as we got to the bottom of a hill.

"We have to go up. Are you good to climb?"

He stood looking up the hill, hands on hips. He seemed pumped and ready to go. I figured if he could do it, then I could do it.

"Sure, I'm game."

I'd no idea what I was getting myself into by agreeing to this adventure. The climb was not an easy one. My knees were getting scraped, my hands were muddy from grabbing roots and trees to pull myself up. I did it though, and without Gray's help. He was leaning against a rock, as I got to the top. He had a bottle of water in a small pack I hadn't noticed he was wearing. He took a sip and handed it to me. I sat beside him and tried to not guzzle down the whole bottle. The difference in gravity really hit me on the climb. I hadn't done anything that taxing until now, and it felt good.

"Where to now, Boss?"

He chuckled. "Are you always this impatient?"

"Yes. Had will vouch for that too." I grinned knowing Hadraniel would find it funny. I had to have a mass of patience in order to complete this job. Collecting souls was a job that couldn't be rushed.

"Well, you see that tree up there?" He pointed to a tree up another small hill that looked to be dying. It was the only tree up there. "We are going to go sit there. The view on the other side of the tree will be like nothing you've ever seen before."

I didn't have the heart to tell him that I was sure I had viewed sights more breathtaking. I was sure I would still love the view. Earth's landscape never failed to bring me happiness. I felt bad that Hadraniel wouldn't see this view with me, but I had gotten some good information, however small it was, about Gray. As we headed to the tree, Gray's face grew pensive, almost solemn.

"Why the face?"

"This was my brother's favorite place to go. His name was Oliver. He was three years older than me. He had Down 's syndrome, and we came here two or three times a week. I usually brought him up with a four-wheeler, because of that climb. He loved it up here. He would describe what he saw to me, and I would draw his world. I had a picture book for him that he would flip through when we couldn't get up here. He's part of the reason I want to study art so much."

"Where's your brother now?"

"He got sick one day. We took him to the hospital after he got really tired and wouldn't answer us. They ran some tests, but couldn't find anything conclusive. We stayed at his bedside every day, rotating between me, Mom, Dad and Hannah. Oliver loved Hannah." He gave a small, sad smile. "After a while, he slipped into a coma, and still we had no answers. I was coming in to relieve dad from his shift when he died. Dad said it was peaceful. One minute he was breathing and the next, he wasn't. My parents decided not to do an autopsy. There was nothing we could do for him. I decided to go into teaching, to teach art, so that kids who couldn't normally express themselves could learn different outlets."

I quickly wiped the tears away before he noticed them. Here I was judging him for being normal, and he was anything but. He had a beautiful soul. Even if he did nothing else important, he deserved to be saved. We reached the top of the hill and I gasped. In front of me was a waterfall, a valley full of the most beautiful flowers, and a creek running through the valley dividing it into two sections.

"Wow."

Gray smiled. "I told you. I love it here, but my purpose today was to actually see if there was any change in the landscape after that quake we had earlier. You see, this place was created almost as an oasis of sorts after a collapse of a cave many, many years ago. It has an eco-system unlike any other, so I figured if anything was changed, it would be here. Because of the recent rumblings we've been having, I started studying the chances of the New Madrid fault line having a catastrophic earthquake, and this place reminds me of what kind of damage could be done."

I was really in shock now. I couldn't say anything to him about the earthquake as that was one of the few restrictions I was given. He seemed knowledgeable about the possibility of the event occurring.

"Does anything seem different?" My shock from him knowing about the earthquake played well into feigning anxiety of any possible damage from the tremor.

"No, everything seems as it was before." He got quiet, staring out into the valley. It was a minute or so before he spoke again. "Well, I guess we should make our way back into town. Before Had starts to worry about you."

"Let him worry!" I laughed, but then nodded that it was time. I now had a renewed sense of purpose, and was ready to jump back into my research. I needed to do further investigation of this valley as well because it could be the ideal camping site if it really couldn't collapse, and I needed to run it by Hadraniel and Father Paul.

I entered the bookstore about two hours after I had left. Before I was even able to get to the back, I was accosted by Declan. I watched as he approached; his eyebrows were drawn down in a frown, nostrils flared, and lips pressed firmly together. He was angry. I wasn't sure why, but he was. I knew whatever he was about to say was not going to be nice.

"Exactly where the hell were you for the past two hours, Bayla?" He asked, nose flaring. I almost giggled.

"I was with Gray, if you must know. I went out to clear my head, and he invited me to go for a walk with him. Which, by the way, ended up being very helpful for me, thank you very much." I glared back at him, all comical enjoyment was gone when he rolled his eyes at me at the mention of Gray's name.

"And you didn't think to tell someone, anyone, where you went?"

"Actually, I did think to do it and decided not to. I am not used to answering to anyone if you recall, Declan, and I definitely do not have to answer to you. I do not have to check in when I choose to do something. Especially when it is helpful for my mission that I happen to know is going to be successful! Now, if you're done interrogating me, I have more research to complete."

I stepped past him and noticed the look of relief on both Mr. Whitstock's and Hadraniel's faces and felt bad. I gave a sheepish shrug and apologized quickly before taking my seat. I hadn't lied to Declan. I wasn't accustomed to having anyone on my missions with me, so I didn't have to think about how my actions would affect others. I needed to remember that while I was upset, it was not Hadraniel's or Father Paul's fault.

"I really am sorry, you two. I just needed to step away for a minute."

"I was worried, but now that I know you're okay, and that it was a useful break, it's all good." Hadraniel smiled. "While you were gone, Jacob" he pointed to Mr. Whitstock, "found a book that he thought you might find of interest. I'm not sure how it is supposed to be helpful. It looks like a fairytale story." Confusion crossed his face, but he handed me the book.

The story was about an angel who helped deliver children to heaven. At first I was confused as well since the story just told of the angel, but as I read, and re-read, I noticed that the angel does something to help the soul be okay with his transition. It was simple, yet it resonated with me completely. As I sat silently, staring at the words yet not quite seeing them, I realized the story was telling me I had to find a way to make the transition to safety something meaningful for Gray and Declan both, something they could see as a good thing and not as a sign of loss. For Gray to lose his family would be something rough to deal with, I got that. But for Declan to be redeemed from Hell, would he feel as if he was making a sacrifice or losing something?

I had a plan on how to use this new information with Gray, using the sight he showed me earlier today, I could explain the need to visit that place. This also meant I needed to figure out a way to spend time with Declan to get to know him a little better. This was not something I looked forward to in the least. I scanned the back area of the store and saw he was still brooding. He was leaning against a shelf, reading something, but the scowl remained. Something inside of me danced, and I mentally scolded it. Now was not the time to feel human emotions towards a demon or any man, for that matter. I hadn't noticed I was staring until he looked up, and his gray eyes met mine. The stare was intense; there was an unfamiliar look in his eyes, and it wasn't entirely unpleasant. I had to look away. I looked over to Mr. Whitstock who curiously was smiling. I stuck my tongue out at him, and he gave a boisterous laugh, startling Hadraniel.

"I'm sorry. I think I may be going a little stir crazy. Shall we break again? This time together," I added that after I was given a very pointed look, "in order to eat supper? I know I am hungry. Let's head to the café."

"Sounds like a good plan to me."

"Oh, Haddy." I teased, "Any plan with food sounds like a good plan to you." I needed to keep up with the brother/sister façade because as far as Had knew, Mr. Whitstock was just Mr. Whitstock.

CHAPTER eight

A man who was completely innocent, offered himself as a sacrifice for the good of others, including his enemies, and became the ransom of the world. It was a perfect act.

~Mahatma Gandhi

Dinner was a fun event. Hannah joined us during her break. It was a nice distraction from my thoughts as we sat around the table at the café having fun and laughing. Declan turned the charm on full blast, regaling us with the adventures of his travels. Whether they were stories made up for the part he was playing or if they were true, they were funny. He was telling us about getting lost in a foreign country, with no real knowledge of the language. After some confusion with the hostel clerk, he was able to procure a bed for the evening. He proceeded to explain that because of the lack of communication, he ended up sharing a bed with a little old lady who thought he was sent as an answer to her prayers, and he had to spend the majority of the night fighting off her advances by hiding in the bathroom of the hostel. We were in tears by the time he finished his story. Hannah had spit water everywhere, and Mr. Whitstock almost fell off his chair. Declan chuckled some at his story, but mostly he looked amused at his ability to make the four of us laugh so hard. We were just calming down when Gray headed our way for his break. Hannah gathered herself and waved bye as she went back to work. Gray took her seat.

"Y'all sound like you're having a great time." he said to no one in particular. He then leaned towards me. "I guess this means you're feeling better than you were earlier?" His forehead wrinkled in concern.

"I am. Thank you for asking." His smile was kind and warm. Gray was special. This I could tell, yet I still didn't know why his kindness made him more worthy than other humans to be saved from the fast approaching earthquake.

"You're welcome. Anytime you need a break from these knuckleheads, you just let me or Hannah know."

Declan was scowling, but Hadraniel had a look of mischief in his eyes. Mr. Whitstock was grinning.

"I'm sure she will be entirely too busy these next few weeks." Declan responded before I could. I shot him a look that warned him to not answer for me again.

"Gray, that is a kind offer. I may take you up on that if I get a chance, but unfortunately, Declan is correct. I have a lot of research to get through before school starts, and our parents will be stopping by to check on us. However, Haddy and I were talking about planning a camping trip for the weekend before classes start. We've narrowed it down to the valley you showed me earlier, and some mountain nearby called Adam's Peak. Do you have a suggestion as to which is a better place? Also, do you and Hannah want to join us? So far it's myself, Declan and Haddy." Both guys knew enough not to challenge me on the invite.

"Adam's Peak is not a great place to camp, and it's a heck of hike to get to, but I'm not sure about the valley either." He looked leery at the thought of camping in his and his brother's special location.

"Well the reason we were looking at those two spots, was because there is supposed to be a wicked meteor shower that night, and both of those offer the best viewing." Declan stated matter-of-factly.

Mr. Whitstock cleared his throat, signaling me to close my mouth at the shock of Declan helping. I was unsure of what this game was that Declan was playing, but I recovered as quickly as possible, praying Gray hadn't noticed my reaction. I was thankful for this input that I was not aware of, making my camping trip more viable. But I began to wonder why he hadn't shared with us that there was going to be a meteor shower that evening.

"Sounds like a great idea, let's do the valley. I'll see if Hannah's brother and his girlfriend want to join us. They always come in to visit that weekend."

"We should meet in the next week or so in order to make concrete plans." Hadraniel suggested.

"How about this coming Saturday? My parents are having a cookout at our house. We can get the plans settled there, and be able to tell Alex and Megan the plans afterwards."

"It's settled then." I smiled. That went a little too easy for my taste, but I would take it.

We spent the rest of his break taking turns telling Declan, Had and Mr. Whitstock about the valley. Gray explained how it was created after a roof of one of the caving systems collapsed. The ecosystem was completely different than that of the land around it. Because of the river and the minerals in the earth, the soil was extremely rich. Gray went on to talk about his studies of the earthquake tremor we had yesterday, as well as the signs he had discovered that a possible bigger earthquake might follow. He finished by telling us that according to historical records, the New Madrid was due for a big quake. Had's eyes widened as he looked between Declan and me. I gave a slight shrug to indicate that as long as we didn't react like we knew anything, it should be fine. Mr. Whitstock looked amazed that Gray was as adept in his studies without any assistance. He began to ask Gray questions.

"Did you study the outlines of where the earthquake would affect if it did happen?" Mr. Whitstock was appropriately concerned as a citizen of the town and storekeeper. I smiled at how well he played the part.

"Actually, I have a map I've drawn here. Would you all like to see?"

I was very interested in comparing it to the map we'd been given, showing where the safe places were for saving Gray when the time came. He pulled out his hand-drawn map, and the details were beautiful. Declan and Had both complimented him on his talent. He gave a sheepish shrug and began pointing out different areas that he felt would be affected. However, the damage he was expecting was nothing compared to what we knew would actually be occurring. Luckily both the places we had indicated for camping we're not going to be affected. The only plus to Adam's Peak compared to the valley was that it was far enough away that when the quake happened, it would take a while to get back in town, and by then the danger would have passed. Camping in the valley gave us the same protection, but the humans would be aware of the quake, and the destruction would be seen, heard, and felt with little they could do to help as they watched their town, friends and family disappear and die. Because my mission was to save the human life that was Gray, my predecessor was going to be collecting the souls of those who didn't survive the catastrophic event, and just then, it struck me. If another angel was going to be taking part, then another demon must be collecting as well. My eyes shot up towards Mr. Whitstock. Apparently the color had drained from my face, because before I knew it, Hadraniel was at my side. The last thing I remember was him calmly telling me that he had me. When I woke up, I was on the stage being fanned by Gray and Hannah. Declan, stone-faced, was leaning against the stage wall.

Mr. Whitstock was telling everyone to give me space. Hadraniel helped me sit up and handed me a glass of water.

"Are you okay?" Hannah asked so quietly, I felt bad for scaring her.

"Yes, I must have gotten too hot." I cast my eyes down, praying no one noticed my fib.

"It's been a busy day for you all. Had, maybe you should take Bayla home to rest?" Mr. Whitstock made the suggestion, but it was more of a command than anything.

I didn't want to leave yet. I wanted to talk to him about all the things that I had learned today. But I realized that he was letting me know that wasn't going to happen and that I needed to trust and rely on Hadraniel to help me with this information. With drooping shoulders, I nodded in agreement. Hadraniel helped me stand, and when I was steady enough to walk, I turned to wave goodbye to Hannah, Gray and Declan. Declan continued to stare at me, no emotions at all. Sadness flooded me. Hannah ran over and gave me a hug.

"Oh, Bayla. I'm so glad you're okay. I know we just met, but I feel like I've known you forever." My heart pulled at her words and the sight of tears unfallen in her eyes. Hannah was so kind and sweet. I could see why she and Gray got along so well. I hugged her back.

"Me too." I smiled, and she gave one in return, wiping the unshed tears away. "We'll catch up tomorrow if you want. I think I need a day of relaxation."

"I'm off, so maybe we can go to the quarry and hang out."

"Ok." I glanced back towards Declan one last time, and he was gone. I scanned the café, but he was nowhere to be seen. Mr. Whitstock gave a wave, and Hadraniel and I headed off to the cottage.

On the walk home, I filled Hadraniel in on all the things that were made clear to me throughout the day, from Gray's brother to the second demon. I kept Father Paul's secret though. I explained that Declan must have been sent so that Mephistopheles would be available to collect the souls that were lost. I explained how evil Meph could be, and how our mission was going to be harder than expected. Angels followed the rules, and I would be receiving no help, other than from Had. However, Meph could easily decide to help Declan and we would have two very strong demons to face. As I was explaining all this to him, I realized now why Hadraniel was sent with me.

"Oh my Grace! They sent you as back up. You're a Blue-In-Training. You're supposed to save Gray in case I fail. The Elder's knew! They knew I might fail, and that I might have to face two demons. Granted usually when souls are collected, there isn't much of a fight. Most souls were already destined for one place or the other. However, with Gray being special, there would be a fight. I can't win against both. We need to come up with a contingency plan, Had. You must promise me now, this instant, that if it looks like I might lose, you will take Gray and Hannah someplace safe. We must have a successful mission no matter the cost! Promise me!"

Hadraniel looked ghostly white, but he nodded.

"I need to hear you say it, please." My voice was barely a whisper.

"I promise." His wasn't much louder. After a moment's pause, he spoke again, a little louder and more confident. "I don't think it will come to that though, Bay. Honestly, I think it will all be okay."

I appreciated his confidence in me, but it only made me more nervous. Once we got inside the cottage, it took everything I had to make it up the steps to my room. I collapsed into a fitful sleep full of dreams and nightmares of what the next few weeks might hold.

CHAPTER
nine

There's no love like the first.

~Nicholas Sparks

The next morning, I was still in bed way past the time I normally woke up. I gathered up my stuff and was heading to the bathroom to shower and get ready for the day when I heard voices from downstairs. I tiptoed to the edge of the steps, knowing whoever was down there couldn't see me, but it gave me a better vantage point to hear what was being said. I could make out Hadraniel's voice but wasn't quite sure to whom he was speaking.

"I've never witnessed Bayla like this, ever. I don't know what to say or do for her. I don't know how to make it better, to ease her mind."

My heart ached at the sweetness that Hadraniel had within him. I knew it was a smart thing to make him promise last night to leave me if needed. What I couldn't say last night to Had was that it wasn't that I was afraid of Meph, as I'd faced him multiple times. It's just that we'd never had to fight over souls before. We rarely even interacted. He collected his, I collected mine, and we went on our merry ways. This was the first time since the birth of the Son that an Angel and a demon would have to battle over the soul of a human who, for whatever unknown reason, was so special. I could fight Declan, if it were just him. I have the training. I could even fight Meph if I must. I wasn't afraid of the fighting..., but I was scared of what could happen if I didn't win, not just for myself, but for both Gray and Hadraniel.

"Just let her rest the next few days, don't do any researching. Just have some fun. She seems like someone who needs to learn how to relax. There's still a few days before Gray's parents' cookout when she'll need a more definite plan. Until then, don't let her near the bookstore."

That was clearly Declan's voice. If I hadn't heard such sincerity in his voice, I would've sworn he was just trying to trick Hadraniel out of learning more about the quake. Declan was full of surprises. Even if the other side's plan all along was to fool me by sending a newbie. I would have thought they would have sent someone more formidable. Someone that would throw me off my game, but not like this. Someone who could be stone cold and scary one minute, and offering a Blue-In-Training advice how to protect his angel the next?

"Yeah. I know she's supposed to meet Hannah later today to spend the day at the quarry, I believe. If she's not up soon, I may have to wake her."

"Good luck with that." Declan chuckled.

"No kidding. I don't know how she would react. She's always the first one up."

With that, I decided to sneak back to my room and very loudly close the door to signal I was up and getting ready. I walked to the bathroom to turn on the shower water. I loved the water as hot as I could tolerate it. I got in and just stood there for what seemed like an eternity. I let the water fall down over me as I prayed. I asked for guidance, strength, and a level head for when the time came. I knew a day with Hannah would be a nice break, but it would still be work. I would still be gathering good information about her and about Gray. I knew I needed to be finishing up soon and getting dressed to go meet her, but the heat felt good on my body. Since yesterday, I had felt chilled to the bone. I gave myself five more minutes before I finished showering.

I decided that for a day at the quarry, my hair didn't need to look cute. I pulled it into a curly, messy bun on top of my head, put on a black two-piece suit with a black sundress over it and headed down to grab a quick bite to eat before leaving for town. Shockingly, Declan was still there, and he was alone in the kitchen. The sight of him relaxing at my table took me aback, and I stopped in my tracks. He gave a lazy grin and nodded before speaking.

"Well Bay, I must say, you look H-O-T hot in black."

I harrumphed in his general direction, mainly because I didn't know how to respond. My lack of response changed his lazy grin into a face-splitting smile. He was beaming at being able to make me speechless. I had to remind myself he was a demon, and he was made to know how to charm people both with personality and looks.

"Where's Haddy?"

Declan stood up and made his way towards me. He kept his eyes on mine the whole time. I felt like I couldn't look away, and it was so intimidating that I needed to take a step back as he approached, causing his to smirk.

"He went out back to grab his gear. We're going to hike to one of the places on the map Mr. Whitstock told us about." My eyes must have widened, because before I could question that decision, he spoke. "Don't worry Bay, I'm not going to hurt your precious Haddy. It's an honest trip. I need to know as much about the layout as you all. After all, I have a bet to win." With that, he winked at me, smacked my butt and headed out back to meet with Hadraniel.

I growled and stamped my foot at him with disgust. "Don't ever do that again. Do you understand me? It will not bode well for you." To which he threw his head back and gave a haughty laugh as the door behind him closed. I was still fuming as I gathered my toast and bags to head to town. I could not believe the nerve of him to touch me, and in such a familiar manner at that!

I must have been angrier than I realized because I made it to town in no time. I was sitting at one of the tables that were outside the café waiting for Hannah. The day was beautiful and hot. It was the perfect day to spend at the quarry with just Hannah. We could lay out, relax and talk. I had never had a connection with other girls, Angel or human. There was something about Hannah that made friendship easy.

"Hey! Want to grab a smoothie before heading to the quarry?"

I turned to see Hannah who had brought Alissa and some other girl I hadn't met yet. I wanted to roll my eyes but smiled instead. I was hoping to get one on one time with her so that I could get one up on Declan, but it appeared it would be no such luck. There was a quick introduction between myself and the new girl, Sadie. She apparently was newer to town too, having just moved here a little over a year ago.

When we walked inside the café, Gray had four banana strawberry smoothies already made. I assumed Hannah must have texted him on her way in, or there was more to him than I knew.

"Psychic mind reader?" I pointed to the smoothies.

"Oh, yes. The great and powerful phone knows all things." he said with a laugh.

I smiled and took the cup he was handing me.

"You girls don't have too much fun today." Gray said to none of us in particular while he handed his jeep keys to Hannah. She gave him a quick peck on the cheek.

Inside the jeep, Hannah insisted I sit up front with her, leading to slight protests from Alissa. Hannah gave her a look that told her it wasn't up for discussing, and she shrugged and climbed in back with Sadie. Gray had taken off the top of the jeep, so the wind was enough distraction that I hoped I could talk to Hannah some before we got there.

"You look better today, Bayla. You really gave us quite a scare yesterday. Declan caught you and carried you to the stage before the rest of us even knew what was happening."

"You mean Had. He caught me and told me he had me." I distinctly remember Hadraniel coming behind me before I passed out.

"No, that was Declan. Had made a move to stand beside you, but Declan caught you. He was whispering something to you as he carried you. You should have seen the look on his face when you passed out. It was like his whole world collapsed. Had pushed him out of the way once you were on the stage which is why he was huffy afterwards I suppose. There was too much commotion after that for me to go check on him. Have you seen him today yet?"

I couldn't quite process what I was hearing. Declan carried me. Declan whispered that he had me. He was mad at Hadraniel for taking over. I must have been thinking about it a little too long because I heard her ask me again if I had seen him yet today.

"Yes, sorry. I just guess I'm still a little off today. I think I just got too hot yesterday with the studying and going with Gray to see the valley." With the word valley, Hannah slammed on the brakes and turned her entire body towards me. Luckily there was no one else on the little side road we were on.

"He what?" She didn't look angry, just shocked, and maybe a little hurt.

"He found me outside of the bookstore and asked if I wanted to join him on a hike. He took me to the top of the hill, told me about his brother and showed me the valley."

"He talked about Oliver?" The tone of her voice had increased almost to a squeal. "He hasn't talked about Oliver since his death!"

"You're not mad are you?" I didn't know if I was supposed to have told her or not.

"No! I'm a little sad he didn't talk to me about Oliver. I miss him a lot too, but it's good for him to talk about him. It was hard on Gray when he died, but it helped him straighten up too. He was on a rough path before all that happened. He was supposed to be staying with Oliver that night he got sick but left him alone for a little bit to practice with a different band he was in. Oliver had stayed alone before, so Gray didn't really think much about it. When he came back, Oliver was sick, and had a fever. Gray called his parents, and they took him to the hospital. He never came home. Gray took it hard. He holed up in his room for a long time. His parents had to threaten him to get him dressed and to the funeral. The whole town showed up. It was months before Gray was somewhat himself again. That's when he decided he was going to be an art teacher. He had seen how his drawing really brought out Oliver's personality, and he wants to be able to help other children in the same way."

There was so much love in the way Hannah spoke about Gray. I didn't know that feeling, but the way she expressed it, made me jealous, made me want to know how it felt to love someone that much. I audibly sighed, making the girls in the back giggle.

"That's how I feel about Gray, too." Hannah giggled.

All these things made Gray special and kind, but still not so astounding that I could figure out why he was more special than other humans that had been kind and caring. Tired of racking my brain as to why I was supposed to save him, I decided to give it a rest. The Elders knew what they were doing, and I had a mission. It didn't matter why he needed to be saved, just that he did. The beach was crowded when we parked the jeep. We decided not to unpack our stuff, but just lather on the sunscreen and head to the floating platform to lay out as there wasn't anyone out there. The swim was nice and refreshing, but I was ready to lay in the sun and sleep by the time we got out there. I could hear Alissa and Sadie discussing how hot Had and Declan were, plotting about how they could try to get dates with them.

"Had actually is talking with someone." I said in a sleepy haze. All this time with these human girls, made me realize that once I was home I needed to give Aniston a chance. Maybe she wasn't so bad to have as a roommate.

"What about Declan?" Alissa asked.

"Declan.is Declan. Who knows what he's doing." I had a twinge of jealousy at the thought of Declan with Alissa. Then I reminded myself that was his false advertisement, and he was using his strengths to play with my mind. If Alissa wanted to date a demon, more power to her. I was here on a mission, and to learn to enjoy myself some, and that's what I was going to do. I stretched and rolled over to tan my back. I glanced over at Hannah and noticed she was smirking at me.

"What's with the face?" I asked grinning. I couldn't help it. She was so bubbly it flowed over to anyone around her.

"You like Declan."

"I do not. I tolerate him."

"Nuh-uh sister, you like him. A lot! Your body language when he's around, your snarky responses to Alissa, the way your eyes widen when I talk to you about him give it away. I think it's fair to say you may even love him."

The absurdity that I could love him without knowing what love really was made me cough out loud and laugh. I had to explain I wasn't laughing at her before I hurt her feelings.

"I have never even had a boyfriend before! Remember we've lived missionary lives, so I highly doubt I could love him. I don't even know what love is."

She smiled. She looked to be plotting something that would not be good for me in the end.

"You don't have to know love to feel it, Bayla. You just wait. You'll see. It's love, and I would bet my next paycheck that he loves you too."

"Save your money, Hannah, for something more worthy." I slipped off the platform, and went for a swim so I could avoid having the rest of that conversation. I didn't want to think about Declan loving me. It wasn't a possibility. Like, ever. Maybe if we were just humans I could see being with Declan. His stormy eyes made him more interesting than any of the angels I knew, and he was definitely steaming hot. I took a deep breath and went under. Maybe the lack of air would reset my brain and my heart. I swam for a quite a distance underwater before coming back up. Hannah was waving at me to head back to the platform.

"You were under for so long, I got worried." She reached her hand down to help pull me up on the platform.

"Sorry." I forgot that sometimes I had to decrease my physical abilities some to not bring attention to myself for the wrong reason.

"We were talking about heading back into to town to get lunch, are you ready to go?"

"Lunch sounds great. Let's go."

Back the café, we were just about to eat our hamburgers when Declan and Hadraniel entered. They were dusty and dirty. I was pretty sure the older lady who was our waitress almost dropped the dishes she had just cleared from the table next to us from the sight of them. It was entertaining to watch others react to their looks so much. Even I had to admit that the dust and dirt looked good on them. Alissa straightened her hair and waved for them to join us at our table. Both boys grabbed a chair before sitting down, Declan between Alissa and me, and Hadraniel safely beside Hannah.

"How was your afternoon, boys?" Alissa almost sung her question.

"It was most educational," Hadraniel said in a seemingly bored tone.

"That doesn't sound fun." Sadie pouted towards Had.

I rolled my eyes causing Hannah to giggle.

"It would have been more fun if the walking encyclopedia over there had shut up even for a minute." Hadraniel pointed towards Declan, who simply shrugged, unconcerned with the jest.

"I know what I know."

Another eye roll from me garnered yet another giggle from Hannah. This one was not unnoticed by Declan.

"Something funny?" He arched his eyebrow.

"Bayla. She's a funny, funny girl who doesn't know how to control her face."

I made a silly face at her and then stuck my tongue out.

"Anyways, Gray and I were talking about a group date," she said, glancing at me before continuing. "Would you all want to team up and go with us?"

"Declan, you can be my date." Alissa was literally bouncing at the chance to have a date with Declan.

"Cool." He was nonchalant, but she didn't seemed fazed.

"Had, you can accompany Sadie. It can be on a friendly manner. Bay told us you were dating someone. I wouldn't want to step on toes."

"What about poor Bay over there? Is she to be left out, or go solo?" Declan asked with a smirk. He was lucky my eyes couldn't do more than glare.

"Actually, Gray has a friend in the band that could accompany Bayla on the outing." She looked very pleased with herself when Declan grunted at her answer.

"Sounds fun to me, I guess. What's the plan?" I asked.

"They're playing a movie on a portable screen downtown on Saturday." Gray stepped up and wrapped his arms around Hannah's neck and rested his head on hers. Again, the texting was something for me to get used to.

"Friday, cookout at your parents, and Saturday, a movie on the square. Right?" I was making sure to reiterate the dates, so that I kept us on a working timeline to get us safely out of town at the right time.

"Yes ma'am."

The rest of the day was spent hanging out with the group, checking out shops together and just enjoying each other's company. Having friends my age was nice. It was different to pretend to be a human teenager, and I could see what Hadraniel was talking about when he said I needed to have a little fun. I was enjoying myself and really letting go. It was late in the evening when we made it back to our cottage, tired but fulfilled.

CHAPTER
ten

Breath is Spirit. The act of breathing is Living.
~Author Unknown

The next morning was Thursday, and I decided we should just hang out around the house most of the day. I explained to Hadraniel that I needed a break to clear my head. He agreed, but thought maybe we should invite the group over to hang out in order to not lose all contact with them, as well as creating an opportunity to learn more about them. I finally agreed. We made the phones calls and decided to order several pizzas. The guy on the other line said he could deliver to us even though he acted like he never even knew a house existed where we were staying.

"So what's on your agenda until they get here later? Are you planning on staying in that chair all day?" Had dropped down on the couch across from me. He seemed to be following my lead for bumming it for the day.

"This is it. I'm going to lie right here and be a lazy human teenage girl until it's time to get dressed." I snickered. The thought of me being lazy, human, or even a teenager was ludicrous. I had never done anything that fit those categories.

"Sounds like a good plan. Do you know any games to play tonight?"

I glanced over to see he had laid down on his back on the couch, staring at the ceiling mimicking me. I wasn't sure if I should admit that I had never played games before or not. I knew we should have something to do when they arrived, but I didn't know what.

"I don't know any games, Haddy…like at all." I slid my eyes back towards him to see him shaking his head and grinning.

"I'm not surprised you're so good at your job. Have you never done anything just for fun or even misbehaved just a bit, ever? I'm not really sure if they have the same kind of games here. Why don't I use the internet and see what some normal games for Earth teenagers to play are?" He pulled the laptop onto his chest and propped himself up some so that he could see what he was typing. Had was adapting well to being a human, quicker than I would have expected.

"Truth or Dare."

"What is that?"

"Apparently, you take turns asking each other to choose either truth or dare. If the person chooses truth they have to answer whatever question they are asked truthfully. If they choose dare, you have to dare them to do something."

"Sounds kind of fun, but we would have to make sure our 'truths' were believable. I'm up for whatever though. Apparently, I'm in need of some fun." I arched my eyebrow at him.

"I figured you heard us talking. The door slam was weird. You never make noise when you move." I made a face at him. "I'm a Blue, remember? We are trained to observe." He winked.

"Thanks for not ratting me out, then. You spent all day with Declan yesterday. What's your take on him? I know I haven't really asked you for much help with the mission. I'm not one for working with others, but you have intel now that could benefit both of us. Since you are so well trained in observation, as you say, he must have given something away."

"First of all, he is really dorky. Like really dorky," he extended the second really out for several seconds. "Second of all, I don't know any other demons, but he just doesn't seem like how we were taught demons should be. Sure, he's clever, and pretty good at making other people like him, but he just doesn't seem to be evil. I don't get it. In training, we are taught that all demons are conniving and that they use their looks to manipulate others to follow them. Declan just doesn't fit those descriptions. Most of the day, he explained the areas we were checking out and asked about you. Not about your job, or your plans, but what you like to eat or do, what makes you laugh. Those kinds of questions."

"It's still probably just his way of getting to me. Maybe he thinks if he can get me to like him, I'll give in to him easier. I am resolved though. I will be kind towards him, but I will treat him like I would have treated Meph. We have a mission to save Gray, and I, WE, will succeed in that mission."

"That's true. He could be trying a different angle, but honestly, I don't think that's it at all. I think he likes you, Bayla, which is just as dangerous. Angels and demons cannot be together. We learned about some that tried in the past. It never worked out well, specifically for the angels." He shuddered at whatever he had learned in class. The Blues are privileged to information most angels are not.

"Rest assured, Had, that I have no interested in trying to have a relationship with Declan or with anyone for that matter. Other than the Elders and Father Paul, I think you're the only angel I've ever spent this much time with outside of mandatory gatherings."

"But you live with Aniston."

"I do. I'm sure you'll find this hard to believe, but I'm not big on chipperness, or friends in general. Well, that is, I wasn't before this trip. After spending time with Hannah and the others, I think I would like to give Aniston a chance. I think I may actually like her, and will probably make her a friend."

"Is she really that bad?" Hadraniel's face fell a little.

"No, not at all actually. It's just I've always liked my alone time, Had. Honestly, it was easier before because if I didn't make connections to others, I wouldn't have feelings. I'm sure you can see why not having feelings would help. At least, that's what I used to think. I think feelings aren't so bad now."

He grinned and nodded. "I'm glad you don't think Aniston is all that bad. I may ask the Elders to see if we would make a good match. If we are, then you'll be stuck with her forever, 'cause you're already stuck with me for life, Bay."

"There are worse fates." I smirked, and he threw a pillow at me. I caught it, put it behind my head and snickered.

"Bayla." He looked at me no longer grinning. "Is your fate worse than that? Is that why you made me promise?"

"Had." I grimaced, "please don't ask me that question. We already discussed what could possibly happen and why. I don't want to think about that right now. I have every intention of saving Gray, and anyone else who may need it as well. So we need to work on making ways to ensure that, not thinking of ways to save me."

"Okay. I know we said we needed to rest some today, so I'm going to put on some music. Care if I do some earthquake and camping research while you relax?"

"As you wish, my dear Blue."

He snickered, turned on some relaxing music, and before I knew it, I had drifted into a deep sleep. My worries seeped into my dreams. I had to fight Meph in my dream. I had to fend him off while Gray was falling. I knew it was just a dream because Gray was falling upwards, but it was still stressful for me. I don't know how long I slept, or fought rather. But I woke up on the floor. Hadraniel was laughing as he was trying to check on me. Once he saw my face though, he stopped laughing.

"What's wrong, Bayla?"

"I was fighting Meph in my sleep. I must have fallen off the chair when I was falling down to Hell. The impact woke me." Fear struck my heart. It had been such a realistic dream. I needed to talk to Father Paul, alone. "I need to run to town and see Fath…...er...Mr. Whitstock before everyone gets here. I'll be back soon, okay?"

"No. You said no working today. The pizza will be here in less than an hour, and everyone else in about thirty minutes. You can't go in today. I know you want to talk to him but save it for the morning." He sounded very Blue and authoritarian. If he didn't make me mad and scare me a tad, I would have fought it. But he wasn't backing down on the eye contact, and after all, I had agreed to no work.

"Fine" I glared. "First thing in the morning though I am going. Alone. You can sleep in. I will be back long before the cookout at Gray's parents."

"Works for me." He smirked at his small victory.

I was still fuming when I decided to head up to the bathroom to shower and get ready. I hadn't changed out of my pajamas for the entirety of the day. I had no intentions of letting anyone see me looking like that other than Hadraniel. The hot water felt great. The water on my head allowed for a different kind of quiet. I used that time to pray and ask for guidance. I needed to come up with some plan for taking the fight with Meph away from where Gray and the group would be. I had faith that Hadraniel could not only save them but defeat Declan if necessary. I needed to get out to where we would be camping before anyone else to scout out the best hiding places. I knew I needed to let Father Paul know my plans tomorrow so that he could find me if something happened once I left the bookstore.

I stayed upstairs longer than I should have, but I needed the time alone. When I went back down, everyone was already there, plus a new guy I had seen in Gray's band the first night. Hannah grabbed his hand and pulled him towards me. At first he looked reluctant until he saw me. I must have been better looking than he hoped, because he broke out into a goofy grin.

"Bayla, this is Everett. He's in Gray's band. He's the one I told you about last night. Everett, this is Bayla."

Admittedly, Everett was easy on the eyes. Tall and lean, with shaggy, dark hair and light brown eyes. I put my hand out to shake his, which seemed foreign to him. He fist-bumped me instead, awkwardly, before handing me a water from the counter. I heard a snort from the corner of the room where Declan was standing. He seemed amused at the events that had just occurred. Ignoring him, I joined the group in the living room, alongside Everett.

"Pizza should be getting here soon." Haddy announced. "Ok, so I have a confession. As kids of missionaries, we didn't play many games growing up. Do you have any suggestions? We looked up some on the internet and found Truth or Dare, but that's about it."

"OMG! I haven't played Truth or Dare in forever! Let's play that!" Hannah giggled.

Looking around, the guys in the group, all had a collective look of annoyance, while the girls had silly grins. After some more coaxing from Hannah, everyone decided that we would play after we had our pizza. Just as Alissa started to explain the rules to Declan, the pizza arrived. It smelled heavenly. Hadraniel looked pretty happy with the choice as well. I knew with the number of boys that were coming two pizzas wouldn't be enough. I'd ordered four, which Hadraniel thought was ridiculous. I think he probably understood why now. I had two slices myself. There wasn't much talking going on while everyone was eating, but as soon as we were finished, Had suggested sitting around the fire outside to play games. It wasn't quite cool enough to need a fire at night, but no one really questioned the suggestion. I sat on a glider, and Everett sat down beside me. Alissa very happily sat beside Declan on the swing, while Hadraniel, Gray, Hannah, and Sadie took the remaining seats around the fire.

"So how's this work? Who goes first?" Had asked.

"I'll go first." Hannah shot me a grin. "Bayla, truth or dare?"

"Crap. Um, truth?" I shot a quick glance at Had to make sure he knew that most of our truths would indeed be untrue.

"Yes!" She high-fived Gray who was sitting next to her. "If you had to kiss one person in this group, who would you choose?" She tried to play innocent, but her mischievous eyes gave her away.

My eyes glided first to Declan, who seemed to have little more than a passing interest in my response, while Everett's cheeks were turning all different shades of red. I'm sure my face matched his. I took a drink, coughed, and delayed so long, she told me I had to answer. I glared at her, causing her to grin even more. "I guess Everett." Declan rolled his eyes, and Hannah just full-on laughed. Hadraniel seemed more than amused as well. Gray high fived Everett this time.

"Your turn now, Bayla. You get to ask someone."

"Alissa, truth or dare?" I had no idea why I chose her. I didn't even really like her.

"Dare, because I'm not afraid of a challenge."

I knew she was poking at me and my choice of truth, but I wasn't going to let her get to me.

"I dare you to go wash off all of your make-up and have a bare face the rest of the day." As much as I disliked her, Alissa was pretty. She just wore make-up all the time. I wasn't sure if it was out of vanity or insecurity. My dare must have caught her off guard.

"Okay." She didn't looked pleased, but after talking such a big game, she had to follow through.

A few minutes later, she came back out. She was prettier without the make-up in my opinion. Everyone else agreed, and even told her so which made her less self-conscious, but not any less annoying. She appeared to be gloating like she had won over me or something.

"Declan. Truth or dare?" No surprise there with her choosing him.

"Dare"

"I dare you to kiss someone in the group." She looked assured that she was going to get kissed.

"Is that the whole dare?" He looked bored.

"Yes."

He stood up, walked over to me and bent forward. My breath caught, and everyone gasped. I couldn't even look up at his eyes. I could feel his eyes upon me, patiently waiting for me to look up, but I couldn't. I could barely breathe. I had never, ever, been kissed, and here he was about to kiss me, with an audience no less. Time seemed to stop. I heard my heartbeat in my chest, I saw his knees bend, going from a bent to a squatting position directly in front of me. Hadraniel had said there were bad consequences when Angels and Demons tried to interact this way. I hope a kiss didn't fall into that category.

"Angel, look at me," he whispered so only I could hear him. He placed his index finger under my chin, lifting it up slightly, so our eyes met. "One kiss, right?" He spoke out loud, never breaking our eye contact. He leaned over, bringing his face closer to mine. My heart was close to breaking free from my rib cage. Just as I felt his breath on my lips, I closed my eyes and then… nothing happened. When I looked up, he was on his butt near the fire. Everett was standing over him.

"Calm down, dude!" Gray had a hold of one of Everett's arms.

Declan was smirking. He stood up, dusted off his pants, and stepped towards Everett, getting very close to his face. "You get that one. Next time you touch me, I don't care who's around, I will retaliate." He winked at me and turned back to sit next to Alissa, who was now pouting.

I glanced at Hannah who was wide-eyed in shock. Hadraniel looked upset. I had no control over what just happened. It was like I forgot how to do anything. He had a hold over me in that moment. I wanted him to kiss me. I had never wanted anything more than I did at that moment. I shook my head and took a drink in hopes that it would help clear my thoughts.

"Okay, seems like Truth or Dare wasn't the best idea after all. Shall we play something else?" Hannah suggested, hoping to cut some of the tension.

"I'm sorry, Bayla." Everett apologized to me. "I know that was not fair of me. I have no rights to dictate who you kiss or who kisses you, but I felt like maybe it was unwanted?" The inflection in his voice made it seem more like a question than a statement.

I simply nodded in agreement. There was no reason to answer it any other way. Even though it might have been wanted, it shouldn't have been. I wouldn't let that happen again. Everett asked if I would like to go for a walk with him. I agreed. As I stood up, I stole a peek at Declan, who was watching me intently while vaguely paying attention to Alissa. That made my heart skip again as a reminder that I had been excited that he had wanted to kiss me. My talk with Father Paul in the morning wasn't coming fast enough. I prayed that he would have some answers or guidance for me. I was quickly falling apart on this mission. The thought that the Elders may have just witnessed that made me groan.

"Are you okay?" Everett looked concerned.

"Yes. No. Sorry, just not feeling well. I think the pizza is getting to me. Would you be too upset if I went up to bed instead of walking with you?"

"If that's what you want, I understand." His shoulders fell slightly in disappointment.

"It is. I'll see you tomorrow night at Gray's parents' house though, right? And Saturday for the movies?"

"Of course, if you still want to go with me."

I smiled at him. I didn't want to lead him on, but he was nice enough, and I needed to keep up the façade. "Absolutely." I raised my fist, and he put his up to meet mine. I said goodbyes to everyone before heading to bed.

CHAPTER
eleven

Reality is merely an illusion, albeit a very persistent one.
~Albert Einstein

Another night of restless sleep had me tired but still rising early. I showered as quickly and quietly as possible so as not to wake Hadraniel. I knew the bookstore would be open today, but I was hoping that I could get there before any customers and get adequate time with Father Paul. I decided that I would stop by the café to get us bagels and coffee. Father Paul loved sweets, so I was sure as the human Mr. Whitstock he still would appreciate the goodies. The walk to town was a great way to get my thoughts gathered. I needed to make sure my conversation with Father Paul went in the way that would both garner me answers but help to calm my fears as well.

The café was almost empty when I entered. Hannah was behind the counter, and another older gentleman from town was sipping on coffee, but that was it. Hannah greeted me, and introduced me to the older man. It was her father, and he barely grunted in my direction. It was strange that someone as sweet as Hannah could come from someone who seemed less than inclined to be social.

"I need two coffees please, with milk and two sugars each, as well as two of those blueberry bagels toasted."

"Are you and Haddy having an early morning?"

"No, actually, I am headed over to the bookstore for some research and decided to bring Mr. Whitstock something for bothering him so early."

"Research? It's still summer."

"Yeah, I know. We have stuff we have to do for mom and dad before they get here in a few weeks to visit. Nothing major."

"Okay, well don't forget about the cookout at Gray's parents' house tonight."

"Of course not. Seven o'clock, right?"

"Yes ma'am." She smiled and handed me the bagels and coffees. "Try not to have too much fun at the bookstore today."

"You know me, wild and crazy Bayla." I laughed as I headed out the door.

The bookstore was on the corner across from the café, and as I was crossing the street, Gray drove by and honked. I lifted my hand in acknowledgement, but didn't stop to talk. I didn't have time. I needed to see Mr. Whistock, plus my stomach had started growling letting me know it was time to eat. The bell above the door jingled as I entered the store. Mr. Whitstock, greeted me from the back.

"I figured I would see you this morning. How are doing, Bayla?" As he was asking me, he went around behind me and flipped the "open" sign to "closed".

"Not good, Father Paul. I have never had so many things going on during a mission like this before, and I'm not sure what to do. Can we talk? I brought breakfast." I sheepishly raised the bags towards him in hopes of getting a grin or a wink or some other normal Father Paul reaction.

"If there's bagel in that bag, you're on." He responded with a chuckle.

"There's blueberry bagels and some coffee for both of us. I hope you still enjoy sweets."

"Earth sweets are my favorite kind of sweets. Let's eat first, then we will talk." He led us to the tables in the back of the store. He grabbed some napkins from somewhere in the back of the store while I took the bagels and cream cheese out of the bag.

"Mmmm. This is a good bagel. Thank you Bayla."

I just nodded, as my mouth was currently full with bagel. We ate in amicable silence. Father Paul was the one angel in Heaven I knew best. He was usually the one to give me my missions and all prep prior to leaving. His knowledge of Earth and humans had always been helpful. He'd never been to Earth with me on my other missions though. With both him and Hadraniel here with me, I was starting to wonder if Elder Michael really had the same faith in me that Father Paul had.

"Ok, Bayla. What's weighing on your mind?"

"Do you want me to just unload completely or can we review each concern separately?"

"There's more than one thing on your mind?" His eyebrows shot up in surprise. I nodded.

"Let's do each thing individually."

"Did Hadraniel get sent as backup in case I fail?"

Father Paul didn't say anything. He just met my eyes and nodded.

"Am I supposed to save both Declan and Gray?"

"Yes."

"Mephistopheles is going to be there, isn't he? I'm going to have to fight him, aren't I?"

"Bayla. I'm not really supposed to be telling you this, you know that." His eyes told me the answer even when his words didn't.

"Father Paul, I'm scared. I've never been scared before, and I have never feared that I wouldn't succeed."

"Maybe you need to decide on a different perception of what success is and plan your mission out for that ending, and not the one you were expecting." Sadness radiating from Father Paul. It was almost if he didn't expect me to survive this mission.

"I've been having dreams..., well more like nightmares. I think I know what I am going to have to do. I'm just not sure I can, or if Hadraniel will follow through. Is there something you can do to make sure Had does his part?"

"No. I can't help out in the end at all."

"Thank you, Father Paul." I walked over to where he was sitting and threw my arms around his neck. My sudden outburst in both emotion and physical contact surprised him, but he quickly rebounded and wrapped his arms around me in a big hug.

"Bayla. You are one of my favorites. You know what to do. You can succeed, but you have to figure out all angles and beat them at their own game. Now, really I cannot say anything more. You can visit if you want to drink coffee or research books, but I will not be talking about this again. Understood?" He was kind but firm.

"Yessir."

"Good girl. If I recall correctly, you have a party to get ready for, yes?"

"Yes, but I think I am going to go to the valley and scout it out before I head back to the cottage."

He walked me to the front and waved goodbye before opening the store again to the public. He'd confirmed my fears, and didn't really help settle my mind. He did however, set me on the path to prepare a way to ensure that both Gray and Declan were with Hadraniel when the quake occurred, no matter what happened to me. Scouting out the area was my first step in coming up with a plan that would lead Meph away from the camp. I was hoping that if he thought Declan only had to deal with Hadraniel that he would be willing to leave their line of sight. As far as the demons were concerned, they probably just thought he was my apprentice and not a Blue-in-Training.

The trek up to where Gray had taken me was just as taxing this time as it was then, but the descent back into the valley was nice and gradual. It was even more beautiful down here than it looked from the hillside. The creek was easily passable, but I could see where it could get rough with enough rain or a change in structure like you would see with an earthquake. There were plenty of meadows dotted randomly throughout the groupings of trees. I found one that was fairly open, with trees completely around it on three sides and the creek on the other. I took a moment to just take in the sights. It was truly amazing. I sat on a rock by the creek and watched the water rush by me. I was so focused on the song the robins were singing above me that I became entranced. I sat there forever, just taking in the world around me and allowing it to relax me. I decided that this was the place to camp. It allowed us some protection, but was calming. If we were going to have to survive a catastrophic event, we at least needed to have some rest beforehand.

Finally, grudgingly, I made myself get up. As I was making my way towards the hill I had come down, movement out of the corner of my eye caught my attention. I turned and noticed a deer about a hundred yards away from me. He watched me, trying to determine if I was a threat before turning and heading in the opposite direction. He leaped across the creek and headed towards a patch of trees. Just before entering, he turned and looked at me again, almost like he was telling me to follow him. Deciding that it wouldn't hurt, I went in the direction he was heading. Once inside the trees, I noticed that I could hear fast-moving water stronger and fuller than the creek. I continued to walk towards the noise before stumbling upon a second waterfall. It dropped off from where I was standing into a hole that looked like a cave of some sort. I dropped a rock down and counted how many seconds it took for it to hit bottom. It had to have been deep, because I never heard the stone hit, not even against water. If worse came to worst, I decided I could lead Meph here in hopes of pushing him down the hole. I made my way back to the clearing to head back, but not before making a cairn to mark the pathway. The climb up was a work-out but not as bad as coming the other way.

By the time I got to the cottage, I decided I should probably take a nap before the cookout. Had was sitting at the table with Declan. They both looked worried. Their looks of relief upon seeing me were made more comical due to the fatigue I was feeling.

"Just where have you been, Bayla?" I was halfway expecting Declan to have stamped his foot.

I giggled. "I was out. You both do realize I am grown, right? This is not my first rodeo. I have done this many, many times and never had any help."

"Yes, but you do have help now. You should have at least told me where you were going." Hadraniel looked crestfallen at my step backwards from depending upon him.

"I'm sorry. I honestly just didn't think....'

"That's the problem though isn't it? You just don't think." Declan glared with his statement.

"Excuse me. First off, you do not get to make a point to make me feel bad. You don't know me, and you are not responsible for me. Last I checked, we're on opposing sides. Secondly, Haddy, I am sorry, but I am quite capable of taking care of myself. I do apologize for worrying you, but I'm fine. I am going to shower and take a nap before we head over to Gray's." I walked way before either of them could respond.

Once upstairs on my bed, I collapsed, not even wanting to shower at the moment. I knew I needed to because I was dirty from all the climbing, but I was exhausted both mentally and physically. I laid there for a few more minutes, then hauled myself up and into the bathroom. I took the laptop with me so that I could stream some music like Hannah had shown me, and took time to enjoy the hot water and music. I walked myself through a plan to get Meph away from the group, if necessary. I thought out how to lead them to the meadow I had found without them knowing I'd scoped out the area beforehand, and also how to explain to them what was going on when the earthquake actually happened. I realized that Hadraniel and I would need to bring all things necessary for the remainder of the mission with us when we camped because the cottage would be gone. The bookstore, the town, my friends' families and homes, all would be gone. My heart began to hurt for them. I was sad that they would know such loss, and even sadder with the knowledge that they would be blaming me for not telling them so they could warn people. It was in my contract for this mission. I could not tell anyone. There were things that were supposed to happen, and I couldn't go out of my way to prevent them unless it was going to be a failure of the mission.

Downstairs, I could hear Declan and Had still moving around, but even once I laid down on the bed, I kept the music playing so that I didn't have to hear what they were saying, about me or anything else. The lyrics from the song playing at the moment was not helping my mood. The words were expressing my feelings of being lost and desperate with little hope of surviving this mission. Tears fell from my eyes without my permission and were still there when I woke up hours later. I must have overslept, because Had was knocking on my door telling me we needed to be leaving soon. I jumped up and quickly dressed. I had picked out a soft pink lace dress prior to falling asleep so I didn't need much time. I pulled my hair to the side and quickly braided it. I found some silver flip flops to throw on. Hadraniel looked nice in a heather gray v-neck and khakis with hideous sandals that the human males were wearing around town. Declan must have left some time ago while I was sleeping. I looked at Had sheepishly hoping that he wasn't still upset with me.

"Still mad?"

"No, I'm not mad Bay. I wasn't mad before, I was just upset. I thought we had gotten past the whole 'I'm Bayla, I don't need help. I'm the queen of all things mission related" mindset. He even had an eye roll with the comment.

"I am sorry. I just saw a chance to go scope out the valley before coming home, so I took it."

"Well, Mr. Whitstock called after you left saying you had seemed a little upset and to be looking for you soon. I probably wouldn't have thought anything about it if he hadn't suggested that you would be home soon. When you didn't arrive, I got nervous. Believe it or not, I care for you, Bayla. You're not just under my protection, I see you as a friend." He stopped very abruptly when he realized he just told me something he wasn't supposed to have shared.

"So, you're my protector, are you?" I narrowed my eyes at him. I was not entirely surprised as he was a Blue, but I thought it was more for the sake of the mission and Gray, and not me.

"Bayla. We need to be leaving. Let's not argue about this right now."

"I'm not arguing, I'm simply going to state that I do not need protection. I have done this for four angel years and thousands of human years, I know how to protect myself. So if you are here as my protector, there are only a few things that could mean. One of which is the most obvious...that somehow I am in danger. Tell me Haddy, am I in danger? Do you have more on the mission than you've shared with me?"

He didn't make eye contact with me. His shoulders slumped, eyebrows furrowed, and there seemed to be some sort of internal struggle going on. I was not going to let this pass, and I stood there in silence. I had learned in my own training that silence, if given time, can become awkward enough to lead others to talk. I had the patience of Job, or so Father Paul had said. He was always the one that would break the silence during our training sessions. He continued to avoid looking at me. It seemed that we had come to an impasse with him refusing to speak and me refusing to drop the subject. He cleared his throat several times.

"Hadraniel" I decided to try a different route. "Look at me Haddy, please. Don't you think if I am going to fail or need protection you should tell me? Don't I deserve a fighting chance?"

"Bayla." He pleaded with me. Just that one word let me know, that he wanted to tell me but couldn't. "Just as you have a contract for what you can and can't do or say, I have one as well. I shouldn't have even slipped up and let that out, and I can't take it back. Please. Please just drop it." Such hurt and anticipation were in his eyes.

"Fine. Let's just go get this cookout over with."

We were the last ones to show up to the cookout. Everyone was hanging out in groups spread throughout the backyard. Gray's parents' house was nice. It was a yellowish tan, with brown shutters and a brown door. They had flower beds all along the edges of the sidewalks, and underneath the windows on either side. Gray met us on the side of the house and let us in through the gate of the white picket fence. Hannah ran up and gave me a hug. She grimaced at the coldness I put off. I was still upset at Hadraniel. I needed to let it go soon. I couldn't let on that something was wrong. Gray took us around the groups introducing us as the twins with missionary parents. His parents, aunts and uncles, cousins and friends were all very friendly. They were so accepting of me and Hadraniel. Here we were, almost complete strangers, and yet they acted like they'd known us forever. My emotions were running high. Tightness was creeping into my chest.

"Come with me." I heard a whisper from behind me, and felt a hand pulling me away gently. When I turned, I saw Everett leading me to the front of the house. He sat on the top step of the porch and patted the area beside him. "You look like you needed to get away. Are you okay?"

"Yeah. You would think with having been a missionary most of my life and dealing with people, I would be better at handling crowds. Obviously, I'm not."

He grinned. "It's okay. I'm not good with a lot of people either. I could tell by your body language you needed an escape. Plus, I get to be a little selfish and have alone time with you."

"A-ha, and now the truth comes out." Holy crap, where did this flirtiness just come from?

"You caught me." His hands raised up, and a smirk lit his face. Everett seemed sweet. I know that this was supposed to be a ruse, one that Hannah concocted, but it didn't seem fair. Not only was I not interested in Everett, I couldn't be if I wanted. He was also another human I wasn't going to be able to save when the time came.

"What do you do, Everett?"

"I'm a mechanic at my dad's shop in town. It's a good job. I'm about to start taking classes at the community college too so that I can take over one day. What about you Miss Bayla? What do you do?"

"I don't really do anything right now. I have plans to go to the college here too, but that's as far as I've thought about it all." A silly grin came on my face because in all honesty that was very close to the actual truth. I hadn't thought past this mission.

"Tell me more about you."

"Well, Had and I are twins. We are nineteen, and our parents are…"

"No, I want to know about you. I know all the superficial information. What are your dreams, what's your favorite food? Your favorite color, season? Things that make you, you."

I opened my mouth and then shut it again. Angel or pretend human, I'd never been asked about myself in that manner. I wasn't even sure if I had answers for those questions.

"Ummm," I giggled. How absurd! It's not like he asked me to solve the quadratic equation. "My favorite food would have to be bacon and eggs. Favorite color, black."

"Black?"

"Yes, black. There's just something completely soothing about it. Favorite season, winter. I love seeing the ground covered completely in the snow. Snow creates a beautiful silence when it blankets the Earth."

"Your dreams?"

"I don't know." That was not a lie. I had never had a dream. I was given a mission, and in between missions, I studied for the next mission.

"What do you want to be when you grow up? It's not that hard of a question."

"I've never really thought about it. I guess I want to be happy in my choices. I want to do something that has meaning to not just me, but to others. I guess I need to look into occupations that will fulfil those requirements."

"Fair enough."

"There you guys are. We've been looking for you." Hannah's face looked pleased to have found us not only together but enjoying each other's' company alone.

"It's time to eat." Gray pulled Everett up. I stood and locked arms with Hannah as we made our way to the back to get food and socialize with the others.

The meal and company was pleasant. There was a lot of laughter and love shared in the group of people I had the privilege of being around for the evening. One by one people started leaving as the sky turned fiery orange with purples and blues dispersed throughout. Gray lit the fire in the pit we were sitting around. The remaining adults had gone inside for coffee and to allow us to have time to discuss our camping trip. By the end of the evening, we had determined who was bringing whom, what each of us needed to pack, how long we had planned on staying out, and the dates. Declan had been quiet throughout the whole night, with barely even a peep when discussing the camping dates. Alissa, too, was quiet with little acknowledgement towards Declan or myself. She did agree to go camping with the group, along with Declan, myself, Had, Everett, Sadie, Gray, Hannah, and her brother and his girlfriend. There were just embers left in the pit by the time we had worked out all the kinks for the trip. I was getting sleepy when Hadraniel suggested we head for home.

"Let me take you guys home. It's too dark to be walking." Everett jumped up.

"It's okay. We enjoy the walk, but thank you." Unexpectedly Had had turned down the offer, that I was gladly about to accept.

Everett looked defeated. "However, if you would like to pick us up tomorrow for the movie, I would greatly appreciate it." Olive branch extended.

"Sounds like a plan. See you all tomorrow."

We hugged and waved goodbye to everyone before leaving. Still, Declan sat quietly, no goodbyes, nothing. If I wasn't so tired, I might have made a big deal about it. Then again, maybe it was for the best. The less I was around him, the less his power was over me. He didn't look mad, just completely bored with the whole thing. Maybe his lackadaisical approach meant I wouldn't have much of a fight after all. This thought woke me up a little more than I had been, and I was ready for the walk home.

"Bay. We need to talk. I need for you to hear me out completely before saying anything. I've been fighting with this all night, but then something Declan said made me decide maybe I should tell you."

My eyes shot up at the mention of Declan having spoken to him. "Declan talked to you?"

Confusion muddled his face. "Yes. Why wouldn't he have?"

"He didn't say anything to me at all."

"Oh. Well. That makes his comment make a little more sense now. Declan told me that part of his mission was to separate you from us towards the end. He wanted me to know so that I could come up with a way to help you. He also reiterated that that doesn't mean he isn't going to fight for Gray, but he didn't see why he would need to hurt you in the process. Right now, I need you to agree not to leave the group while we are camping unless someone is with you. Please."

"I cannot agree to that. I cannot even tell you why I can't agree to that. I will say this. Until the time comes that I may have to take certain actions, I promise I will let you know where I will be at all times. Is that an agreeable compromise for you?"

"If that's the best you can give me, then yes. I will accept that compromise."

CHAPTER
twelve

If you know the enemy and know yourself, you need not fear the result of a hundred battles.

~Sun Tzu, The Art of War

Hannah arrived at the house super early to help me get ready for my first date. She brought bags of clothes, shoes, hair products and makeup. It was frightening that this was all needed just to get prepped for a date. Hadraniel looked just as scared as I had felt when she came in and had made himself scarce ever since. My bedroom looked like a tornado had swept through, leaving a mess of scattered debris of "girl". I tried on four outfits before Hannah found one that she thought was appropriate for our date. I was happy to find it comfortable so I wouldn't be focused on what I was wearing. Everyone knows that clothes can definitely affect your mood, especially when it is something uncomfortable. We ended up choosing a cream colored maxi dress that had navy colored anchors all over it, paired with navy colored sandals. She had braided my hair across the crown, and left the back down in loose curls. We were now on my bed facing each other as she applied makeup to my face. I had never worn makeup as it really wasn't something that had interested me before. When she finished, I looked in the mirror.

"What do you think?" She was almost bouncing on the bed awaiting my response.

"Oh my Grace! I look beautiful! Thank you!" I didn't look like me, but I did at the same time. Hannah had accentuated my eyes and lips with her application techniques, bringing out the best of those features. It was tasteful makeup, not caked on like Alissa wore hers.

"Yay! I'm glad you like it. I was a little worried that you wouldn't. I know you're not a fan of makeup. My turn now, and then we'll be ready for when Gray and Everett get here."

"What about Had?"

"Sadie was supposed to pick him up already. I had a chat with her about behaving, and she agreed. She also may have a little bit of a thing for Everett now after having seen him take on Declan." She rolled her eyes while giggling.

"I don't understand girls."

"Neither do I." She bumped against my shoulder before heading over to finish her makeup. She had chosen white shorts and a pretty yellow tank top that was billowy. Hannah was pretty without the makeup too, but she did the same thing to herself as she had done to me using just enough makeup to make her eyes and cheekbones pop. "We never had a chance to talk about the kiss."

"Almost kiss. Everett put an end to it before it started, remember?"

"Yes. I've never seen Everett react that way about anything before, not that I think he's in love with you. I just think he felt the need to protect you. We all do really. It's strange. I see you, and you look strong, but I feel this compulsive need to protect you. Does that bother you, me saying that?"

"Bother me? No. It makes me chuckle a little. I have never needed to be protected before, so it's a strange feeling. A feeling that's not all that unwanted, I can say, just different. Everett seems nice. I will try to find a way to let him know that if he has some interest in Sadie that he can be free to hang out with her this evening."

"Hoping to get a chance to see Declan again? Maybe finish what was started?" She waggled her eyebrows at me, causing me to blush. "Your face says yes." She grinned.

"I don't want to kiss Declan. He makes me feel powerless when I'm around him."

"I get it. Gray takes my breath away, and I feel giddy around him, still."

"You two are so sweet together."

"Thank you. We've really fought to get to this point. We had a lot of miscommunications in the beginning, but we made promises to each other to always put in the effort to stay together. It's worked for us, so far. I can see myself marrying him, having his babies, and just growing old together." Wherever she was in her mind right now was light years away from my messy bedroom.

I felt jealous at her hopes of a future but was happy that I knew I was going to be someone who was going to help her get to that old age. If I got to go back home, I was going to have to show Aniston all the new things I had learned. She would find it funny, me acting so girly. I knew she would be happy too, though. She was always interested in Earth and the humans. I got lost in my thoughts wondering how she was doing. I wished I could tell Aniston I missed her now, and could tell her goodbye somehow, in case I failed my mission. That I could somehow let her know that I did miss her, and would miss her if I failed. I could write her a letter, I suppose, and place it somewhere in Hadraniel's things so that he would find it. I was plotting where I could hide it when I heard honking

"Looks like they have good timing. I just finished. How do I look?" Hannah raised her arms out to the side and did a quick twirl for me.

"Marvelous."

She giggled. "Ditto"

They honked a second time.

"Let's go. Our very charming princes await." Hannah rolled her eyes. Sarcasm from her was something new. I found it completely hysterical, and I fell into a fit of giggles that took a minute to get over.

Everett had graciously gotten out of the Jeep to open my door and even had a single rose for me. Gray, on the other hand, was just chilling, waiting on us. Hannah faked being annoyed, but couldn't help but giggle when he leaned over to nuzzle her into forgiveness for not opening her door or having flowers for her. The drive into town was fun. We were getting close, and I was still struggling, trying to figure out how to broach the subject of Sadie to Everett. Gray opened the topic up, like one rips a band aid off, quick with little pain.

"Everett, dude, have you heard that Sadie is mad crushing you right now?"

Everett looked at Gray, eyes widened, then to me and back to Gray again, unsure if he was allowed to respond, or even how to respond.

"It's okay. I already know. If you have any interest in her, and the chance comes up, please take it. I appreciate you talking to me and taking me tonight, but I don't want you to feel obligated."

"I don't feel obligated at all." He furrowed his brows. "Have I made you feel like you're an obligation, Bayla?"

Realizing I must have said something wrong, I quickly tried to recover. "Not at all. You have been more than kind to me. I enjoy hanging out with you. I just didn't want you to feel stuck with me if you wanted to be with Sadie."

"Okay, because you are not an obligation. I like you, and I like hanging out with you too." He smiled timidly.

I returned the smile, turning his into a full-blown grin. I could have fun tonight. I could do this dating thing. There was nothing I could do tonight to change the fates for any of us, so I might as well let loose and have some fun.

"What's this movie about, the one showing tonight?" I asked to no one in particular.

"It's some old black and white movie. I'm not really sure. I'm more excited for the food trucks that are going to be out." Gray responded.

"Gray is always more excited about food than anything." Hannah laughed. She placed her hand on his arm, in such a nonchalant way, you could tell it was more of a habitual act than one of purpose.

"Not true, I love music more than food."

"Yeah, until you're hungry again." Everett winked at me as he joined in on the banter.

"You got me there."

The looks they shared were very deep and sincere. It was fun to watch. On all of my other missions, I never got to observe a couple so in love. It was good research for me on human emotions. Father Paul would be pleased that I was getting such knowledge when I returned. The thoughts came out before I could stop them. I wouldn't be telling Father Paul these things. He would never know how much I had grown. He was another one I needed to write a note for Had to give to when things were all over.

"Do you like funnel cakes?" Hannah had shifted in her seat to talk to me.

"I can't say that I've ever had one."

All three were gawking at me incredulously.

"This is something we have to remedy as soon as we park. It's a tragedy that you haven't had one before now. Deep fried, doughy, powdered sugary goodness. It's like a taste of heaven. You'll be sad for the chances you could have had them before, and didn't." Hannah looked to be off in some far away land, and there was such conviction in her voice it was borderline hysterical.

"Okay, Hannah. Bayla, you'll need to excuse this weirdo over here. She may or may not be a sugar fiend." Gray said between laughs.

"It's true! I'm in Sugarholics Anonymous."

"Guess you're not anonymous anymore, huh?" Everett was proving to be somewhat witty.

"It's okay. I'll have a new member after tonight." She sent a very pointed look in my direction.

"Let's hurry and park so we can go get these tiny pieces of heaven." Just as we were parking, Sadie and Had pulled in beside us. On the other side of them was Declan and Alissa. Declan's ignoring of me continued which was fine with me. I didn't need him distracting me from the fun I was planning to have.

"Bayla! You look great." Sadie sounded shocked.

"She always looks great." Declan said in passing, almost as if he was bored with the whole situation already.

"Thank you. Everett, I believe we have a mission to complete with Hannah." I wrapped my arm around his and allowed him to lead me towards the food truck that had the funnel cakes. The smell that was coming from the direction of the truck was intoxicating. Rounding the corner, I saw Mr. Whitstock in line for the funnel cakes too.

"I see someone has a sweet tooth." I winked.

"Oh, yes. I must say, these may be one of Earth's greatest inventions." Mr. Whitstock closed his eyes and took a deep breath.

"Do you want a plain one or one with a topping?" Everett asked.

"I'm not sure. Should we get one plain and one with a topping of your choice?"

"I knew we were going to be good friends!" Hannah came up from behind me. She put her hand up for a high five at my suggestion of getting two.

The four of us gathered at a picnic table with our four funnel cakes. We got a plain one, one with strawberries on top, one with chocolate on top, and what Hannah declared as her favorite, one with cinnamon sugar sprinkled on it. I tried a bite from each. They really were as good as Hannah had described. The amount of sugar I had in me was going to make for even more fun. I started to get giggly by the time I had finished my last bite.

"We need to go back to the Jeep and grab our blankets. The movie will be starting soon." Hannah was clearing the table while hustling us up and away from the table.

Hannah had brought two large flannel blankets for us to use. We spread them out directly behind where the rest of the group had picked to sit. We had a great view of the screen that had been erected just for the event. It seemed as if most of the town had come out for the evening. I noticed Gray's parents and shot them a quick wave. This atmosphere was something I had never witnessed. Everyone knew each other. Each person seemed to be enjoying the opportunity to spend this evening with their community. I was caught up in the mood when the first small tremor occurred. I barely noticed it. No one else seemed to either...except for Declan.

"Bay, did you feel that? How sure are you of the timing?"

"I am certain of the timing, you should know that. But that doesn't mean there might not be other smaller ones beforehand."

"Should we be concerned?"

I was shaking my head, about to answer, when the next tremor began. This one was not as small as the first. The screen began to shake. Declan realized at the same time as I that the screen was going to come down. We took off in full sprint towards the front to warn the people to move back. The others caught on quick and were yelling for people to move away. The quake continued for longer than it should have and moving was getting more and more difficult. We barely got the last of the people away when the screen collapsed. The jolt of it hitting the ground was barely felt with the continuous tremor. Finally after a good five minutes, the earth settled. Everyone was in an uproar. The local cops got everyone together in order to take a head count. After several failed attempts, the sheriff suggested people just take their own counts to ensure everyone in their group was safe, and if not, to report to someone from his office.

"That wasn't supposed to happen." I whispered to Hadraniel.

"I know." He was leaning towards me to continuing telling me whatever he was thinking when I saw Mr. Whitstock trying to get my attention.

"Hold that thought...I need to go check on Mr. Whitstock." I made my way through the crowd to where he was standing waiting for me.

"What was that?"

"I have been told to let you know that things have changed. You have this week to rearrange plans. The earthquake will happen this Saturday evening, seven days from today. Now, go Bayla. Go do what you do best, plan and succeed. I'm leaving tonight." He gave me a quick hug and was gone.

Hadraniel had a funny look on his face as I made my way back to him. The crowd was beginning to thin as each group reported to the Sheriff. I grabbed Hadraniel and Declan and pulled them off to the side to let them know what I had been told. I was going to have to out Father Paul to them. I just didn't know any other way around it.

"Father Paul just told me that something went wrong. We have until next Saturday night. That's when the earthquake is going to happen. We need to come up with a plan, and soon, for how to change the camping trip. Let's get back to the group. Declan, just come by tomorrow so we can talk about this more?"

"Yeah, I'll come by first thing in the morning. Someone said the church got damaged, so you won't be attending anyway."

I started to walk back to the group with Declan when Hadraniel put his hand on my shoulder.

"Has Father Paul been Mr. Whitstock this whole time?"

"Yes."

"You didn't think to share that with me?"

"He strictly forbade me. He is my commanding angel when I am on a mission. I had to obey."

"The secrets just have no end with you do they?"

His words caught me off guard. I couldn't move as I watched him stomp back towards the group. I wasn't sure what other secrets I had kept from him that made him react that way. He couldn't know about my plan to get Meph alone, and I had already apologized for the trek to the valley. With nothing to say to him, I made my way back to the group too. Hannah had calmed down and was trying to help keep Alissa calm. Everett was beside Sadie, calming her down and looking very content beside her. Declan was scanning the crowd almost as if he was expecting to find someone else there.

"Do you have your entire group here?" someone from the Sheriff's office asked as he passed me.

"Yes sir. We are all here."

"You all can leave the area then."

"Thank you." I turned towards the group. "Hey, we can go home now."

"I don't think I can go home just yet. My nerves are just a little shook up. Can we just go hang out at the cottage for a while?" Hannah's voice cracked a little.

"That's fine, but maybe you should at least let your parent's know you're okay first." Hadraniel spoke before I could.

"I spoke to mine already." Gray said, and the rest of the group murmured something along the same lines.

"Well then, let's pile into the cars and head over."

"Declan, are you coming?" Alissa looked hopeful.

"Nah, I have an early morning. You all have fun."

Everett rode over with Sadie, leaving Hadraniel in the back with me. I could feel his anger rolling off of him. I still could not even imagine what he was so mad at me about. Before I could get my emotions under control, tears started rolling down my cheeks. The stress of this mission, and now with Had mad and Father Paul gone..., it just got to be too much. The slow tears soon came faster, and before I knew it, I was sobbing. Hadraniel wrapped his arms around me and pulled me closer. He was rubbing my hair trying to calm me. Somewhere in the fog of my break down, I heard him giving Gray and Hannah some explanation of adrenaline and being scared. They seemed to understand and allowed me to have my break down while Hadraniel soothed me.

"I'm sorry." I whispered between sobs.

"It's fine, Bayla. It wasn't fair for me to get mad. There are things I can't tell you either. However, it would have been a significant asset knowing he was here and could have helped us."

"I know, but he made me promise."

"I know. Just calm down, you don't want the others to see you upset. We're almost to the cottage now."

I nodded, wiped my face, sat away from Had and took a few deep breaths. My body would still shake every few breaths, but I was calmer now. Hadraniel was really someone I had learned to rely on without even realizing it. He had been there for me since the mission started, and he was really making great strides. He would make a great Blue Angel one day. I had a feeling his graduation to full Blue would come sooner than expected once he returned with a successful mission under his belt. Everyone else was in their cars waiting for us by the time we pulled into the driveway.

"Are you okay?" There was love and concern in Hannah's voice. She had come around to my side of the car when we got out to hug me and check on me.

"I am. I think it all just got to me. Thank you." I hugged her back. "Let's go in and join everyone else." I shot her a smile that I had hoped was convincing and sincere.

CHAPTER
thirteen

Be strong and courageous! Do not fear or tremble before them, for the Lord your God is the one who is going with you. He will not fail you nor abandon you.
~Deuteronomy 31:6

With little luck sleeping, I was up early setting the table when Hadraniel came downstairs. I had a variety of fruits and bagels on the table because I wasn't in a frame of mind to cook. The coffee had just finished brewing as Declan came in through the front door. The formality of knocking seemed to be lost on him. Pouring the coffee became the most important task at hand in order to avoid staring at Declan, who was watching me. I was beginning to feel like I was some fragile little thing with the way I was being treated lately.

"Delaying this conversation any longer isn't going to make the situation go away." Declan said. He seemed to be more brooding than normal today.

"You are correct, however without food, my brain can't function." I responded in a similar tone, to which Hadraniel raised his cup of coffee up in agreeance.

"Fine. You two eat, and I'll tell you what I've come up with so far. So your Father Paul said the date has been moved up a week sooner but didn't say why? Do we focus on that as well as how to move the camping date up or just not even worry about that anymore? I figured we can say that your 'folks' were coming in that weekend instead, so we needed to move the dates. Finally, this isn't really a pressing need, but I need to make a shopping trip for camping gear, and I assume you two do too, so why not go together. I've never been camping and will need all the help I can get even if it's from you two angels."

I was still chewing a bagel and couldn't respond, but I nodded at the suggestion of shopping together. Time spent with Declan was never a bad thing, even when it was a really bad thing at the same time. He seemed to have put some thought into this situation. What was curious was that he had never said anything outright demonic. He was smooth like the demons, definitely had the great looks necessary to persuade the humans to follow him, and sure he could be moody, but he never seemed to present himself as evil, not even once. What a strange demon.

"We can't use the parent idea. I was thinking about this most of last night. If we say that they're coming in, they will want to meet them. The guys might even want them to come camping with us or put the trip off until the following weekend so Had and I could spend time with our parents. We need to come up with a plan that eliminates any option other than this Saturday. As for the reason why the timetable changed, I can't even begin to speculate. In Heaven, we have been taught not to question the big decisions. We definitely need to go shopping for gear. Maybe while we are at the store, something will come to us. Should we invite the others to come with us?"

"No, I think we need to do this alone so if we do get ideas along the way, we can discuss them freely." Hadraniel still sounded groggy.

"Do we walk?" I was never one to shy away from walking, but the thought of having to carry any gear we bought on the way back wasn't going to be as fun.

"I borrowed Alissa's car this morning." Declan said with a smirk.

He knew that that would elicit an eye roll from me. However, I was secretly praising Alissa and her inability to say no to him because now I wouldn't have to walk all day. While the boys finished eating, I ran upstairs to change. Yoga pants, a baggy sweater and flip flops seemed appropriate enough for the local sportsman store we were heading to for the gear. At home, I would never have left with my hair up in these messy buns that are popular here, but I love them now.

"Bayla, let's go!" Declan hollered up to me. Hadraniel must have changed while I was in my room as they were both waiting for me outside.

"What's the rush?"

"Just want to get there and get our stuff before noon. I have to meet Alissa for lunch and to return her car. She has to work tonight."

Groan.

The drive to the store was spent in silence. I was beginning to feel awkward towards Hadraniel after my meltdown yesterday. No wonder he felt he needed to protect me. Here I was the Soul Collector, the angel that had never failed a mission, and I was having a breakdown over a little change of events. These thoughts were consuming my mind even more than the need to create a concrete plan for getting the group to camp out this weekend. I had a surefire way in my head that I could use, but it broke all the rules. However, if the time came, there may be no choice. Had would get the success for the mission, Gray and Declan could be saved, and my breaking the rules wouldn't be of consequence. Inside, the store was bustling. We looked at a list of camping essentials that were provided on a slip of paper given to us by an associate of the store. We each took a list and divided up the items so we could make quick work gathering everything.

I was standing in an aisle that was full of lanterns, grills and fire accelerants for the grills, when I heard footsteps. I looked up to see Declan standing beside me. I froze. We had never been alone, at least not alone like this before. I wasn't sure what to do. It felt like my surroundings were suspended in time. I was watching him, watching me. My breath seemed to quicken, and while I wanted to look away, to do anything but stare at him, I couldn't. I was locked on his eyes. They were brooding and dark, but there was something else going on there too.

"Dance with me, Angel."

"What? Dance with you? Here?"

"Yes, why not here? There's music. We're alone. Dance with me." He stepped closer to me.

I inhaled sharply when he placed his hand on my hip and pulled me closer. "We're in a store, in the middle of an aisle, with things to do. Don't be ridiculous."

"I'm not being ridiculous." We were swaying to the music. "Bayla, I need to tell you some things. There will come a time when you may want or need to ask me something. I may not be able to answer it truthfully or even at all, so I want to answer you now. Since the beginning. Remember that for me, okay?" The deep emotion in his voice and pleading in his eyes made it hard for me to swallow.

"Okay." I whispered.

"What do you need to remember?"

"Since the beginning."

"That's right. You keep that with you always, okay?"

He leaned forward and placed his lips softly on mine. Everything went dark and silent. I heard nothing but the sound of our feet on the floor as we circled to the song talking about loving someone so much they felt stoned. We were alone in the universe. I had no thoughts about the consequence of this kiss, just that it was the most wonderful thing that had ever happened to me. When he pulled back, I must have pouted a little, making him chuckle.

"Haddy is on his way here, and I need to go." Just like that, I was once again alone in the middle of a camping aisle having just had the most romantic experience ever.

"Bay, did you get the items for the list yet?" Had stood there for a minute. I saw his mouth moving but didn't process a word he said. "Uh, hello? Earth to Bayla? Did you get your items yet?"

"What? Oh, no, not yet. Sorry. I must have spaced." Sheepishly, I shrugged. I gathered the items quickly and followed Hadraniel to the front to purchase our stuff.

Declan was already in line with two tents. Hadraniel had the sleeping bags and grills, while I had the lanterns, and fire accelerant. We decided we just needed the very basics.

"Did anyone come up with something?"

With that kiss and its implications still reverberating in my brain, I hadn't thought anymore about how we were going to get them to go camping this weekend. Since the kiss, I had barely thought of anything but that. I needed to get my head in the game, but I could still remember how his lips felt against mine.

"Let's tell them I have to go away that weekend. Alissa alone can make the case that we need to move the date so that I will be there."

I glared at him, but he didn't seem to notice. "That will only work if, and only if, you are planning on saying you're going to be gone for a few weekends."

"I can be gone for a few weekends if need be." His smirking lips didn't quite irritate me as much as they had.

"That can work, I suppose." Hadraniel looked between me and Declan, his expression a little leery.

"That's three issues solved, and before noon at that." Declan declared, looking somewhat proud.

"Three?" Had asked

Declan gave a full-blown grin. It made me giggle, but one look from Had shut it down quickly. I didn't need to be explaining a kiss from Declan to him anytime soon that's for sure. He would never leave me alone again if that was the case.

"Three: a place to sleep, when to sleep, and schmoozing with Alissa." I replied, failing miserably at sounding as annoyed as before.

I don't think Hadraniel believed me, but he let it slide for the time being. "Shall we head back to the cottage so Declan can make his lunch date?"

Back at the cottage, we unloaded our gear, keeping Declan's items with us. After Declan left, I had time to discuss some other things with Hadraniel without his ever-present demon ears listening in. I grabbed us some sodas and plopped down on the couch, legs criss-crossed facing him. He turned his body to face me.

"Since we won't be back here after the camping trip, we need to make sure we pack everything we will need from that point. All of our mission notes and folders need to come with us as well."

"I thought about that, too. I also think we need to go the campsite together and hide things we may need should the occasion arise."

"Like what?"

"Like food if we get stuck there a few extra days, swords to fight Declan and Meph, water, first aid kits for the humans." He slid the swords in there nonchalantly.

"Why would I need swords?"

"Not just you"

"No, you are not fighting. If it comes to that, I am fighting. You are to save Gray and Declan," I said, adamant.

"Declan? Why would I save Declan?"

"Oh my Grace!…Have you not figured it out yet? That's why we have to work with him, I don't know why, but for some reason we need to make sure he survives this too. You cannot kill Declan."

"I'm sorry Bayla, but I have strict commands to ensure that you survive no matter what. If I have to choose between you and Declan, I will choose you."

"Haddy, I'm so glad I got to meet you." There was no point in arguing with this man. He was loyal to a fault, and I appreciated it. It was going to be hard walking away from him when it came time. He would save Declan though, I knew he would. Just as I knew he would give the letters I had planned to write later today to Aniston and Father Paul when he found them.

"Should we go walk to the grocery store to get the items now or just go do some scouting? I need to have some time later to do a few things alone, but I'm good to go there now."

"Let's go then."

The walk to the valley was something I had completed several times. I was beginning to notice familiar areas on the way up where we could stow away some items. I needed to make sure that once we were in the valley, I kept Hadraniel out of sight of the cairn I had created. I didn't need him to find the hole, or take the chance of him figuring out my plans, especially after his revelation of not saving Declan over me. Because of all his training to be a Blue, Had was not out of breath like I was once we made it to the top. I sat down on a rock to take some nice deep breaths before continuing down into the valley.

"The valley was created by an earthquake thousands of years ago. According to Declan, the walking Encyclopedia, the reason it's the safest place this weekend is because this used to be a cavern in the caving system so there's no way it'll sink or split. Declan thinks there's a possibility that the hill we are standing on may collapse though. You came here scouting before. Did you find any place to set camp that would be far enough away from the hill if it did indeed go with the quake?"

"I did, actually. You just can't see it from here; we'll have to go into the valley to get there. Maybe you can decide if you agree with the spot I selected. You have a more trained eye and the information that Declan provided."

I led the way down the path towards the valley. The creek was moving a little quicker than before, making me wonder if the earthquake last night hadn't changed something with the sinkhole I had found. I needed to find a way to go check on it without Had. There hadn't been any rain lately that would cause the creek to be moving that fast which meant there had to be a change in the landscape somewhere.

"This way." We crossed the creek at a narrow area, too afraid that the quick water might knock us down. "This meadow is the perfect spot because we will have access to the creek as well as be surrounded by trees that will help block any debris from the hillside collapsing, and possibly keep them from knowing what's going on. I'm fairly sure once they realize what is happening, they'll want to head back to town to check on everyone. We need to make it as difficult as we can for them to get back. I have an inkling that Meph will be coming while we are in the valley, which may be to our advantage if he does. There would be less people to witness what is going to happen." We entered into the meadow I'd found last time just as I finished talking about witnesses.

"Looks like as good a spot as any. It's got enough space for all of us to put our tents up and still have a place for a fire. Let's spread out and mark some good places for stowing items away." Hadraniel reached into his pocket and handed me a piece of chalk, "Here, use this to mark trees or stones, or whatever."

Getting away from him was easier than I had hoped. He gave me the out I needed. I made my way towards the direction of the sinkhole, making sure to look as though I was just randomly searching the area and not heading to a known location. I marked a few places on my way that were actually convenient for both food and water. I could hear a loud rushing sound as I neared the cairn I had created two days earlier. I made my way through the trees at a quicker pace once I was sure that Had couldn't see me. The sinkhole had increased, as I had suspected. It was a good ten feet wider at the opening than it had been previously. I was beginning to doubt the safety of the valley. If there was this sinkhole here then what's to say there weren't others that just hadn't collapsed yet. I decided to do a larger search, since maybe this was just a fluke area. I carefully walked around the opening, checking for edges that may be less than safe so that I was prepared for Saturday. I headed in the opposite direction of Had to see if there were any more sinkholes like this one.

As I exited out the other side of the trees, I suddenly stopped. I was in awe of what was in front of me. There was another waterfall coming off the hillside on the back of the valley. This one was much higher, and the meadow here was further from the town side of the valley. Forgetting about looking for any other sinkholes, I headed back towards Hadraniel. He needed to see this place. I was sure he would agree that this area was an even better camping spot than the first. Just as I passed the cairn, I saw him exit the area. There was something wrong. I ran over to him just as he was collapsing to the ground. I caught his head before it hit.

"Haddy, what is wrong?" My voice was caught in my throat.

"Something's not right, Bayla."

I pulled his hand away from his chest, and there was blood everywhere. "What happened?" Panic started to set in as I began to scan the area. I wasn't sure if we were safe.

"I don't know. I was heading in the direction you were shouting when something hit me from behind."

"I don't understand Had, I wasn't yelling for you."

"I heard you. I was coming to help."

"Who could have done this? What's happening?" Sobs began to escape.

"I don't know. We can't die, right?" Fear was in his eyes as he awaited my answer.

Looking down at him, trying to find a way to comfort him, I was lost. Before I could answer, the Elder Blue showed up with a team of other Blues. Hadraniel had lost consciousness before he saw them.

"Help him!" I yelled. I was angry that this could happen to him. This was not in the plans. Had was good. He was strong. Why would someone target him other than to get at me? How did anyone even find us, if they hadn't followed us here?

The Elder began to examine the wound. His eyebrows furrowed, and he turned towards me. "How did this happen?"

"I don't know, Elder. We were separated. He said he heard me calling out for him, but I wasn't. I was across the valley. Is he going to be okay?"

"We have to take him back with us. It doesn't look good. There are only a few things that can erase an angel. You know that. Without taking a further look, I don't know if he will be okay or not. I'm sorry, but you're now on your own with this mission. Good luck." He stood, saluted me, and with the group of Blues and Had they disappeared.

"What am I supposed to do now?" I was yelling at thin air as they were already gone. "How am I supposed to succeed now?" My voice was now no more than a whisper. I was alone.

I sat down where Had had been lying, my tears flowing freely. I couldn't fathom how I was going to succeed now. Worrying about Had, who had become such a big part of this mission, of *me*, was overwhelming. I was stuck. I couldn't move. The sadness was so powerful. I had never felt such emotion. I couldn't even worry about coming up with a story to tell the others for why there was no more Hadraniel. I had no idea what to do next. All of my plans were contingent on having Hadraniel to save Gray while I fought Meph. Even if I could get Meph away from the group, I had no one that knew what we were doing and no way of saving them. I would either have to fight Meph, and then hope I had time to save them or give up on the mission. I knew that wasn't really an option, but at this point I was hopeless. It was close to dark before I decided I should head back to the cottage. I was so glad I was able to tell Hadraniel that I was glad I met him earlier. It was only a small comfort, but it gave me something to hang on to. I don't know how long it took me to get there, or even how I got there, but when I reached the cottage, I was afraid to go in. I didn't want to see reminders of Had everywhere. How did this day go from one of the greatest to one of the worst with no explanation? I needed to know what happened to Hadraniel, but right now, I needed sleep. I walked into Had's room. I'd never been in there before, but it smelled like him. I wrapped my arms around his pillow and waited for sleep to take over.

My dreams were filled with snippets of Hadraniel and things that he had said to me since the beginning of the mission. I finally gave up trying to sleep, and spent the evening writing down everything he had said, such as making sure I survived, to see if I could make sense of them. When I tired from that, I took time to write the letters to Aniston and Father Paul. I figured I could put them in the mission files. No matter the end results, I knew the files would be returned automatically for review to make sure everything was done that could be. The letter to Aniston was easiest, the letter to Father Paul not so much. It took some time, and several rewrites to get it exactly as I wanted, with as little tear stains as possible. I wanted them both to think of me with love and not sadness.

"Hello?"

"Declan?"

"Hey, what are you doing here? Where's Haddy?"

Before I could stop the barrage of tears, I fell into Declan's arms. I was so glad there was someone I could share my tears with.

"Hey, what's this now? What's going on?" He was rocking side to side and petting my hair.

"Hadraniel is gone." Then it hit me, suddenly and hard, he was why I was home. I pushed him away. "What do you mean, what am I doing here? Did you not expect me here? Did you kill Had expecting it to be me?"

"Kill Had? Hadraniel's dead?" He faked the shocked look well.

I should have known. He was trying to one-up the playing field except he got Had instead of me. "Where were you yesterday afternoon?" I squinted at him with hard accusation.

"I had lunch with Alissa, I told you already." He grabbed my shoulders. "What do you mean Had is dead?"

"Someone shot him, or something. Elder Blue came and took him. They weren't sure if he was going to survive or be erased completely. You did this, didn't you? You followed us to the valley!" I was screaming at him at this point.

"Are you kidding me right now, Bayla? Why would I do that? Do you want to go see Alissa right now? She will tell you that I was with her."

"You could have charmed her into saying whatever you wanted her to say, you're good at that!"

He looked like I had just slapped him.

"I see. I'm sorry about Haddy. I didn't do anything to hurt him, but I'm glad I know your true feelings about me. See ya Saturday, Bayla." He closed the door behind him, never looking back at me.

I was seething, and more tears fell. He had to have been the one to do this. Who else would have known we were there? I was pacing, biting my bottom lip, when I heard a knock at the door.

"Go away Declan!"

"It's Hannah."

I ran over to open the door for her. "Sorry."

"Lover's tiff?"

"Don't arch your eyebrows at me!"

"You look like you've been crying; are you okay?"

"Yes. No. Maybe." It dawned on me that she may be able to help me. "Would you like something to drink and maybe let me lament?"

"Sure, got any coffee?"

"Of course. Let me get some brewing, come sit in the kitchen. Did you come to visit or to talk to me about something specific?"

"I was coming by to invite you out with us today. Alissa said she had told Declan we were having a girls day, and he should go hang out with Had. I guess he's already been here and left?"

I dropped my coffee mug sending it shattering everywhere. Not only was I guilt-stricken about the possibility that Declan wasn't lying, but now I had to confess that Had was no longer here. I bent down to pick up the broken pieces. Hannah came over with the broom to help get the smaller pieces.

"Had is gone."

"Gone where?" She looked confused.

My Grace. I hadn't thought that far yet. I was too busy doing everything else this morning. "Oh...uh, our parent's called, and he had to go out of town for a while. So it's just me for now."

"That sucks."

I handed her a cup of coffee and sat across from her. I was silent for a while, trying to figure out what I could say to have her listen and help without revealing too much. "Hannah..."

"Bayla, you look to be struggling with what to say, or not to say for that manner. I want you to know you can tell me anything. I promise. Whatever it is, I'm here."

"I have never had many friends before, and what I'm about to say, I'm not even allowed to say. I have no choice though at this point, so before I go on I want you to listen very carefully for what I need from you. I need you to swear, promise, shake hands on it, whatever you need to do, but you have to assure me that what I'm going to tell you stays here. You cannot tell anyone, not even Gray, and actually, especially not Gray. I will need your complete silence. IF you can't promise me that, I cannot go on any further..."

"I agree." She stated without hesitation.

"No, wait. I need to let you know what agreeing means first. You might change your mind, and I won't hold it against you if you do. There are very serious consequences for both of us if you agree and don't follow through, life-changing consequences. I'm not trying to scare you, Hannah. I just want you to know the truth before you get yourself into anything." She looked pale, but she hadn't run out screaming. She nodded that she understood. "If you agree to help me, you must understand that you have to do some things you may

TARA BENHAM

not want to do, things that might hurt more than you can ever imagine, both physically and mentally. Know this that I am asking you for help because I need it. With Had gone, some things have changed. Do you agree?"

"Yes." Her voice was shaky.

I mashed my lips into a grim smile. "Are you sure?"

"Yes. I am sure."

"I am an angel. I am on a mission from Heaven. My target is to save Gray from a massive earthquake that is going to destroy the majority of this town and almost all of its inhabitants. Had was my protector and assistant with this task. For all intents and purposes, he is gone. That's all I can tell you. You, Alissa, Sadie, Everett, Gray and Declan were invited to come camping with us as a way to ensure your safety from the event. You cannot tell anyone, in hopes of saving them. Not even your family, to save them. This event has already been predestined. You cannot change the course of events without major catastrophic consequences." I paused to let her process and to see how she was doing with the news.

"My parents are going to die?" Unshed tears welled up in her eyes.

"Yes."

"Gray is going to live?"

"He will if you will continue to help me. You and the rest of the group will too, it'll just be a little trickier without Had's help. You can't tell anyone you are helping me. Do you still agree?"

"Yes. What makes Gray so special?"

"I don't know. I'm not given all the information. I'm given a task to complete. I am only a soul collector. I am given the information I need to complete the mission and nothing more. I am not here to collect Gray's soul though. I'm here to make sure he lives. I will be collecting the souls of those lost after the earthquake."

"Okay." She began to sob.

"Hannah. I'm sorry. If this is too much, you can walk away now. I won't blame you."

"How can I walk away, Bayla? You have no one to help you, and this sounds like an important task."

"It is the most important mission I have ever been assigned. I'm breaking so many rules right now by telling you." I was kind of shocked that she was not only still sitting there but she seemed to believe me so quickly without any real proof. I was starting to get curious if maybe she wasn't all she appeared to be.

"I understand." She did at least seem scared, but I would have felt better if she was skeptical. "I want to help however I can."

She called and canceled her plans with the other two girls so we could spend the evening talking through everything and making plans. I left out the information about Declan being a demon. She didn't need to be afraid of him, plus I didn't need him knowing I had recruited help. He might not have been lying about being with Alissa, but that doesn't mean he wasn't getting help from someone else. We had decided that we would go to the meadow I'd found yesterday afternoon. We decided we could stow away food and drinks as Had and I had planned. After hours of solidifying our plans, we parted ways.

"I'll see you Friday to help prepare everything. I think I'm going to go ask the café for this week off to spend as much time with my parents as I can." She pulled me into a tight embrace. "I don't know if I was a part of the original plan to be saved, but thank you for including me, and thank you for saving my Gray. He is really more special than any of us know, I guess." She didn't let go for a few more seconds, and then she was gone. I was exhausted. It was close to bedtime already.

I went to Hadraniel's room and laid on his bed again. It made me feel safe. I decided I better snoop around and see if his files were left behind, or had been retrieved when Had was taken. I went through his closet, and drawers. This guy was entirely too organized. How did he have time to do anything else with his day? It was funny how little I knew about him really. I was closing the very last door when something caught my eye. There was a manila folder labeled

Bayla. I know that was not given to him by Father Paul for this mission, so it must have been something he was doing under his commander's direction or for himself. I pulled it out and sat on his bed.

Bayla-19 years old.
Duty: Collector of Souls
Race: Possible Angel

I closed the folder quickly before finishing. What in the Grace did "Possible Angel" even mean? I opened the folder back up to continue reading.

Mission: To save human and fallen angel from earthquake. To earn her wings as a real angel.

I was completely lost now. I was a real angel. I had wings. I hadn't stretched them since coming here, but I had them. At the thought of my wings, they expanded out behind me. I loved my wings. They were solid white without a speck of any other coloring like most had. The tips were almost iridescent they were so white. They looked delicate too, but they were strong. I don't know what this folder was, but I decided it was pointless. I didn't even bother looking through the rest of it. I left it on the bed, and went back to searching for his mission files. He had them in his desk draw, of course, because where else would you keep files. I rolled my eyes at this man and his organization.

The files were not only in the drawers, he'd put them in hanging files, and they were labeled too. Gray, Missions, Earthquake Research, Valley, Humans and How to Kill Demons. I grabbed them all and once again plopped down on his bed. It made me grin a little knowing it would annoy him that I wasn't using the desk for its purpose, and instead was using his bed. I started with the Gray file, thinking I wouldn't find much new in this one. He had taken notes on Gray's personality, his job, looks, mannerism and people important to him. I scanned each of the pages in this file and found nothing new or necessary to the mission. I looked through the Mission's file next. Again it had the same information from the original reviews we had done together. I looked through each page just in case. The earthquake research didn't really have anything I hadn't already learned from Had in it other than a map of all the towns that would be lost with the quake. Approximately half of the state of Kentucky would be gone, and under water after Saturday. Moving on through the files, I found nothing of interest, until I got the Human's file. There was information on each of them except for Sadie. He had a section with her name and age written, what she looked like, but there was no background information. It was like she didn't exist before we got here. He even made a note about how it was suspicious that there was nothing on her. Everyone seemed to know her. I knew that this was my mission tomorrow. I had to seek her out and see what all I could uncover.

CHAPTER
fourteen

Any emotion, if it is sincere, is involuntary.
~Mark Twain

The walk into town was made quicker with the knowledge I had a lot to do with only five days left to do it all. I didn't know where Sadie lived or how to get in touch with her. I knew I could probably get the information from Everett, and I remembered that he said his dad's shop was in town. I didn't know exactly where the shop was located, but I figured if I stayed on Main Street I would run across it. My heart hurt a little as I passed by the bookshop and saw the "Closed" sign. I wanted so badly to stop in and talk with Father Paul, to just see the twinkling eyes, even if only to get a sense of comfort. But then I got angry. I had never relied on anyone for missions before. They were making me feel weak. I took a deep breath, straightened my shoulders, and headed down the street in search of Everett. I barely made it another block when I heard my name. I turned to see Everett waving.

"Everett, hi! Just the person I was looking for. How are you today?"

"I'm good. What can I help you with?"

"Do you have a way for me to get in touch with Sadie? I was going to see if she wanted to go shopping with me today? Hannah is hanging out with her parents today."

"Yeah, she should be here any minute. She said she was going to bring me some breakfast." He looked down, red creeping up his neck into his cheeks.

"That's very sweet of her." I smiled.

"So, no hard feelings then?"

"None."

He smiled.

"Sadie. Hi!"

"Hi, Bayla." She looked at me oddly.

"Would you want to go to the store with me? I just need a few groceries and some clothes for camping."

"Sure."

She gave Everett the food she brought him and gave him a kiss on the cheek. She looked sideways at me to see if I reacted. I had no interest in Everett, so I didn't mind that they were dating now. He thanked her, gave me a quick wave, and turned to go back into the shop. Sadie turned back towards me, giving me a grin that I could tell was fake. I had a feeling that this day was going to be fruitful. She looked like someone who would want to brag about herself given the opportunity.

"Shall we go shop until we drop?"

"Of course. Where's Haddy today?"

"He had to go out of town. My parents needed him to do some things for them before they come to visit. So I'm here alone." Her eyes lit up. I wasn't sure if it was the prospect of me being alone, but something I had said was of interest to her.

"That's too bad. I know he was looking forward to the camping trip next Saturday."

"That's right." I snapped my fingers, pretending to have just remembered. "We need to move the camping trip to this Saturday." Her nose flared a little, but then she regained her composure. "Declan has to go out of town next weekend, and he'll be gone for a few weekends, too. You know Alissa will want him to be here for the trip." Honey was oozing from me.

"Yes, I'm sure she will want to change everything." She seemed to be spitting venom.

"Everything okay between you two?"

"Yes. Sorry. She's just obsessed with that boy, and I don't know why."

"Have you seen him? I can understand." I giggled.

She rolled her eyes.

"Looks aren't everything. That's why I liked Had." Her mentioning his name caused a physical ache inside of me. "He was kind and smart, not just handsome. Declan seems to be full of hot air."

"I won't argue with that." I managed between laughs.

The store was fairly empty. I got a basket for the essentials that Hannah and I had decided we would need to have hidden, and headed towards the food area. We figured granola bars, bottles of water, and fruits like apples would be best to have. They would keep fairly well and would have better nutritional value than the junk food we would actually bring to the camp site Friday evening. After getting the few essentials from the grocery section, we headed over so I could get some clothing items I would need for the trip. I probably didn't need most of what I was getting, but I needed a reason to be there with her.

"Are you starting college here in the fall too?"

"No, I'm going to a university in Tennessee. I actually leave in three weeks to get ready for classes to start. I plan on becoming a doctor. What do you want to do? I heard you moved here to go to college?"

"I'm not sure yet, but that was why we came here. My parents felt the programs here were the best for what we would need, if and when we started doing missionary work with them. Are you from here originally?"

"No, I moved here during my senior year. I am from Tennessee. My dad got a job here working for the parks doing seismology research." She seemed to be paying close attention to my reactions. I made sure not to let my face give anything away.

"So I guess he's been really busy here lately with all the activity that's been going on?"

"Yeah. He's been having me go out with him. It's really interesting. I think he's hoping that I will decide to follow his footsteps instead of being a doctor." She rolled her eyes, but I could tell she enjoyed hanging out with her dad.

"That sounds really interesting. Has he made any conclusions to why we've been having so many?" I tried to make it sound like casual conversation. I needed to know if she knew anything that would help me.

"He thinks we are going to have a big one soon." She got closer, like she was telling some big secret. "Actually he thinks it's going to be catastrophic. He plans on monitoring it from the valley we are going camping in. He has it happening in a month or so, which is a good thing since my momma and I will be in Tennessee by then. He thinks the whole town will be gone afterwards." Her eyes were open wide in fear, or maybe in anticipation even. I couldn't get a good read on her at all.

"That's very scary! Is he planning on warning people so they will have time to evacuate?" I knew his timing was off, and that it wouldn't matter, but as a concerned human, I needed to pretend to be frightened.

"Daddy has sent emails to the council, but they haven't responded." She shrugged slightly, as if to say it doesn't affect me so who cares.

"Well, I think I'll make sure Haddy and I are away then." I widened my eyes, and she nodded like she agreed that was a good idea. "I think I have everything I need. Are you ready?" I decided I had no need to worry about her. She was new to the area which is why there was no information on her in the file.

"I am. After this, do you want to go by the café and get coffee or something else to drink? I know it's too early for lunch, but I thought we could hang out some more. Other than Hannah and Alissa I don't have any friends."

"Coffee sounds great. Let's go pay for these items and head to the café. Maybe we'll see Gray there, and we can tell him about changing the camping trip dates."

"So, I bet Haddy is not very happy about having to miss the trip."

"He wasn't but, we knew before we came here that it wouldn't be all fun. We had things we needed to do to help out our parents."

Gray was at the coffee shop and gave us a wave as we sat at a table near the window. We could watch for Everett from where we sat, which is why Sadie chose the location. She was barely paying attention to me as I prattled on about random things to make it seem Had would just be gone for a few weeks. I wished that the Blues would send someone to at least let me know if he had survived. It was getting harder to pretend everything was ok as the day progressed. The longer I sat at this table making up random nonsense to entertain Sadie, the more anxious I became.

Gray had brought over two coffees for us without asking. "So Hannah said we were moving the camping trip to this weekend. Do you know if that works for the others yet?" he asked as we each doctored our cups appropriately.

"I'm good, and I know Everett is off work this weekend, so he should be good to go, too." Sadie chimed in.

"I haven't had a chance to ask Alissa or Declan yet."

Gray glanced up outside, and my gaze followed. "Looks like we're about to get the chance. Before they get here, can I talk to you Bayla? Alone?"

I was hesitant but had no good reason not to talk to him. "Sure." I responded as I got up to follow him over to the counter.

"Hannah told me."

My heart started pounding. "Told you what?"

"About Had having to leave, and why you need to move the dates up. She said you seemed pretty upset."

I exhaled, without realizing I had been holding my breath. "Yeah, thank you."

"If you need anything you make sure you let me or Hannah know, okay?"

"I will."

He pulled me into a big hug. When I turned around, Declan was glaring, and Alissa and Sadie seemed shocked. Gray didn't seem to have noticed or was unfazed by the looks if he did. "Listen, before you head back over, I need to let you know that I saw Declan with Alissa all day Sunday. I know you don't like her and that there may be something going on with you two."

"There's nothing going on between us, but thank you."

"The death glares he is sending us right now beg to differ." Gray chuckled, and he made his way back to the group.

"So, camping this weekend, guys?"

"Yeah that's fine with me." There was little inflection in Declan's voice.

Alissa glanced at us, then at Declan and just shrugged. I'm pretty sure she didn't have anything else better to do anyway. Plus wherever Declan was going to be, she was going to make sure to be there too. The silence between Declan and myself almost seemed palpable. I should probably apologize, but I was finding it easier not having to talk to him. Seeing him reminded me of Hadraniel and what I had lost. I needed to do something, anything to get away from him and my thoughts. I needed to get back to the valley and see if there was something I missed when Had got shot. Maybe I would find some clue as to who or why. I decided I needed to excuse myself so I could sneak away, so I feigned a yawn.

"I'm getting really tired guys. I have all this stuff I bought earlier that I need to get back to the cottage, so I think I'm going to head out."

"Let me drive you."

"No thank you, Declan. I think I'll walk."

"Oh, I insist." There was a staring contest occurring with neither of us wanting to give in to the other.

"You should let him, Bay." Gray, ever the voice of reason, spoke. "That's a lot of stuff to carry, and if you're already yawning, you'll be exhausted by the time you get home."

Declan gloated. He had won by default only, as I really couldn't argue with Gray. I had just told them I was tired, so anything I could come up with would negate my previous statement. Gray put his keys out towards Declan, but Declan just declined. He said he had his own keys. I'm sure they were for Alissa's car, but if they were, she didn't seem to mind him using them. I said goodbye to the group without acknowledging Declan. I stood outside the café waiting for him to finish saying bye to Alissa.

"Lover's tiff?"

He rolled his eyes. "No. She's not anyone to me. She was just making sure I knew she needed her car back before she went home later."

"Hmmm."

"You weren't going home were you?" It was more of a statement than a question.

"Why does it matter?"

"You were going to go the valley. It's obviously not safe for you. What is wrong with you? Do you have a death wish?" His voice increased in volume with each word.

"What do you care? If I go and something happens to me, then you have your first mission success - and not just that, but you will have defeated the undefeated Bayla."

"Are you serious? Do you think I care about some dumb mission? Whether Gray lives or dies? I couldn't care less. You are incredibly dense, Angel." He was seething.

"Can we not do this out in the open?" I stomped off towards Alissa's car. I refused to out myself to the town because this demon couldn't control his temper. I sat down in the passenger seat and waited for him. I watched as he seemed to argue with himself.

"Let's go to the valley." Declan climbed in on the driver's side, but wouldn't look at me.

I could feel my face heating up. I didn't want to feel any emotions because of Declan, and I definitely did not want to show them in front of him. "Why are you helping me, Declan? I don't understand. I lost Haddy and Father Paul. You should be elated." I swallowed, feeling the tightness in my throat.

"Bayla..." There was so much unspoken yearning and pleading in just my name. "Please, trust me. I know I am not on your side but that doesn't mean I want you to be erased, or harmed. I didn't hurt Hadraniel. He's the first guy that I could talk to honestly without fear that what I said would get back to Mephistopheles. Seriously, where is this weakness coming from? You are the Soul Collector for all of Heaven. Your name is revered as someone to be afraid of in Hell. What's so different this mission?"

Tears sat unshed on my lashes. I couldn't answer, and all I could do was look at him. I couldn't respond. He stared for a minute before pressing his lips together. His eyes lit up with understanding. He was what was different. I had been fighting that truth since the first time I saw him. His gray eyes, moody face, dark hair, his smirk, his laugh, even his stupid man bun. He made everything different. I had some weird connection to him. He made me feel both off and whole, at the same time.

"After this trip to the valley, I'm leaving. I'll come on the camping trip so it doesn't look suspicious, but I cannot be the reason you fail. If I win, I want to win because I was better than you at a hundred percent. He paused, and seemed to collect himself before he continued. "Do you know what you're even looking for up here?"

I just shook my head, still afraid that if I spoke, I would lose control of my emotions. The drive to the parking area before climbing up the hill into the valley wasn't that far, and I was out the car and heading up before he had completely stopped. I couldn't be in the car with him another second. I felt like I was suffocating. I didn't need to be reprimanded by a demon. I was angry with myself and with him. I was angry at the Elders for changing the timeline. I was angry at Hadraniel. A Blue Angel, even one in training, should be aware of his surroundings. There was no reason he should have been taken by surprise. I got up to the top in record time, barely out of breath. I stopped and waited for Declan who was huffing and puffing by the time he joined me.

"We need to get into the valley and check out the areas Hadraniel marked to stow food and drinks. Those markings will help identify the path he took. I know where he was when the Blues came, and I know where we started, but we need to find the in between places."

"Lead the way." His breath was slowly returning to normal. At a different time or place, I might have found it comical, seeing him struggle this way.

Once in the meadow, I turned in the direction I had seen Hadraniel heading as I was walking towards the sinkhole. We had walked about three hundred feet when Declan pointed out the first "X" on a tree. It had a hole at the bottom that could be used to hold water. I soon realized I should have brought the stash of supplies I bought today. It would have made for one less trip out here. . It was another hundred feet when we found another "x", this one more hastily drawn than the first.

"He seemed to draw this one with less precision." My face contorted some in confusion. Did he think he was being followed?

"Didn't you say he thought you were hollering for him? Time wise, could this have been when he first heard "you"?"

"It's possible, but I had walked a far distance away and was heading to the same spot he was when he was hit. Let's continue on this path a bit to see if we can find another X."

I headed towards the edge of the tree line and was just about to step out when I was slammed against a tree with a hand covering my mouth. I opened my eyes to see Declan pressing his body against mine, his finger to his lips. I nodded. I didn't know what was happening, but I was enjoying his body against me. I listened, trying to hear something, anything that may have triggered this sudden hiding we were doing. He peeked around the tree and was quickly scooting us to my right, keeping us as close to the tree as possible. He pointed to his eyes, then to something behind us. I made a move to turn to see what he was looking at, but he shook his head quickly. Another few seconds passed, and we scooted to the right some more. Whatever we were hiding from must have been moving more into the trees. We stayed motionless for another minute or so before he pushed away from me. He indicated to continue to be quiet. He reached for my hand and led me out of the tree line. Once out of site of the tree, he took off running. He was easy to keep up with, but he wasn't slowing down. We ran into the creek, and then behind the waterfall. Inside the falls was a cavern. It was large and well hidden. I had to lean against the wall for support while I gasped for air. I was drenched.

"What in the Grace was that? Did you see someone?"

"Meph was out there. I don't know how he didn't detect me. He was searching the ground for something." He genuinely didn't look happy.

"Mephistopheles is here? Already? If he hurt Hadraniel, I will erase him. I have the swords to do it."

"Bayla. Don't tell me where the swords are! Do you understand me?"

"Why would I ever tell you that?"

He chuckled. "Good girl. I'm not saying Meph had anything to do with Hadraniel being shot, but it would make sense. Had was strong. He knew he could be a big help to you. I swear to you that I don't know Meph's plan, but it's not that hard to guess he would want the two of us against you. I'm going to go check and see if he's gone. Stay here. If I'm not back in twenty minutes or so, head out towards the car."

"Following the commands of a demon," I mumbled under my breath. I noticed him looking at me, slightly amused with his eyebrow arched awaiting my answer. "Yes, fine. Go."

If Meph had done this to Had, then I would need to make sure I had a small sword on me at all times from now on and have the two others hidden around the valley. Also, knowing this cavern was back here might come in handy if I needed to hide the others safely. I was beginning to feel a spark of hope. My mission would be completed if I could keep Gray alive until after the quake and keep him away from Meph. With the help of Hannah, I had no doubt I could do this. Declan didn't seem like he would fight me if it came to it. I could use that knowledge to my benefit. I sat down on the floor while waiting for Declan. I used the time to draw a map of the valley in the dirt. If we could get to the meadow I had found, it would provide us protection from the hill if it were to collapse, but we would be further away from this cavern. Plus, we would be closer to where I was hoping to push Meph into the sinkhole if need be. From the papers I had found in Had's room, I knew this cliff and waterfall to be safe from the quake's aftermath.

I was just finishing plotting the two X's on the map, when the water parted. Declan was standing there drenched. I wiped the map clean and stood up. "Ready to go?"

He continued to stare at me.

"Declan?"

Before I could get another word out, he was there, inches in front of me. I was staring into his eyes. They looked stormy. "I heard you screaming, Angel"

"I wasn't screaming. I was in here in the whole time. I swear." I spread my arms to show him no harm had been done. "See?"

"I heard you though. It must have been what Hadraniel heard. I never, ever want to hear that sound again!" He pushed me against the wall and kissed me. It was hard and rough at first, but then turned deeper. It was like he was drowning, and I was his air. I was breathless when he finally stepped away.

"What the Graces was that for Declan?"

He didn't answer. He reached for my hand and hastily made towards the hillside. We didn't talk the whole way up. He kept searching the area for someone or something, but we never saw anything. We made it up the hill and back down to the car in record time. He opened my door, then made sure I was in with the door closed before he would even walk to his side. "I don't want you at the cottage alone. I'm going to drop you off at Hannah's."

"You can't. She's spending time with her family this week."

"Why?"

"Because...I told her. I needed her help."

"YOU TOLD HER WHAT?"

"Everything. Well, almost everything. I didn't tell her about you or where Haddy really was because I didn't want to stress her out more. I needed her to know so if I needed help, I would have someone."

"And you thought a teenage human girl was your best bet? You probably put her in danger. What the hell, Bayla? Did you even stop to think about the consequences for you when they find out you told her?" He smacked his hand against the steering wheel causing me to jump.

"I made a decision based on the facts that I had. I didn't tell her every single detail. I know the consequences." What I didn't say was that I doubted I would live long enough to have to deal with the consequences.

"Well, I guess I'll take you to the cottage, drop of Alissa's car to her and then walk back to stay with you."

"I can stay alone."

"No you cannot. Look at what you've already gotten yourself into. I'm coming over. End of story."

"Declan."

"Don't 'Declan' me. I'm not arguing this point. Hadraniel would agree with me, and you know it!"

"Cheap shot." I shrunk into the seat and rode in silence for the remainder of the trip to the cottage. I got out, slammed the door, went inside and locked the door. I knew locking the door wouldn't make any difference, but it made me feel better. Upstairs, I quickly hid all of Had's files in my room. I didn't need Declan snooping while I slept. Once I was sure everything was hidden well, I changed into my pajamas and went into the living room to wait for Declan. The next thing I remembered was the feeling of being carried, and someone whispering, "Sleep, Angel. You're safe."

CHAPTER *fifteen*

I always seem to have a vague feeling that he is a Satan among musicians, a fallen angel in the darkness who is perpetually seeking to fight his way back to happiness.

~Havelock Ellis

The next morning I felt lighter, freer. I had slept well. My mind was made up and my path was clear. I dressed quickly so I could get down before Declan woke up. I wasn't sure what I planned on doing today. I needed to give exploring the valley a break just in case Meph was lurking around. I pulled on yoga pants that Hannah had left, a sweater and put my hair up into my favorite messy bun. Downstairs was very quiet, so I assumed Declan was still sleeping. I crept into the kitchen and started a pot of coffee. I put two bagels into the toaster and went to find where he had passed out so that I could get him up. I searched throughout the whole first floor and didn't find him. He must have slept in Had's room. Upstairs, I quietly opened the door to peek in on him, only to find the room empty. Where in the world could he be? I was making my way downstairs when I heard someone knock on the front door.

"Declan, what are you doing out there?"

His face contorted in confusion. "You told me not to come back."

"I did not. After you used Had as a cheap shot, I didn't say anything. Besides you carried me up to my room last night."

"Someone carried you to your room?" Panic seemed to be rising in him.

"You did. You said 'Sleep, Angel. You're Safe.'" I frowned. Surely I knew his voice by now, even in my sleep.

He grabbed my hand and pulled me to the front porch. "Don't move."

He went inside like he was some cop inspecting a break in. I had just completed a full sweep while searching for him. There was no one in the house. I didn't feel unsafe. He was overreacting about the whole situation. I stood outside for a few minutes before he returned.

"I think it's safe."

"I could have told you that. I just searched the entire house looking for you. I knew no one was in the house. So if it wasn't you, who could it have been? I felt at ease. I had the best sleep I had had in ages." I led him into the kitchen to finish preparing our breakfast. "Have a seat, I was just making bagels and coffee."

"I'm not sure who it was, but I won't make the mistake of leaving you alone again. If you don't want it to be me, then I'll get Alissa or Sadie to stay with you."

I snorted at the thought of Alissa or Sadie staying here, especially if Meph showed up. He would probably laugh at the thought that either of those human teenage girls was supposed to be a threat. "No, you can stay. But I will continue to do what I want for my mission."

"That's fine with me. I have things I need to do too. What's your plan for the day?"

"I actually have nothing planned. Yet. I figured it would be better to stay away from the valley for now. Just in case Meph was prowling around there seeing if I would return. You?"

"No plans, but if I'm going to be staying with you, I need to get my stuff. You can ride with me to my place." He was talking between bites.

His hair was pulled back messily, and he seemed tired. I could study his face forever and not get bored. Even just eating he made so many different expressions. I wanted to know them all. I wondered if all demons had this power. I knew they had these looks. Mephistopheles was handsome too, but he carried himself to be powerful and scary. Certainly no one drooled over him, as they were usually too frightened and kept their distance. I had never been afraid of him, but I could see why he would be feared. He was second only to Lucifer. Some rumors have him as his son, which would make Declan his son as well. I had a hard time seeing Declan as Lucifer's son. If I made it back, the Elders and I were going to have to discuss training the angels more about the demons and fallen angels. We needed to be better prepared for the fact that some were not just out-and-out evil.

"What's going on in that mind of yours Bay?" He looked amused.

"Just thinking how all my training about fallen angels and demons had not prepared me for you."

He laughed out loud. "Fallen angels, huh? I assure you I am not one of the fallen, but I would be happy to answer any questions you may have about us demons."

I grinned. I liked playful Declan. "I'm formulating my own answers, thank you very much. Shall we head to your place?"

"That's awful forward of you, don't you think angel?"

I blushed. I didn't think of it in that manner. My embarrassment only made his laugh deepen.

"Come on, let's go. Sorry for tainting your delicate mind."

I made sure to lock all the doors this time and had already hidden most of my files the night before when I thought Declan was coming, so I was reassured that we were good to go. I turned, half expecting to see a car there. "What? No schmoozing with Alissa this morning to get her car?"

"Nah. She can be a bit too much sometimes. I decided a nice walk would be good. This place is really beautiful. I've been to a lot of places on Earth, but anywhere with trees is ranked high on my list. I love the outside. When I'm not doing my duties, I am always studying nature."

"You are nothing like I would expect." I was shaking my head but grinning.

"What does that mean?"

"Just that you are so unlike Meph. Unlike anything I have learned. You don't portray evil. According to Had, you're nerdy and full of knowledge. You just make it hard to remember that you're a demon."

"Maybe I'm not a demon." He looked at me very seriously. "Maybe I'm one of those Fallen Angels you mentioned earlier."

"I could believe that more easily if you had not outright laughed at me when I mentioned them. I know they exist, and you would seem to be more like them than a demon, but who am I to judge. You say you're not a fallen, and you're not a demon. What could you be?"

"Maybe I'm just someone in the wrong place at the wrong time? Or maybe I'm an alien." He waggled his eyebrows at me, causing me to giggle.

"Ah yes, an alien. I can see it now. The bun gives it away."

"You like my bun." His stride perked up, and his chest popped out some.

"I would argue, but you wouldn't believe me anyway."

"In all seriousness Bay, not everything is black and white, good and evil. Sometimes there's some gray in there too."

"Nice pun."

He shook his head at me in exacerbation. "I'm being serious."

"Okay. You're being serious. So are you saying that as an angel, I haven't been taught everything?"

"I'm saying, as an angel, you should know that not everything is as it seems."

This made me think about whether I was missing something. When I got back to the cottage, I needed to review both mine and Hadraniel's files as one set. Maybe I wasn't seeing something. Black and white mission was to save Gray from the earthquake...and Declan, too. What could be the gray part that I was missing? I didn't say anything the rest of the walk. I was surprised when we stopped. I looked up and saw just a tent.

"Home, sweet home."

"Oh, Declan. We had room at the cottage. Why didn't you come stay with us?"

"And miss out on camping in this glorious land? I think not. Besides, it wasn't really that bad. I showered at Alissa's. She's not as bad as you think. She's a sweet girl."

"If you say so. Where's the rest of your stuff?" He pulled a backpack out and started rolling up the tent.

"This is it. My clothes are in my backpack. I have this tent. I didn't need anything else."

"No files or notes?"

He tapped the side of his head. "It's all up here Bay."

"Let's get back to the cottage. You can stay in Haddy's room."

"I'm sorry about Hadraniel. He told me that you had a hard time in the beginning accepting him being sent with you. It seemed that you two had learned how to work together well. I can see you are hurting. Have you heard anything back yet?"

I shook my head no, and tried to swallow the lump that suddenly appeared in my throat at the mention of Had.

"That doesn't mean it's bad news. Any number of things could be happening right now that would keep them from bringing you news."

"I keep telling myself that. My fear is that he was erased, and they don't want me distracted from my mission."

"Hadraniel is strong. Only a few demons even have the power or the necessary weapons that will erase an angel. You know that."

"I do. Mephistopheles is one of those demons. He was in the valley yesterday, looking like he was on some kind of separate mission."

The conversation switched to Meph on the way back to the cottage. Declan wouldn't divulge too much, but he painted a picture that showed growing up with Mephistopheles as not being pleasant for him. Apparently Meph was mean all the time and not just when doing his duties. Not that I expected him to have had a soft side, but Declan was his brother. Surely demons had some sort of love for their kin? I had no siblings…but then again, I'm sure life in Heaven is nothing comparable to life in Hell. There was a slight breeze forming in the woods on our walk home and it brought up the smells of the earth. It was comforting. I could see why the humans loved this place. There were just so many things to experience. I wouldn't choose to live here, but visiting Earth was my personal favorite part of my job. I glanced at Declan, and he seemed to appreciate Earth too. He was taking in the sights and sounds of everything around us as we spoke. He was careful to avoid beautifully created spider-webs or stepping on visible anthills. Watching him was entrancing.

Once at the cottage, I led Declan up to Had's room. He chuckled at his obsessive neatness too. I excused myself and went to my room to start studying the files. Not long afterwards, I heard music coming from Hadraniel's room. Normally it would have irritated me or distracted me, but I was enjoying it. Declan had great taste in music. Hours of studying would be made easier with the melodic sounds creeping under my door from across the hall.

I started with our files on Gray, scanning through both what was provided to us and what we had written. Nothing stood out as different or overly important that would make it obvious as to why he was the target. It just provided the information of where he worked, his interests, Hannah and his parents. I was just about to close the file when I realized we hadn't been told about his brother. You would think that with his brother playing such as big part of his story and his path that it would have been mentioned in the files. Why would it have been left out? I created a list on a notebook I had brought with me to make notes on any discrepancies.

Possible Clues

1) No mention of Oliver

I scanned once more, before closing and moving onto the mission files themselves. I had to ensure that Gray lived through the earthquake. I had to make sure that once he was safe from the quake, all I had left to do was to collect the souls of those that would make the journey to Heaven. There was no mention of keeping Gray away from Meph or any demon for that matter. Did that mean he just had to live through the earthquake? How long did he have to survive the event for the mission to be considered a success? I added it to the list.

2) How long does Gray need to actually survive?

I moved on to the file Hadraniel had kept hidden. Before, I didn't get past the first few sentences as it had all seemed absurd to me. Now, I needed to review the whole file. Was there something in there that I didn't know about myself? Could there even be something about me that I didn't know? My wings ached at the memory. I allowed them to stretch out. Keeping them in didn't necessarily hurt, but Angels loved their wings, and mine were used to being out more often than they had been lately. Sitting crossed-legged on the bed, pencil between teeth, wings stretching, I should be relaxed, but I just couldn't get comfortable. The file again listed about me earning my wings, but there was something in there about my family. It explained that I was an only child, but it also stated that my parents were forbidden to have other children. It was no secret that the angel population was highly guarded. What was surprising was that it was listed specifically in my file. There really wasn't much else of great importance, so I added that to my list. I didn't even bother to question the earning of my wings.

3) Why was it important that I was the only child born to my parents?

By the time I had read through all the files, I had about ten items on the list that I needed to find answers to, but I just wasn't sure how. I'd thought about asking Hannah, but Declan was right. I should have never involved her in this whole mess. I was shocked at how quickly she believed me, didn't ask questions or anything. Maybe I had scared her into thinking I was so crazy she was afraid to ask any questions or doubt whether or not I was telling the truth.

"What are you shaking your head about?" I hadn't even heard his knock.

"Just at Hannah. Bless her heart."

"Nice wings."

I blushed. Demons and humans were not really supposed to see our wings. I quickly retracted them. I should have been more careful. "What can I do for you?"

"I was coming in to ask if you would like lunch. I thought about making something for us. You've been up here for about three hours now, you have to be hungry."

"Thank you. I would appreciate that. Hopefully you're better at cooking than Haddy."

"I manage." He gave me a quick grin. "I'll let you get back to whatever it is that you're doing. I'll holler up when the food is ready."

Possible Clues

1) No mention of Oliver

2) How long does Gray need to actually to survive?

3) Why was it important that I was the only child born to my parents?

4) Why was Declan sent to be saved for this mission specifically?

5) Why was saving a Fallen Angel so important now?

6) Why was there no mention of Sadie in any of the files?

7) How was I going to collect the souls in a timely manner while battling with Meph?

8) Who else would be knowledgeable of how to erase an Angel?

9) What effects would the quake have on the valley, if any?

10) Why would an event set in "history" be able to be moved up?

I had three days to come up with answers to these questions. Some I may be able to get from Declan without him knowing what I was up to, and the others would require some researching and praying. I could ask Gray more about Oliver if necessary. I was pretty sure that I wouldn't find an answer for why I was only child. I only added it since it was in the file. I didn't feel it was that pertinent to the mission as a whole. I was just reviewing the list one last time when Declan called me downstairs to eat.

There were candles on the table, soft music playing, and the lights were dimmed. It may have just been the middle of the day, but he made sure to set the mood, for certain. He had set two place settings across from each other at opposite ends of the table. He told me to have a seat while he finished making plates for the both of us. A passing thought that it might not be safe to allow him to serve my food was gone as soon as I smelled the delicious aroma of whatever was on the plates. He made an obvious show of mixing the food up when he placed things on our plates; I assumed it was his attempt to assure me that he had not tried to poison me.

"It's safe. I assure you."

I smirked. "You a mind reader?"

"No, but I could see you assessing the situation. Want to tell me what you were doing upstairs?"

"Mission research."

"Anything I can help with?"

"Maybe. I mainly just ended up with more questions than answers."

"Well let me hear some of these 'maybes', we'll see if it's something I know."

"Okay, I'll ask them all at once; you answer where you can. What effect will there be on the valley during the earthquake? How much are demons taught about fallen angels? Who would know how to erase an Angel? Are you given mission files? And if so, what do yours say about Gray's brother, Oliver?"

He took a few bites. I couldn't tell if he was trying to decide which questions to answer, or how to answer them. I joined him in eating. I could wait for the answers. He took a few more bites, this time I think it was more because it was delicious. I understood completely. I was filling myself on venison. I hadn't had deer before, but it was quickly becoming a favorite. I reached for my glass of water just as he was beginning to answer.

"I'll answer the easiest question first. Depending upon where in the valley you are, it should be completely safe. However, I came upon a sink hole when doing land navigation with Had that could be a potential hazard. As for Gray's brother, I didn't know he had one. Do you have information in your files?" He genuinely looked like he had no clue about Oliver.

"Gray was telling me about him one day last week." It wasn't an inadvertent side step from the question.

"Almost any fallen angel would know how to erase an Angel seeing as they were once Angels themselves. Depending on the level of duty of the demon, they would know too. What is the obsession with the Fallen? This is the second time you've brought them up."

"Not really an obsession so much as a theory. Is Meph a Fallen?"

Declan's laughter was loud, and he had laid his head on the table and was wiping tears from his eyes. That was my answer I suppose.

"Mephistopheles is most definitely not a Fallen. He was trained strictly to be a soul collector. As for learning about Fallen Angels, there really isn't much to learn. They were once Angels, and now they are not. On rare occasions, new ones will show up. Angels that made mistakes or chose to leave on their own accord. There are also Fallens who don't associate with us in Hell at all, and just roam Earth doing as they please. Usually they don't cause any harm, but sometimes they do. That's when we have the responsibility of taking them down. As a matter of fact, that was my duty before I was assigned this mission."

"Had you completed your prior mission before getting assigned this one?"

"Ah-ah, Bay. I cannot reveal all of my secrets, just like you are not revealing all of yours."

This was new information. I needed to add a side note to my list to see if his prior duties were why he was in need of saving. Maybe he had completed enough good deeds to allow him to be saved? From all of my research and confirmation from Father Paul, Declan had to be a Fallen. Did he either not know it, or did he refuse to admit it for whatever reason? I had never met a Fallen Angel before, but from all of our teachings, they usually are quick to brag about being one. I finished the lunch he had made us and excused myself back to my room, grabbing the laptop on my way up. I needed to complete more research. Declan didn't seem to mind that I was leaving him to fend for himself. For all I knew, he may have started doing his own research from the small bits of information he had gotten from me during lunch.

CHAPTER
sixteen

The weak fall, but the strong will remain and never go under!
~Anne Frank,

My research last night had only gotten me so far, and by the time I went to sleep, I was unable to see clearly. I needed to go to the bookstore and check out some of the books that might help as well as talk to Gray again. Maybe I could get some insight about Oliver without giving away too much. I hoped I would be able to see Hannah as well. I wanted to see how she was doing. I hadn't heard from her since the first night I told her about my mission. I know she had gone to spend time with her family, but surely she would want to know about the progress of everything. I went to the café first, but Gray was not in yet. At the bookstore, there was a new owner. He was not friendly and seemed more concerned with reading than with helping the customers. I wandered down the aisle to the Natural Science section to find any books on earthquakes that maybe we had missed the first time. Scanning up and down the shelves, all I was finding were books that we had already read through. Finally, I found a book about seismology and predicting earthquakes and decided that I would start there. I headed to the back table area when I realized the tables had been taken out.

"This is a bookstore, not a library. If you want to read a book, you need to buy it."

"Okay, then I need to buy this book." How annoying. I missed Mr. Whitstock. I headed towards the front of the store with the stocky man following behind me, breathing heavily.

"This place would have closed soon if I hadn't taken it over from that old Whitstock. For years he treated this place more like a library. He was running it into the dirt, and I'm glad he had to leave."

His words struck a chord with me. It had never occurred to me that Mr. Whitstock might have been placed in people's memories if Father Paul created him, or that Father Paul could have overtaken his body temporarily. This gave me an entirely new theory about Oliver. I really needed to find Gray or Hannah, or both. I quickly paid for the book and made my way towards the café. Just as I was about to cross the street, I heard my name. Hannah was making her way towards me in a hastened manner.

"Hey! Bayla! I'm so glad that I found you. Listen, my grandmother fell and is in the hospital in Ohio. We are heading to visit her, but I wanted to let you know I will be back for Friday. I gave you my word. I don't know if I necessarily believe everything about what you told me, but I believe in you. I didn't want you to think I was running away or had shared the secret." Before I could say another word, she hugged me and made her way back down the street to where her parents were waiting for her.

Hopefully she was telling the truth. Inside the café, Gray was tying his apron around his waist. I headed to the bar area to sit, so I wouldn't have to share a table with anyone who might show up. Plus, this would give me a bit of privacy when discussing Oliver with Gray. He put a cup of coffee in front of me and indicated he would be back after doing some waiting duties. He had taken to covering for

Hannah this week. The place was slowly filling up with the usual morning crowd, and I knew I would have limited time with him. I didn't really have anything else to do, so I decided I could wait around. Listening to the talk of the town might provide some much needed input.

Before, on other missions, when I worked alone, I spent a lot of time in open places such as cafes, market places, or whatever public gathering area was popular for the era I was in. I found that people usually wanted to talk, to me, to each other, just in general. Given time and patience, you could almost always learn something new or helpful. If my theory of memories being altered was correct, then Oliver might never have existed. If that were the case, then why would Gray be so special? I had been banking on the fact that maybe his future work with children was what was going to make him some major historical figure, but if the whole backstory wasn't real, what was the purpose?

"Did Hannah find you?"

"She did. I was sorry to hear about her grandmother."

"Yeah. She was not happy about having to leave. She had to beg her parents to be able to get back by Friday. I told her I didn't think anyone would fault her for missing the camping trip and that we would have more, but she was adamant."

"That's what she said to me, too." I shrugged. I didn't want him to think I knew too much about why she was stressed about the whole weekend. "While we are alone, I wanted to make sure with you that it was still okay to camp in Oliver's valley."

"It's fine. I think Ollie would have loved to camp down there. I've thought about bringing my sketchpad and pencils with me. Maybe I could find some inspiration over the weekend."

"I think that sounds like an excellent idea."

"I'll be back. The customers await!" He bowed and winked before making his way to a table that had just been occupied by some of the locals.

"Can I join you, Angel?"

"Mephistopheles!" I almost fell off the stool. I realized everyone had turned to stare at me after my outburst. I lowered my voice. "What are you doing here?"

"Just doing a friendly check-up on my little brother. Have you seen him lately?"

"Not since yesterday afternoon. Afraid he's going to fail this mission?"

"Not at all. I have complete faith in his talents and abilities. I can see he has already been able to win you over." He shook his head amused. "My little brother may be more evil than I have ever been, wouldn't you agree?"

"I don't know what you mean." His words stung.

"Of course you do, Angel. You just don't want to admit it. Well, good luck. I'll see you on Saturday to collect my souls."

With that he was gone, and everyone was still staring at me. Meph was beyond humanly handsome, especially to those not used to seeing a full-fledged demon. Had Declan really pulled the wool over my eyes? Was he using his charms to completely enamor me? This mission couldn't end soon enough. I was getting tired of the mental game that was being played and I didn't understand. That is probably the most Meph has ever spoken to me in the years that we have been collecting souls side by side.

"Who was that guy?"

Gray's voice startled me. He must have made his way towards me some time ago, because he was really close. "I don't have a word to define him. He's just someone with whom I have had the displeasure of meeting occasionally on various missions with my parents."

"Are you okay? You seem really shaky."

"I'm fine. I just wasn't expecting to find him here. I really need to get back to my cottage. I'll catch you later. Bye, Gray."

"Bye, Bayla. Be careful on your way home."

I waited until I was out of sight of the main street of the town before I took off running towards the cottage. The further I could get away from Meph and his words, the better I would feel. He didn't seem to be wanting to frighten me or attack me. It was almost as if he was warning me, which made it that much worse. He was in the woods that day we went searching for details about Haddy. Had he been there to meet someone? Was he looking for me? I just didn't know anymore. I was almost to the cottage when I realized that Declan was probably still there. I wasn't ready to face him yet either. I stopped, looked around my surroundings and decided to walk towards the waterfalls. I needed time to process everything. Plus, it might do me some good to read outside for a while. A different view could give me a different perspective on things.

I made my way to the waterfalls that ran through the woods. I found a nice sunny spot where I could prop up against a tree. I pulled out my book and took a seat. Between the sound of the falls and the heat from the sun, I was starting to relax. The book wasn't really that interesting of a read, and before long, I could feel my eyelids getting heavy. I closed my eyes, listening to the sounds of everything around me. I knew it wasn't safe to sleep, but I could rest. I was thinking about earthquakes, and how caves are supposedly a safe place to be. I remember how I had read about a river south of here reversing directions from an earthquake many Earth years ago, creating a lake. A lake...water! My eyes flew open. Why hadn't I thought about that before now? The mission files stated that the whole area was going to flood. The water would have to come from somewhere. I got up too quick and had to use the tree as balance until I was no longer dizzy. I left the book there, knowing I would have to come back by this spot to get home. I followed the creek upstream, trying to find its source.

It seemed to take forever before I came upon a large river. It was fast-moving and quite wide. Prior research of the state let me know it was the Green River, but I didn't remember seeing that it was so close to this area. If the river flow were to reverse direction, it could definitely flood this area if the ground collapsed. Since this area would be lower, the water would be trapped, keeping the river from returning to its original direction of flow. I needed to follow the path and see if this would also affect our valley. We did not need to be trapped down there if it were to start to flood.

As I made my way back to where I had started, I noticed something that sounded like footsteps. I stopped to listen, and they seemed to stop too. I turned to see if maybe there was some kind of animal, but I didn't see one. As I turned back around, I came face to face with menacing gray eyes. He looked angry. His eyes were blazing, nostrils flaring, and his lips were almost white, they were mashed so tightly together.

"What are you doing Bayla? Why are you out here traipsing around in the woods alone? I heard about Meph coming into town looking for me. Do you not understand the trouble you could have gotten into out here alone?" He didn't step away from me, so I backed up.

"This whole scene is getting old, Declan. It's like déjà vu every time you find me out by myself. I have done so many missions alone and have yet to get myself killed. Besides, you could win, and this whole matter would be over." I pushed past him. I needed to follow the creek to see if it led to our valley.

"You're right. I don't know why I even bother. I guess I should just leave you alone. I mean obviously you protected Hadraniel so well.'

I stopped. I was seething. How dare he even think of blaming me for what happened to Had! "Go to hell, Declan."

"Fine by me. It's where I'm from anyway, so I know it's not any worse than being stuck here with you."

"UGH!"

I was pretty sure I broke every branch on the ground on my way to the falls. I was so angry that anyone could have easily tracked me if they'd had the notion. I didn't care. He was infuriating. I tried to save Hadraniel. I couldn't. I wasn't to blame though for him getting hurt. I was nowhere near him when he was injured. Both of us had been to the valley before without incident so neither of us thought it was unsafe. I would never have intentionally let anyone hurt Hadraniel. I was fighting tears by the time I reached the second set of waterfalls that fell into our valley.

I sat at the edge watching the waterfall. The creek was back to a slower pace than it was when Had and I were here just a few days earlier. It seemed like ages ago. I knew that the cave was behind the falls now, and I knew from what I had read in the book that caves were one of the safest places to be, but would the cave be high enough if the valley started to flood? Would the group be able to get there quick enough to save themselves? I needed to be able to get them there without having to rely on Hannah. She was brave for taking on this challenge, but if things went bad, I didn't need her feeling guilty. Just as I was planning on heading back, I had a thought about rerouting the creek into the sinkhole. Surely it was a possibility that would keep the valley from flooding. But that would be a lot of work for only one full day. I just didn't see how that was a viable plan. No, I needed to get back to the cottage and research the lake that formed a century ago to see if there was something there that would be of help. Answers were coming, but so were more questions.

CHAPTER
seventeen

First say to yourself what you would be; and then do what you have to do.
~Epictetus

Back at the cottage Declan was stomping around, slamming cabinet doors and banging things on the counter as he cooked dinner. I don't know why he stayed. *He knows Meph is still out there. He's probably just worried about me, but I've told him several times that I can take care of myself.* Stupid conscience was nagging at me to remember that while what Meph had said rang true to that theory. However, Declan's actions had never been anything but helpful. I sat at the table with my laptop stealing glances as I researched the lake and the backflow of rivers. Occasionally, I would glance up at him over the top of the screen. He was cute when he was mad. His brow furrowed and his face scowled.

"You can make your own plate this time." He harrumphed as he sat at the far end of the table from me.

"Thank you." It took everything I had not to laugh at him. Here was this big, evil demon that Meph was warning me about, and he was pouting.

"What are you researching?" he asked. I thought it was telling that even though he was cranky with me, he was too curious to mind his own business.

"Rivers that flow backwards."

"Is that even possible?"

"Yes. It's happened before not far from here."

"What's the reason behind this research?"

"The river here could reverse and flow into the valley. Because I know the town floods and becomes an inland sea of sorts, I assumed that it would be because of the river. If we are in the valley and it floods, we have little hope."

"Were you at the last event?"

"I didn't have any mission for that earthquake, so I didn't know the effects. Usually I don't have humans to save. I only have to collect the souls and ensure that the event happens as history has written it."

"How does history write something that hasn't happened yet?"

"Well, on Earth it may not have happened yet, but in Heaven time moves differently. I have only technically worked this job for four years, but thousands of years have passed."

"What was your first mission?"

"I worked the destruction of Pompeii. I had to ensure that no one survived."

"Wow. Did you lose friends?"

"No, I don't usually make friends...for good reason. Well, I never made friends before this mission. Haddy changed my perspective on things. I was detached from all emotion and feelings from this job. It was the best way to keep from letting any of those feelings get in the way. I had a mission to make the event stay the course, collect the souls afterwards. Today, at the café, that's the most that I have ever spoken to Meph in all the years of doing this job. In Heaven, my roommate is this perky Delivery Angel. I always assumed we were roomed together so that we got to see both ends of human life. She brought new life and I brought them out at the end of their life. Now, I'm starting to see they were hoping she would teach me how to connect with others. I must say I preferred the other way better. Less stress, less turmoil over whether I was doing something correctly."

"Must have been a lonely existence."

"I had Father Paul." I shrugged. "I didn't feel lonely. I was content. Now, I feel sadness because I miss Hadraniel. I feel anger because people I have learned to like will lose loved ones. I feel stress because I don't know what is real anymore. I feel gladness because of new feelings. I feel too human."

"I like feeling human. I loved my job before I got assigned this task. I lived here on Earth most of the time. I loved getting to travel while seeking out rogue Fallens. I got to see birth, death and everything in between. I must say, the in-between is my favorite."

"I was able to see glimpses of the in-between, but I never focused on them. I was more focused on the death and aftermath. Don't get me wrong, I enjoyed my natural surroundings. I love the stars, the views of the different lands of Earth. That helps ease the hardness of dealing with death on a regular basis."

"Is there anything in your past that can help you with whatever it is you're fighting against with this mission? I'm on the other side, but that doesn't mean I can't give you a different way of seeing things maybe. When…"

"You mean if?"

"*When* I succeed, I want to win because I defeated the best Bayla possible, not because you gave up."

"I have a perfect record. Don't let this current moment of distress fool you. I may be having human feelings and emotions, but I refuse to let them affect my job or let me fail those I call friends." Declan had a point though, I needed to think back to each of my missions to see if there was something in them that I could pull from along with all the new research. "Can I ask you a question? "

"You can ask, doesn't mean I'll answer...or that my answer will be truthful." He held back a grin, and I knew he was no longer upset about our fight earlier in the woods.

"Have you witnessed angels or demons altering the memories of humans or overtaking someone's body?"

"A lot of rogues change the memories of people to fit their needs. I know a few demons use this strategy too. From my experience, Angels are the ones that will overtake a human's body for short periods of times like your Father Paul did. Why?"

"I was in the book store earlier today, and the new owner was talking about Mr. Whitstock. I'm curious as to how people could remember him if he was Father Paul." I hadn't learned about being able to overtake a human's body. Only certain Angels must have the knowledge and skills. It sounded like it was with good reason too, especially if there were rogue Fallens. That was also news to me. Why were we not responsible for them?

"Hey, where'd you go?" He waved his hands in front of me.

"Wondering why demons were the ones to have to handle the rogues, that's all."

"In order to be a Fallen, you have to have turned your back on Heaven and all that it means. That's what makes you one. So once that occurs, you belong to our side, and you become ours to deal with. There are many Fallen Angels that choose to live among the humans who never do anything evil. They just no longer want to be in Heaven, for a variety of reasons. The main reason is usually because they fall in love with a human. There are some that harbor anger against someone, and that's when the rogues are made. I have met a few that were more evil than any of the demons I know."

"We are taught very little about Fallen Angels. Probably because they don't want it to seem like an option, especially among our young Angels, or at least that's what I think. Who am I to question what we are taught?"

"That is why you are a good angel. You do as you're told, never questioning things. It makes you successful."

"You make that sound like a bad thing."

"It's not necessarily a bad thing. Just, do you have a mind of your own?"

"Obviously. The mistakes I've been making should tell you that I question and think for myself. For Grace's sakes, I told a human about my mission!" I dropped my head on the table, and he just chuckled.

"Touché. Has any of this helped you so far in changing your plans for the mission?"

"Nah. Haddy and I made very concrete plans with a lot of research. I think it's still the best course of action. There may be some modifications needed to ensure people are safe throughout, but the trip is still on. Unless you have a reason that you think is valid enough to make me change my mind?"

"I have nothing. Especially now that Meph has been showing up, I think that continuing the trip will let things play out the way, as you say, history has written them."

"I agree, except history has already been rewritten with the earthquake happening a week earlier than it should have."

"Hmm. If everything is already written, then why would the timeline have changed?"

"Who knows? Father Paul wasn't allowed to explain anymore before he left, so we might not ever know why it was changed or even how it was changed. I need to get back to my research so I think I'm going to take the laptop upstairs and leave you to whatever you do."

"Good luck."

In my room, I sat on my bed; files spread all around me, laptop open, and music playing. Music was beginning to be a necessity for me to focus. It helped provide me with stimuli while I was reading through what could be very mundane information at times. From my research, I had learned that the conditions here were similar to those in the eighteen hundreds that allowed the river to flow backwards. I decided that this was the least of the concerns for the moment. I needed to figure out who could possibly be a rogue Fallen that would have created Oliver. That's the only reason I could think of that my files would have no information on him. Oliver seemed to make Gray a better person though so why would a Fallen want to help save him? Was it their way of trying to redeem themselves? What purpose could there be to help? I needed to figure out who the rogue was, and if they were still around? Could it be the Fallen that I'm after and not Declan? No, I knew I had to save Declan. Father Paul had confirmed that. I pulled up research on Fallen Angels, but the information was very limited. I couldn't go ask Declan for any more information either, or he would start to get suspicious. I grabbed all of Had's files again. I needed to review those closest to Gray. With all my new theories and information, maybe something would jump out at me that could help.

The first file was Hannah, and reading through everything again didn't reveal anything new. She was kind and caring and had been a part of Gray's life for years. Not that she couldn't be a Fallen, but there was a lot of history in her files. In fact, everyone except for Sadie had a lot of history in their files. I had spoken to her and while she was strange, nothing was out right wrong. I looked up her dad online. If he was a seismologist, surely there would be research papers he had done, articles on his findings, something that would validate her story. I wasn't sure of the power of a rogue, but I didn't think that they would be able to completely fabricate a person the entire world would have known.

I was coming up with nothing. I put her name into the search bar and still no information, no social media pages, no links, nothing at all. It was as if she didn't exist. If she was a rogue, why had she stayed around for the main event? Had she created Oliver for everyone to remember? Causing a brother to die was cruel, even if it guided things to turn out well. No longer able to keep this to myself, I went searching for Declan. He would know how to handle her, and whether or not she would be something else to watch for during the earthquake.

"Declan?" He wasn't in Had's room so I headed downstairs. "Declan, where are you?"

"In the living room. Sadie is here. She stopped by to see if we've heard anything about Hannah's grandmother."

I stopped at the bottom of the stairs in order compose my thoughts. I didn't know if she was dangerous, and if so, to what extent. So I needed to not let on that I knew anything. A few more deep breaths, and I turned the corner into the living room. I chose a seat closer to Sadie than Declan. With everything else going on, I really didn't need rumors getting back that something was going on between us.

"I haven't heard anything since this morning. Hannah said her grandma had fallen and was in the hospital, but that's it. Have you heard anything more?" I was silently kicking myself for using the word fallen.

She shook her head solemnly. "No, that's all I had heard too."

"Hey, while you're here, has your dad found out anything else about the upcoming earthquake?"

Declan did well hiding his shock. I hadn't told him about Sadie, my previous theory or what her dad did. "Does your dad study earthquakes?" he asked, with curiosity and interest. He was good at this.

"He does. He's noticed some really strange readings, but he still has his predictions for a month from now. He did hear back from the council though. They asked him to do further research before they plan a mass evacuation."

"Well, if you hear more about Hannah's grandma or a mass evacuation let me know. I can tell my parents not to come out here if I need to, and can have our trips planned accordingly." I replied.

"I will. Well, you two have a good night, and I'll see y'all later."

Declan escorted her to the door. He waited around until she was gone before coming back with a look of questioning. "Her dad is a seismologist?"

"Actually, I don't think she has a dad. I think she's a rogue. I just can't figure out why. That's why I was going to ask you a few things. Like why would a Fallen seemingly try to make something better?"

"In order to redeem themselves, in order to play games with people's emotions, and simply because they can. But I don't think she's a Fallen. Besides, she's close to your age. You would know her as an Angel if she had been one right?"

"Depends. I don't know all the angels, and as for her aging, here on Earth where everything moves at a different pace, there's no way of knowing really." I stated, but I was more focused on trying to remember if I had seen her face in Heaven before.

"I read Fallen Angels can't be redeemed so that doesn't seem like a viable reason. I need something more reasonable. Give me a day to do some snooping around and see what I can find. Until then, I wouldn't act any differently towards her. If she is in fact rogue, she could be more dangerous than we know.'

"Aye-aye, sir." I saluted him in response so that he knew I had heard him.

"You can be such a weirdo!"

"Such love. And you were so angry at me before."

"Still am."

"Whatevs." I snorted at myself for using vernacular that was common among Hannah and her friends. Tomorrow was another long day of planning so I crashed with little thought of everything that had happened today.

CHAPTER
eighteen

The only true wisdom is knowing that you know nothing.
~Socrates

The next morning as I was passing the kitchen, I saw some movement outside. I stopped to watch and saw it again. It looked like Father Paul was trying to sneak closer to the cottage. I wasn't sure why he would be here, or why he would be sneaking, but I was certain it was him. I didn't want Declan to know he was out there, so I went as quietly as possible to the back door, pressed my hand against it while turning the knob and slowly pushed it open. It creaked, and I froze, hoping it wasn't as loud as it sounded. When I didn't hear any movement, I opened the door the rest of the way and snuck out. I took as much care closing it behind me as I did opening it.

"Father Paul" I whispered barely above an audible level.

"Bayla."

"Agh! Father Paul" I gave him a quick smack on his arm.

He chuckled. "I couldn't resist."

"What are you doing here? How's Hadraniel?

"I am strictly forbidden by Elder Michael to discuss Hadraniel with you. I am on a direct mission for him with a message you are to receive and respond to immediately."

"Ok…"

"You are commanded to stop all research unless it is directly related to keeping Gray and Declan safe. Elder Michael says it is not your job or mission to understand the why, just the what and how. The what, is Gray and Declan being saved from dying during the earthquake. He said the how is up to you as you are the expert. He also said to tell you that you were wrong in telling Hannah, but he would forgive you because he understood why you did it. Now, I cannot leave until you send your word with me to Elder Michael you will abandon this need for answers, and spend the remainder of your mission focusing on the mission itself." He had a way of making you feel reprimanded in a kind way.

"I promise." I sulked.

"I can say this, not everything is always as it seems my sweet Bayla. Some things are better not being known. I have faith that you will succeed in this mission just as you have in all of the others. Focus on the what and how, and you will do fine." He pulled me into a hug.

I wrapped my arms around him, sighed and then in an instant he was gone. He was just doing as he was commanded, but some word about Haddy would have helped. The not knowing was killing me. I wish he had left a clue or made a slip of the tongue, but he didn't. Father Paul was good at following strict commands. I wondered why, and then remembered I was no longer to ask the why. I suppose whatever reason they had for not telling me about Had was reason enough to not ask any further questions. On my way back into the kitchen, I took the list I had created and dropped it into the trash bin. I needed to make a new list.

"Hey, good morning. What were you doing outside?"

"Just needed some fresh air."

"You look upset. Are you okay?"

"Yes, just need to make a list of things to do between now and when we leave tomorrow. I know for sure I need to get out and hide the water and food I bought with Sadie the other day in the areas that Hadraniel and I marked in the valley."

"Make your list, and I'll go with you."

I rolled my eyes but didn't argue. I knew it would be pointless to try, and I really wasn't in the mood to deal with Meph alone today. I made a mental list of what else I needed to do before tomorrow. I knew I needed to gather all of the camping gear and pack up the remaining essentials for my mission, because once we left the cottage we wouldn't be returning. I needed to get in some training with the swords somehow. I needed to make sure they were hidden, without Declan's knowledge, in convenient areas in the valley. I needed to stretch my wings. That was not necessarily a requirement, but they were getting achy. Declan had already had the privilege of seeing them, so I didn't think anything about letting them stretch while I was seated at the kitchen table. Just as they were at full length, I heard a gasp and turned to see Hannah standing in the door of the cottage.

"Oh, Hannah. Hi…" It was awkward having a human see me in Angel form. It had never happened before, and I quickly retracted my wings. "I thought you would still be in Ohio with your family."

"I came back early. I wanted to see if I could help you with anything." She looked pale. The sight of my wings confirmed my story but would be intimidating I'm sure.

"There are a few things I could use help with, if you're sure you don't mind."

"I don't mind. You really are an Angel, aren't you?"

"Yes, I'm sorry if my wings frightened you."

"It's okay. I just didn't expect to see a full on actual Angel sitting at the table. What can I help you with today?"

I hesitated a little, knowing there were some things I couldn't ask her to help with, even if I had wanted to. It would just not be safe. "I need to get the camping gear packed and placed by the door, and my clothes and necessary items put into a bag so they're ready to just grab tomorrow. I think that's the main thing I need to do right now."

"Hannah, what brings you to the cottage?" Declan eyed me suspiciously. I'm sure he thought I was telling her more than I already had told her.

"I thought I would come see if Bay needed some help packing her gear. What are you doing here?" She arched her eyebrow and switched between looking at me and him.

"I'm staying in Had's room while he is gone. He asked me to before he left, to make sure our Bay was safe."

He ruffled my hair as he passed and went into the kitchen. Lying seemed to come second nature to him, although at this time, I was thankful for that skill. I wouldn't have had a good answer as to why he was here. He seemed as cool as a cucumber for the most part, unless it had something to do with me not doing what he thought I should. Any other time, it might be fun to goad him, but I knew the stakes were too high right now to do that.

"Do you have all your gear ready yet? It might be a good thing to do this morning before we go run those errands you were talking about earlier." I spoke loud enough for Declan to hear me from the kitchen.

"My gear is indeed ready. I can take care of the water and food for now, if you trust me." Declan responded, almost in a challenging voice in front of Hannah. I couldn't necessarily tell him no, because she would want to know why I didn't trust him.

"Unconditionally." My response must have stunned him. He cocked his head sideways, opened and closed his mouth a few times, before nodding and heading out the back door. I wasn't lying either. For some odd reason, at that moment, I did trust him. Even if he didn't hide the items in the spots Haddy or I had chosen, I believed he would put them in appropriate places. He had been to the valley as many times as I had, at least. He knew areas that were more suitable for us. I just wished I had told him to make sure to hide a few things in the cave. Most of my how, as Father Paul had put it, was depending upon that cave leading to higher ground somewhere or at least providing a decent hiding place until I was able to defeat Mephistopheles.

"Shall we head upstairs to let the fun that is packing begin?" I smiled, hoping to continue to ease her fear of me.

She nodded that she was ready. "Does he know?

"Know what?"

"That you're an Angel. I mean, you had your wings out in the open like you weren't concerned if he saw them? Wait...is he an Angel too? Is Had an Angel too?"

"Yes Declan knows I am an Angel. I shouldn't have had my wings out, but they just were aching to be stretched. I'm sorry they scared you. Declan is most definitely not an Angel, and yes, Hadraniel is...was...an Angel too."

"Can I touch your wings? They are beautiful. I think I was more in awe of them than truly frightened."

"Unfortunately, you can't touch my wings. I'm sorry."

"Why, is it bad luck?"

"No," I shook my head before I continued, "Nothing like that. They're just tender, and touching them could be a little overstimulating."

"Can I ask one more Angel question before we start packing your clothes? Are all Angel's wings white like that?"

I grinned proudly. "No. My wings are very unique. My roommate's wings are white, but they have speckles of brown and black throughout them."

"Do you know why yours are different?"

I frowned. I had never thought of them as different. I had been conceited in my thinking actually. I had been proud that they were so beautiful. I thought they were special. "No, I hadn't put much thought into it."

"Are you in trouble for telling me?"

"Yes, but that's a choice I made when I asked you."

"I hate for you to get in trouble for me." She tossed me a bag to put the stuff I was folding into as she sorted what she thought I would need and wouldn't need for the weekend.

While she wasn't looking, I put the folders from the mission into the bottom of the bag. I needed to make sure they went with me, so I could debrief if I survived, and if I didn't, they needed to be easily located by whomever was sent to collect them. She was packing clothes that could be layered because we weren't sure how cold the valley would get in the evenings. We would only be there for one night, but I didn't want to bring this up right now. I wasn't sure what time the earthquake was going to happen, only that it was going to be Saturday. We had planned to be camping until Sunday so I knew we would be in the area whenever it happened. We worked in silence until we had packed all my clothes, toiletries and such. We were also able to pile the sleeping bags, tents, lanterns and cooking essentials Had, Declan and I had gotten on the shopping trip. That seemed to have been ages ago, not just five short days ago.

"Is that everything?" Hannah plopped down on the couch.

"I do believe so." I took the chair across from her, "Hopefully Declan gets Alissa's car tomorrow. I am really not looking forward to having to carry all of that."

She giggled. "I wouldn't be either."

"Hannah, why was it so easy to believe me?" It was something I had been dying to ask her since our first conversation about her helping me.

"I don't know. You seemed sincere. Besides, if you were lying, you sounded entirely too crazy to contradict, especially being in the cottage alone with you."

"UH!" I giggled as I tossed a couch pillow at her.

"Must be nice to be such lazy bums."

Whack! We both had direct hits to Declan's head with pillows after his bold statement.

"Hey! That's not fair. Two against one."

"I'll have you know. We are taking a much needed break, which we earned, if I do say so myself. And I do say so." She stuck her tongue out at him.

"Here! Here!" I cheered, sharing my agreement with her statement.

He shook his head looking somewhat bewildered. "Well, I got all the water and food stowed. What else is on the list?" He'd sat down at the foot of the couch where Hannah was lying.

I looked at him hoping that he could see I didn't really want to tell him in front of Hannah. I actually didn't want to tell him either. How could I ask him to help me practice my fighting skills, when it could be him I ended up fighting? How could I practice without help though? I couldn't sword fight alone; I could only practice evasion techniques, kicking and striking the air.

"I can tell she's hiding something. What do you think, Hannah?"

She sat up beside Declan, hand on her chin and observed me. I tried to keep a straight face, but Declan moved to mimic her, making me laugh.

"I think you are right, dear Declan." Hannah declared, her eyes alight with laughter.

"This is a serious situation, you two. Maybe I am hiding something because I don't think either of you could, or should have to help with what I need to do next. That's what Had was supposed to do." My shoulders dropped some at the thought of Had. The ache was all over, not just in my heart. I wished Father Paul could've given me information about him.

"Bayla, at this point is there any reason to not tell us?" I looked up at Hannah and saw such earnestness in her eyes. I had made this her mission too.

"I need to train." I glanced at Declan from the side of my eyes. "Like full on, hardcore train."

His face went serious. "Then let's train. I can help. It'll help each of us to know the other's weaknesses."

If Hannah caught on to what was being said, she didn't let on. I had told her Declan wasn't an Angel, but I hadn't said he was a human either. I didn't want her to necessarily be afraid of him, but if she found out he was a demon, and on the side that did not want Gray to survive, she would not be very happy with me for allowing him to join in the planning of the camping trip. Or the event at all for that matter. It was a fine line between knowing and not. I decided that unless she directly asked, I wouldn't bring it up.

"Do we have wooden swords?"

"We can use sticks."

"If you say so." I smirked at the thought of fighting with sticks. When we were trained in battle techniques as young Angels, we first used wooden swords and then moved to hard plastic ones, before advancing to the real things. We had to be able to fight and lift real swords in order to pass our training. Hadraniel had been the best in our class with Aniston being the worst. Even at her worst, she was still good enough to have passed.

"Hannah, would you like to judge this battle please?"

"I wouldn't know how to tell who won."

"You will." We spoke at the same time.

She shook her head at us but agreed. We headed to the back of the cottage to an area that was decently cleared. Declan scanned the wood line for similarly sized and shaped sticks. He brought back two that were thin enough to hold and maneuver, but were thick enough they shouldn't break easily and would be felt if we got hit by them. I took hold of mine and gave a few quick movements to get used to the balance and feel. It was different than the swords that I would have hidden in the valley and bigger than the one that I would be storing in my boots, but I could manage.

"You ready, Bay?" He sort of snarled. He looked hungry to battle me.

"You better believe it." I grinned.

He stepped forward, presenting the first defensive move. I stepped to the right and struck his arm. He winced and backed out of reach. He presented again, this time stepping opposite of what I had expected, and he was able to strike my thigh. It was painful, but not unbearable. In a real match, it would definitely give him the advantage more than my arm strike would have. We continued this dance for a while, one of us advancing and taking turns landing strikes. Towards the end, he was beginning to show fatigue. I stepped towards the right as he advanced, but at the last minute, I pivoted into his reach and was able to tag his chest. I pulled back making sure not to truly injure him.

"Bayla wins with a heart strike!" Hannah clapped until realization struck her. "You're training for a real fight, aren't you?" Both Declan, and I turned towards her. Grim faces met her stare as she awaited an answer. "Are y'all going to be fighting each other?" I could see she gulped.

"Not necessarily." I didn't want to lie so I answered as honest as possible without giving away too much. "Shall we continue?" I glanced towards Declan.

"No, I don't think there's much you need to learn. Practicing too much can fatigue you. Maybe you need to go with Hannah and do something fun, like see a movie or shop, or whatever girls do." He was not happy that I won, but he didn't seem angry either.

"I think that sounds like a wonderful idea! Bayla?" She seemed eager to do anything that would get her away from this awkward situation.

"I suppose a movie wouldn't hurt. We would still have time to come back and finish up things, and I might be able to get a few more hours of training in before bedtime. It helps clear my head."

Hannah clapped, jumped off the tree stump she had been perched on and followed behind us into the cottage. I quickly showered and changed for the movies. At the top of the steps, Declan caught me. He wanted to make sure he hadn't bruised me or injured me in anyway. I had to reassure him several times before he would let me go. I told him I would be back before dark to do some more training. He simply nodded and headed into Hadraniel's room. Downstairs, Hannah was waiting for me.

"Let's go watch some silly meaningless chick flick or comedy. Maybe it'll help clear your mind and let you relax some."

"You choose, I'll watch." I responded. I haven't really ever been into movies, but it might prove to be a good distraction.

CHAPTER nineteen

We may encounter many defeats but we must not be defeated.
~Maya Angelou

Those few hours of relaxation did wonders. Hannah had picked out some comedy full of nonsense that allowed us both to forget the impending events, even if just for a moment. After the movie, we headed over for a late lunch with Gray at the café. Gray was in good spirits and glad to see Hannah back. We regaled him with the silliness from the movie and created a story about needing some girl time before spending a whole weekend with the boys, Sadie and Alissa to explain her coming back to the cottage with me. She drove at a slow pace to give us time to enjoy the last few minutes of the fun we'd had this afternoon. Pulling up to the cottage, I noticed Alissa's car was gone.

"Hopefully that means Declan isn't home. That way I can get some more physical training in. I really need to be up on my game."

"Why do you need to fight, Bayla? Or should I ask who?"

"I can't tell you. I'm sorry. If you want to go home and spend the evening alone, or with Gray, I understand." I checked out the cottage, and Declan was nowhere to be found.

"No, I promised to help. Let me help you train."

"Ok, but this could get interesting!"

To keep from hurting her, I had her put on multiple layers of clothes from Had's room. I promised to keep from striking her at full force, but she wasn't having any of it. She held her finger up, indicating for me to wait where I was, while she ran back inside. When she emerged from the cottage, she had taped pillows around her arms, legs and waist. It took some time for me to regain my composure enough to stop laughing. She looked like a marshmallow or poorly made doll. She picked up her stick and mimicked the en-garde stance that fencers used during fighting. I returned the stance and grinned.

She circled, doing what she had watched Declan do earlier this morning. I had instructed her in the way to hold the sword which would allow me to get the best training, then proceeded to have her circle me, stepping and out at random times. She was a quick learner, and before long was providing me a decent challenge for a beginner. I learned that even though she was little, she was fast. She had good evasive moves, and she was making me think outside of the box. She might have provided me better training than Declan. His motivation was to strike while hers was to avoid getting hit. I had to get creative in my approach. I started taking fake-out steps, backward strikes and sneak attacks when possible.

"Okay, okay...I need a break. My pillow armor isn't as effective as it had been." She was breathing heavy and chuckling. She plopped down, using the pillows as cushions to rest on.

"That's fine. I think I'm good to go anyways. You were really making me change how I think when I'm battling. Honestly, it helped a lot. Thank you."

"It was quite fun actually. I'm glad I could be of help. What else do we need to do?" She wasn't even looking at me, as she spoke.

"There is something I do need to do without Declan, if you want to accompany me."

"Let's do it, I mean I'm officially a pro swordsman... swordswoman?"

"Swordswoman sounds great!" I couldn't remember the last time I had laughed this much during a mission. Or ever, for that matter. "I need to hide my two real swords somewhere in the valley."

"What if you can't get to them?" She sat up, stretching as if she was achy.

"I will have one hidden on me at all times, but it's small, and I need to have the bigger ones somewhere easily accessible."

"Well, we better head over there soon then before it gets too dark."

"Care to walk? I don't want to give away where we are, just in case. I think I found a shortcut anyway." I asked, as I reached down to pull her up from the ground.

"Sure, why not. I'm feeling more rested now than I was, especially since I used my pillow armor as an outdoor bed." She giggled again, waving her still covered arms and legs.

"Let me just go get the swords, and we'll be on our way." I ran upstairs, lifted my mattress, and noticed that only one of the swords were under there. I put the mattress down in confusion. I lifted it again thinking maybe I just overlooked it, but it was gone. Frowning, I headed over to Had's room to see if I had left his under his bed and just thought I had moved it. I lifted his mattress, but it was gone too. Where in the world could the second sword have gone? I met Hannah outside with the one sword. "I cannot find the second sword. Declan has had to have taken it. There's no other explanation."

"Why would he take your sword?"

"I don't really know. I don't have time to deal with that though. We need to get to the valley."

"Lead the way. You're the one that knows the shortcut."

We chatted about her parents and her childhood as we followed the creek to the falls. There was a lot of love for her family and this town. Occasionally I heard sadness seep into her voice, but then she quickly hid it.

The last time I went to the valley, when I was checking out the chance of the valley flooding, I noticed a way down that wouldn't be too treacherous if taken slowly. As we neared the falls, I could hear that the water seemed to have slowed down some from the last time. I wasn't sure why, since it had seemed to have sped up due to the tremor last Saturday, but I was following Father Paul's command of not asking why.

"There's a path leading down this hill. We'll have to go slow, but it shouldn't be too bad."

I pointed where it started, just on the other side of the tree where we had stopped. She nodded. I took the sword that she had been carrying so that she would have both her hands free to climb down as needed. I headed down first to allow her to follow my footsteps. It took some time and some pretty nimble movements, but we finally made it into the valley, right beside the falls where the cave was hidden.

"So where are we hiding this thing?"

"I don't know for certain. I do know where we are not hiding it though. There's a cave behind those falls, and I want to use that as a potential hiding place for you all. Which would make that a bad place to hide his lovely piece of steel."

"What about in an abandoned tree somewhere?"

"Maybe. Let's head over to the meadow where we will be camping and see if we find something on the way there."

There was a lot of activity in the meadow this afternoon. The songs of the birds helped ease my worry that Meph might be around. Animals seemed to be aware when demons were in their presence and quit making noises. I had used this to my advantage before to make sure I stayed in my lane when collecting souls. Hannah was taking in the sights of the area as this was her first time in the valley.

She seemed in awe of the place, turning every so often, making sure to drink it all in.

"I can see why Ollie loved to observe the area. There's so much beauty to take in." My interest was piqued at the mention of Oliver. I hoped she would freely offer more information. "He loved nature, and there are a lot of different sights here. You would have loved Ollie."

"I'm sad I never got to meet him. He must have been special."

"He was. I'm glad we are camping here. It's a beautiful way to honor him, and almost poetic that it's the last place we'll be when the rest of the town is destroyed." She seemed almost shocked at her words. "I'm sorry to be so morose."

"Don't apologize. It's your right to be sad, mad, upset, morose, however you choose to feel."

"How do you do it? Keep yourself so calm?"

"It's just a part of my job. I'm used to death and destruction. Not to change the subject, but what about this tree? Think it'll work?" I picked up the sword to see if it would be hidden inside the crevice of the trunk. It fit well, and when we circled around from all angles, it remained hidden from sight. "I think this will do."

"What should we do now?" Hannah asked.

"We still have a few hours before darkness falls. Let's go explore the cave to see if it's just a small opening or if it leads to other places."

"Oh, an adventure. Sounds fun! I wish we had flashlights with us."

This made me grin. "I think we'll be okay."

Hannah gave me a strange look before shrugging and walking towards the falls. The last time I was in the cave, Declan had kissed me. And oh, what a kiss it was. I could feel flutters in my stomach just recalling how his lips felt against mine and how he had pressed my body between his and the wall. I could feel heat rising in my face. Oh my Grace! What was he doing to me?

"What are you thinking about over there? You look like a silly girl in love."

"What? No. I just…" I didn't know what to say. Did I love Declan? I didn't think I did. "I was just being dreamy. Sorry."

"Declan?"

I blushed, "Yeah."

She released an audible sigh. "Y'all are like a real life Romeo and Juliet, doomed to not be able to be together. I don't like it."

"Shakespeare, now that was a fun guy."

"You've met Shakespeare?" She stopped in her tracks staring at me incredulously.

"No, but I have read him. I did meet John Astor though, on the Titanic."

"Shut. Up. You were on the Titanic?"

"I was. I had a mission to collect the souls of those that didn't survive."

"Is that your job? To collect souls?"

"It's a part of my duties. I'm a collector of souls, but I also make sure that all events happen as they have been written. Some people need to survive, such as Gray, for some purpose. Others are destined to die. The souls who die and belong to us follow me at the end of the event." She seemed to be pondering this information. I jumped behind the falls into the cavern, and not much longer after that, Hannah followed. I brought my wings out, just enough for them to illuminate the area but not to overtake the space.

"That's awesome!"

"I thought you might like that. Shall we go see where this tunnel leads?"

"I hope it's safe."

"If not, I have my short sword on me, and you are behind me and can run to the exit if necessary."

"Not the reassurance I was looking for, but I'll take it. Can you tell me about some of your other missions? It might help calm the jitters I have going on right now."

"I have been to every major event since Pompeii. Before that my predecessor took care of them. There's only one collector at a time. My most memorable mission may have been the fall of Rome. The ancient Romans were a lively people. I loved walking through the street markets watching them interact with each other. I didn't socialize with humans back then. I only observed to make sure things went as planned."

"How old are you?"

"The same age as you technically. I really shouldn't be telling you all of this. I could get into big trouble."

"Then let's discuss something else. How about Declan?"

"I can actually hear the smile on your face. You think you're slick huh?" There was humor in my voice. "There's nothing to discuss. He's handsome, he's charming, and he is a major distraction."

"Not to mention a demon."

"Figured that one out, huh?"

"I put two and two together. What I don't get is why he is so willing to help you?"

"Me neither." About 100 yards from the main cavern, we came into a second cavern area which had a rotunda roof. The room could comfortably fit about twenty people, and the roof was at least ten feet high. It was a great place to hide the group if needed. I could hear water trickling down the sides of the walls. We had to be under the creek, and with the roof that tall, it was likely there wasn't too much ground between the bottom of the creek and the top of the roof. My research had told me that inside a cave was safe during earthquakes and that the movement of the ground would barely be felt. "I think this would be a great place to camp if it was cooler outside."

"You're avoiding the topic of Declan too, huh?"

I grinned at her. She shook her head. There just wasn't much I could say to her. Even when I didn't say anything, she was smart and would figure things out. I liked Hannah. I'm glad that she'll be with us and safe, or safer than she would be in town. "I know you think I'm being coy. I honestly can't reveal everything. I just can't."

"I understand. That doesn't mean that it isn't fun to tease you about Declan."

"Yeah, yeah. Let's head back. If you had to, do you think you could find your way here to this place again?"

"Yes, without any doubt. We didn't really run into any other tunnels that would cause too much confusion. I should be good. I will probably pack a flashlight in case you're not around the next time."

"Probably smart, unless you're hiding wings I don't know about."

"Is it possible for humans to get wings?" Her eyes widened.

"No. Father Paul is the only human in history to be granted Angel status."

She pouted a little but was quickly back to her happy self as we returned to the opening of the tunnel. She made sure to observe and note which turns we made and trailed her fingers along the walls to help identify her location, in case she had to do it in the dark. These were all things she decided upon herself. She was smart and quick, and even though she was a human, I couldn't have a better partner to help with all this planning.

The roaring of the falls grew louder the closer we got to the opening, and with one final turn, we could see the opening as well as the sky that had started darkening some. I went to the falls, slipped out to make sure we were in the clear and signaled for Hannah to follow. We made the climb back up the same path we came down. The way up was a bit more challenging. I had to occasionally turn and help pull her up, and we were both breathless by the time we reached the top.

"If I survive this, I totally need to get in shape." she said between gasps.

"You'll survive, but I agree." I sat beside her and lamented that we hadn't brought a bottle of water with us. I wasn't sure what effects there would be of drinking from the creek so all the water was just teasing my thirst. "We need to be heading back to the cottage. We need a lot of rest before tomorrow gets here and the fun begins."

"Five more minutes."

I chuckled, stood up and pulled her up to her feet. "You can stay with me tonight if you want."

"I think I'm going to spend my last night in my home. Is it okay if I pack some things I would like to keep?"

Even in the pending darkness, there was light shining off the tears sliding down her cheeks. I had spent the whole day doing what I needed to do, yet I hadn't even stopped to think about what she needed. "Since I'm all packed, why don't I go to your house with you, help you pack what you want, and then in the morning, we can bring it over with my stuff before we meet the group."

"I would like that. Thank you. I know my parents will be okay. They're still in Ohio with my grandma, but I'm still nervous. Doesn't it change the course of history for them to not be here?"

"Things have a way of working out." I gave her a side hug as we came around the corner of the cottage.

"I seriously cannot fathom what you have to deal with, but you are so strong. Thank you."

"It's nothing, really. Let's go find Declan so he'll know where I'm going."

The cottage was dark inside, but all of his stuff was piled next to mine by the door. He must still have been running whatever last minute errands he needed. I wrote a quick note to let him know I'd be back in the morning, but I didn't say where I was going to be, just in case it got into the wrong hands. Hannah was going to be in enough danger tomorrow, and I didn't want to needlessly add to that. I grabbed an overnight bag, threw in some things that I would need before the morning, and we headed to her house.

CHAPTER twenty

Secrets are made to be found out with time.
~Charles Sanford

Hannah's house was small and cozy. We spent the whole night talking and going through her things, as well as some of her parents' items that she thought they might want in case she was able to find them again after the earthquake occurred. She showed me pictures of her childhood, of her and Gray throughout their relationship, and other friends. She even showed me a picture of Oliver. She packed up the albums and put them in the trunk of her car. She was hoping that maybe they would be safe in the plastic sealed tub even if we didn't have time to bring them into the valley. I reassured her several times that none of her friends would hate her for knowing, and we created a story of why she had packed them up just in case she didn't want to tell them when the time came. We didn't sleep the whole night. Neither of us wanted to waste her last night in her home sleeping. There was lots of laughter and tears throughout the evening. She spoke to her parents on the phone, and they confirmed they'd be up there until Sunday evening. By the time the sun was rising, we had gotten our second wind of energy. We were loading the remainder of her things in the back of her car when Declan pulled up with Alissa.

"Hey guys, we were going to head the café for breakfast. Do y'all want to join us?" Alissa seemed super perky this early in the morning

I thought I noticed Hannah roll her eyes before turning and presenting them with a grin. "Sure. We'll meet you there after we drop some things off at Bayla's cottage."

"See you there. Sadie and Everett are heading there now too so don't take too long." I could only hear her gleeful squeal as Declan speed off.

"She can be annoying." I stated in a matter of fact voice.

"I agree. Let's go drop this off and head to the café." Hannah responded as we climbed into her car.

We made good time getting to my cottage, unloading her things and getting back to the café. Gray already had coffees waiting for us at the table. He didn't have to work this morning, but he was still behind the counter helping so that we didn't cause too much extra work. Everyone else had already ordered their breakfast before we got there. Neither Hannah nor I were very hungry, so we just grabbed muffins before joining them.

The mood was light, and soon Hannah and I were able to adapt and join in the fun. Declan didn't seem to be able to let go and relax any. I knew he had reasons to be stressed too, but I had made a deal with myself to relax until necessary. I would remain alert and ready, but I wasn't going to let this last chance of real teenage fun pass me by. I knew tomorrow would begin the fight of a lifetime. I was as prepared as I could be, and there was no point of over-stressing about it.

"What's the plan for when we are going to head out?" Sadie was the first to bring up the camping trip.

"We need to grab the rest of our stuff from the cottage," I pointed to both Hannah and Declan, "and then we can go."

"Didn't you *just* come from there?" Alissa said, oozing the snark.

"Well let's finish eating, and then we can all gather up our gear. How about we meet at the parking area just south of the hill in about twenty minutes?" Gray jumped in before anything else could be said.

We waved our goodbyes as we each headed our separate directions. Hannah and I made sure to get to the cottage before Declan and Alissa in order to get her extra stuff put up before Alissa noticed. We had gone out to the woods, and lowered it halfway down the falls so that it was there in the tub for safe keeping. We quickly got back to the cottage and put the camping gear and bags in her trunk just as Alissa and Declan were pulling in. We helped them load Declan's stuff into Alissa's car. I didn't notice anything that was shaped like my sword. He must have hidden it somewhere yesterday when he was out on his own.

I went into the kitchen gathering up the remaining waters from the refrigerator as well as some quick foods like chips, marshmallows and cookies from the pantry. As I closed the door, Declan was right in front of me. I dropped all of the things in my arms.

"Didn't mean to scare you, Angel." He bent down to help me retrieve everything I had dropped.

"It's fine. I was just going over a mental list and not focusing on the present reality."

"Are you okay?" Declan whispered.

Our heads were very close in the position, it made it hard from me to process my thought. "I am, just trying to make sure I haven't forgotten anything I might need since this is the last time I'll see the cottage. I know it's not really my home, but it still feels weird. How about you? Are you ready for all of this?

We both stood up, my arms were full, but neither made a move for what seemed like an eternity.

"Since the beginning." He winked and turned to leave the cottage.

As I got to the door, I turned and took a glance around one last time at the place I had learned to feel. This cottage reminded of the last memories I would have of Hadraniel, not knowing if he had survived, made this all the more bittersweet. I had to blink back the tears that were burning my eyes. I closed them, took a deep breath, counted to ten and then walked through the door, closing it one last time behind me. It was meant to be symbolic, but it just made me feel sadder. Today would be the last day of normalcy for any of my friends for a long time. I needed to hold it together.

As I climbed into Hannah's car, I heard her singing something silly. "Don't judge me, but I need to relax, and this song helps."

"As I am not familiar with what is cool or not, there will be no judging done here."

"This is why you're awesome."

"Well, I'm glad to have finally found a reason." I gave her a deadpan look.

She laughed and proceeded to sing at the top of her lungs. She had rolled all of her windows down and opened her sun roof. Since it was starting to be a little chilly in the mornings, she had the heat blowing on our feet. I didn't know the music, but I was enjoying the fun she seemed to be having, and her mood became contagious. By the time we pulled into the parking lot, we were both dancing in our seats to our heart's desire. Gray was shaking his head.

"Confirmation that my band and I have no competition in this town." he said with a laugh. He was quick to open and unload the trunk of Hannah's car.

We got out and unloaded the back seat making sure that we had our tents, sleeping bags and bags of food. We had strategically placed some items inside our rolled tents and bags to help hide the amount of items we were bringing. I threw on my backpack, picked up my supplies and headed to the hill. It was a difficult walk when not carrying anything so the trek with all the gear was going to be almost grueling. Gray led the way up, followed by me, Hannah and Declan. Everett was in front of Sadie with Alissa bringing up the back.

Declan carried Alissa's extra stuff in an attempt to keep her whining to a minimum. It didn't work. We had to stop several times so she could catch her breath. Even Sadie seemed to be getting annoyed with her, but no one said anything. It was getting warmer as the day advanced, and during one of our breaks I had to shed the long sleeved t-shirt I'd put on this morning. I noticed Hannah had taken hers off too, leaving us both in tanks. Gray, Declan, and Everett had removed their shirts too. Hannah was having fun teasing Gray who took it in good stride, flexing his muscles and posing.

It took every ounce of restraint I had not to just stare at Declan with his shirt off. He was in excellent shape, and he looked good shirtless. I started watching my feet as a distraction. Hannah was giggling at me profusely every time she looked at me. I could feel my face change from pink to deep crimson. Thankfully, I knew if anyone else asked, I could blame the flush of my cheeks on the exertion of the climb. Once we reached the top, Alissa needed another break, which at this time elicited a collective groan from the whole group. We were so close to the valley that none of us wanted to stop, but we did. Once people got over the grumbling and looked around, they noticed the valley. Everyone was remarking how beautiful it looked. Everyone but Gray, that is.

"You sure you're ready for this?" I asked Gray in a hushed tone, in order to avoid drawing too much attention to our conversation.

"I'm ready, but try to imagine if something had happened to Had. That's how I'm feeling right now. I'm happy to have this opportunity, but it's bittersweet."

It was a like a shock of pain shooting through me because Had was my brother, even if not by blood. Therefore, I understood him completely. I couldn't speak, so I nodded, and gave him a quick hug which he returned.

"Bay, you're kind of awesome." Gray said. His voice was filled with sincerity.

"Hannah, we now have two reasons!" I hollered back trying to lighten the mood some.

She shot me a thumbs up, eliciting a look of confusion from Gray. "With you two, I don't even think I want to know."

"Probably safest." Declan added.

"Hey, Michelangelo called, he needs his model back." Hannah threw back at him in response, causing the entire group to fall into a fit of tired laughter. Even Declan laughed at the jab at his perfectly chiseled body.

"We need to be heading down into the valley, so we can get our tents set up. We need to find some firewood too." Declan reined us all back in.

Gathering all the gear we had dropped during our rest, we trudged on back down the other side and into the valley. It was fun watching everyone else see this place for the first time. Everyone seemed genuinely taken by the beauty. Gray was smiling, but I could see some sadness there too. Hannah had moved closer to him to provide silent support. They moved very well together, giving each other what they each needed with little to no words exchanged. It made me happy to know they would continue on together even if I would not. I led them into the valley, and everyone agreed it was a great place to set up camp.

Declan put up Alissa's tent first before setting up his, and Everett helped Sadie get hers up. Hannah showed up the rest of us girls by putting her tent up alone and even came over to help me while Gray was setting up his. We made fast work, mainly because Hannah knew what she was doing. I was of little help to her. I had never even really seen a tent before, let alone put one up correctly. She was telling about camping with her parents and Gray growing up.

"It's one of the perks of growing up around here, lots of places to camp. I don't know why we never came here though. It's perfect." Hannah stated.

"I agree. There's so much exploring I want to do." Everett replied as he finished putting up his tent with the help of Sadie.

I wasn't too sure about Sadie still, but at least she was willing to put in some work. Alissa, on the other hand, was sitting in the chair she had brought while Declan did all the work. She seemed bored with the whole thing. She was surprisingly sans make up for the trip. I'm not sure if she did this on her own accord or if Declan had played some part in it. Declan asked her for a hand, but she just waved her hands to show she was painting her nails. Hannah coughed to cover the laugh that had bubbled up.

"Here, you tell me what I need to do, and I'll help." I offered, walking over to where Declan was setting up.

"Thanks."

"How'd you get the tent up before when you were camping at the other location?"

"It was a different tent. I brought this one hoping it wouldn't be easily identifiable to Meph." he whispered.

"That was smart. It's kind of why I went for a regular colored tent as well. Hopefully, he isn't planning on pulling any tricks until tomorrow." My voice wasn't much louder than his.

"There's a lot of whispering going on between you two." Alissa's snarky voice interrupted Declan before he could answer.

"You could have been whispering with him if you had helped." My remark slipped out before I could stop it.

"Burn." Everett shouted out, providing another good laugh for the group.

"I can't help it that my nails were wet. I take pride in my appearance...unlike some of us." The last bit was under her breath, but I still heard her.

"Some people have more important things to do." Hannah chimed in this time.

"This is supposed to be a fun camping trip, guys. Besides, we need to go see if there's any fish in the creek. We need to get everything prepared for lunch later." Gray sounded a little like a parent, but I'm glad he said it. I wasn't one for quipping with others much.

The remaining tents were up in no time, and Gray was showing us how to make fishing poles with the string, sticks and hooks he had packed. We made a trek to the pool that was underneath the falls and separated around the edges, each with a pole...except for Alissa, of course. She plopped down beside Declan, and stretched out like she was tanning. It had to be exhausting to be her. She was in character at all times, it seemed. That was one side of the human teenage girl experience that I was glad I hadn't adapted.

Fishing with a pole like this was something I could finally do without much assistance, as it was similar to the fishing I had done on previous missions. Sadie was the first one to get a bite. She was able to hook the fish, and was pretty excited about it. Everett ended up catching the second fish fairly soon after Sadie, but those were the only two catches of the day.

"Two should be enough for us, along with the bags of food Hannah and Bayla brought. Everett, take Declan and Sadie and collect some wood for the fire, please. While Hannah and Bayla get the other food ready, I'll skin and fillet these."

Alissa didn't even bother to act shocked that she wasn't given a task. Instead, she continued to sunbathe as the rest of us set out to do whatever tasks we needed to do. Lunch was going to be pretty light. We wanted to save some of the other food for this evening. We divided grapes out on the plates we'd brought and gave everyone a bag of chips and I got out the bottles of water. Just as we were finishing setting out blankets for us to sit on around the fire, Declan and the others were returning. They'd gathered what looked to be enough wood to last through the night. Gray was putting the fish on the grill that I had brought. It didn't take long for the aroma of the fish to get everyone's stomach rumbling. Even Alissa made a comment about how good it smelled.

Lunch was spent telling different stories from childhood. I shared some that were true for the most part, and from the way Declan's sounded, his were based on some sort of reality as well. After lunch, everyone agreed that napping in the sun was a good idea before going out and exploring the valley. I was quick to sleep. The sound of the birds and winds in the leaves helped lull me into a dreamless slumber. I was awakened by voices discussing something rather heatedly, even if it was in whispered tones. Turning my head in the direction of the voices, I could barely make out Declan and Sadie by the tree line. I couldn't for the life of me figure out why they would be arguing. I was debating on joining them when they both looked in my direction. Sadie looked completely stricken. Declan waved me over when he noticed I was awake.

"Tell her what you just told me." He was gripping her arm so she wouldn't escape.

"I thought it was Meph." Sadie saying his name took me aback some.

"That *who* was Meph?" I said between my teeth.

"Hadraniel." She broke down in sobs. "I didn't mean to shoot him, I thought it was Meph. He had been following me around town. I was trying to get rid of him."

I was seething. I wanted to kill her right there. I didn't even know why she knew who Meph was or how to kill one of us. Rage was building in me as she continued to sob. She had no right to cry. "Why?" I could barely contain myself as I awaited her answer.

"I'm a Fallen. My real name is Lailah. I was a delivery Angel. I left for reasons that don't even matter anymore. I wasn't on Declan's radar because technically I'm not rogue. I came here when the Watcher was living with Gray. I wanted to seek out redemption. Even if I was going to have to stay a Fallen, I could still do something good. Meph found me. He was the leader of the Rogues. He gave them the ideas for the things they were doing. He approached me to help him with this mission. I agreed, but not for the reasons he thought. I knew that if he thought I was on his side, he wouldn't go looking for another Rogue, one who might actually try to hurt Gray. I was doing everything I could to help keep him safe until you got here. The Watcher told me about you."

"Who's this Watcher?" I interrupted.

"Nathaniel. He was posing as Oliver." She looked confused that I didn't know all of this.

I glanced to Declan who shook his head. He wasn't aware of any of this until now either. "Continue." I was still mad, but I needed to hear this.

"The Watcher did what he needed to do to get Gray back on the right path. After that, I did enough 'evil' to keep Meph away. However, when you all showed up for your mission, he started getting antsy. Especially when he found out that you had Hadraniel with you. He was pushing me to kill Gray. I was here in the valley when you and Had were here, but I didn't know it was you all. I saw him from the back. He looks a lot like Meph from the back. I swear I thought it was Meph. I saw my chance, I started throwing my voice to sound like you in danger. I knew Meph wouldn't resist the chance of getting you early if he could. When he got into my range, I shot him. I didn't stay around to see it wasn't him." She dropped her face into her hands. Her shoulders were shaking with what seemed like overwhelming remorse.

"What did you shoot him with?" It was important to know. If I knew, I would know if he had been erased or not.

"I don't know. Something I found at your cottage, in Had's room."

I froze. I knew what she was talking about. It was one of his Blue's weapons meant to erase demons. If that hit his heart there was no chance of him surviving. I dropped to the ground. There weren't even tears. I was numb. Had was dead, he had to be.

"I'm sorry Bayla. I was trying to help you. I didn't know it was Haddy. I would…"

"Get her away from me. Now!" My tone was harsh, and I was louder than I should have been.

I watched as Declan pulled her back towards the group. Most had woken up but weren't paying much attention to us thankfully. I sat there for a long time, trying to work out in my mind how Hadraniel could maybe have survived a wound from that weapon. I couldn't come up with a way. That's probably why Father Paul couldn't discuss him. They didn't want me distracted. Well, that would have been a good plan, if not for Sadie, or Lailah, or whomever. I wasn't familiar with a Watcher, or an Angel named Nathaniel. Father Paul didn't mention him either. I took some deep breaths, closed my eyes and visualized the last meeting with him. I listened to his words again. After one more deep breath, I stood. I couldn't focus on the why right now. Declan was heading towards me, I raised my hand. I didn't need him to come over here. I didn't want to talk about it right now.

"Keep her away from me." I said in passing.

He nodded solemnly.

"Bayla! Just the person we were waiting for. We want to explore. You in?" Everett said, almost bouncing with excitement.

I quickly placed a smile on my face, "I'm game. Lead the way."

"I'm just going to hang here, maybe read or something." Alissa said to no one really in particular.

"I'll stay with you." Sadie volunteered. She was smart enough not to try to talk to me or make eye contact.

We gathered our packs and headed in the opposite direction of where we came into the valley. I knew we would find the second falls eventually if we kept going in that direction. It might be fun to go swimming if the pool was deep enough. Hannah came up beside me and locked our arms as we walked through the woods. Declan, being the nerd that he was, lectured the others about the surrounding trees and wildlife. Gray was up front with him, enjoying the little tidbits. Everett was between them and us, just observing the happenings. Hannah slowed us down some so that we were out of earshot of the others.

"What was going on earlier?" Hannah asked.

"Please. I can't. Not right now." My throat felt like sandpaper. I was barely containing the emotions right now. If I said the words out loud, I would lose the tenuous hold I had on them at the moment.

Hannah stopped walking, pulled me back, and gave me a comforting hug. I returned it quickly, but had to pull away. The last thread was vibrating, close to breaking. "Thank you. We better hurry so we can catch up with the boys." I appreciated the hug.

Not one to dwell too long, she quickly changed topics. "Have you been in this direction of the valley?"

"I have. I think you might like what we're going to find when we exit these woods."

Declan and Gray were in the clearing before us, and I could hear when Everett saw the falls too. He was as excited as I had expected. These falls completely dwarfed the ones close to our campsite. I picked up our pace, wanting Hannah to see them too. Declan had the same idea I had and was already in the process of removing his shirt and jeans to go swimming. Gray and Everett didn't need any convincing to join him. The hollering from the boys after they emerged from underwater let me and Hannah know that the water was going to be freezing. I needed the shock. I was quick to take off my tank and shorts. Thankfully Hannah had suggested wearing our swimsuits underneath, just in case. I waited at the edge for her, grabbed her hand, and when she counted to three, we both jumped in. It was beyond freezing. I came up quickly gasping for air. Hannah was doing the same.

"Holy Grace!" I sputtered, gasping from the cold.

"No kidding. Maybe if we stay under for the most part, we will adjust. Let's swim over to the falls. There might be a cave behind it as well."

She didn't wait for me to answer but just headed over with me in tow. She was right about the water getting warmer or at least feeling warmer, as long as we stayed submerged. The guys must have noticed that we were heading towards the falls and followed us. Taking a deep breath, I dove under. I wanted the burning of my lungs. Physical pain at the moment was like a gift. I stayed under until I couldn't take it anymore. I came up, and noticed Declan had come up beside me. He didn't say anything. The look he gave me let me know he knew what I feeling.

Hannah was treading water near the falls waiting for us to catch up. I wasn't sure I wanted to get out of the water to check if there was a cave or not as I had just gotten warm. I indicated I was going to go under the falls to see what was on the other side. I took a deep breath and dove. After swimming several feet, I could feel the falls over me, and after a few more feet, there was stillness of the water. I surfaced and looked around. As I'd suspected, on the other side of the falls was a cave. We could just swim the length of the cave from what I could tell. The others quickly made appearances on my side of the falls.

"Wow, this is awesome!" Everett was the first to come through. "We should see if we can swim back a ways."

"We should wait for the others first. We don't want to take of chance of getting separated."

Hannah, Gray and Declan were quick to follow Everett, and soon we were on our way. I couldn't use my wings as light this time, but thankfully Gray had brought a waterproof flashlight that fit on his head. He swam up to the front and guided us for about a hundred yards. There the water seemed to get more swallow, and we were able to stand and walk. The cave led back another fifty feet or so before it became too narrow and short to pass through. This was not an ideal place for hiding them, but it was better than no option. I peeked at Hannah and noticed she was doing the same as she had in the other cave. She was making sure to feel along the walls, paying attention to the turns we made. We turned back, letting Hannah lead us out.

Back outside of the falls, I climbed up on the banks and laid out, letting the sun dry me. Hannah and the boys joined me. We were all pretty content. It was a great way to spend an afternoon. What made it even better was that Sadie wasn't in my line of sight. I couldn't believe she didn't even bother to stay around to make sure it was Meph. I didn't remember a delivery Angel by the name of Lailah, but she could have chosen to become a Fallen before I was of age to know many other Angels. If her story was true, then what could make her want to be a Fallen, only want to do good once she was here? I knew I would need to talk to her again and ask her about Meph's plans. I was running out of time, and it had to be today or never.

Rumble. We all looked around to see whose stomach was the culprit for the loud noise.

"Seriously, who released the Kraken?" Everett said, making the group laugh.

"I think I might be hungry." Hannah giggled.

"You think? I'm pretty sure people in other countries are now aware of your hunger," Gray teased.

"Let's head to camp. We can have some junk food before our dinner. We'll be total rebels."

"I like the way you think, Bay." Everett was already up and partially dressed at the mention of food.

We were all more intent on getting back to camp than observing the trees and wildlife this time. Swimming was a great way to make someone hungry. I was dreaming about the marshmallows and cookies. Hannah and I started discussing our favorite desserts, and the boys joined in. The talk of food seemed to urge us on enough to make it back before we starved. I wasn't really sure what happened on a camping trip, but if we went on another adventure again later, I was going to pack a granola bar or something.

Sadie and Alissa were each engrossed in their own books. While the others were getting food, I decided to use this time to talk with Sadie some more.

I tapped her on her shoulder. "Follow me, please." She didn't respond, but closed her book and followed.

"I need more answers."

"What kind of answers?" she asked, looking hesitant.

"Why didn't the Watcher stay until I was here? What do you know about Meph and his plan?"

"The Watcher had to leave when his mission was completed, or at least that's what he told me. Nathaniel was one that followed the rules to the tee. Meph never shared his plans with me for this part. He wanted me to kill Gray and collect his soul for Hell before any of these events happened. He didn't say why he was so important, or why he didn't want to wait to battle it out with you. He was the one who told Lucifer to send Declan, or so he told me. He wanted it to be on the down low, fighting dirty. He had been hunting for me in the valley just a few hours earlier that day and that's why I thought Had was him. He was upset that I hadn't followed his command and was planning on erasing me."

"If you chose to fall, then why are you trying to help me or my side?"

"Who said I chose to fall?" She paused for a minute. Sighing, she spoke again. "Besides, it's a long story, Bayla. One that happened long before you were the Collector. Just know that I will help you however I can tomorrow."

"I'm not sure I need your help. I cannot forgive you right now for Haddy either. I just can't." Her statement of not choosing really threw me, but I didn't have the time or energy to even think about that part right now.

"I understand." Her shoulders drooped.

"Let's get back before they get suspicious."

Back at camp, Hannah had gotten us both apples and a water, so much for cookies. I knew the apple was better for me especially having just spent the entire afternoon exploring, but I wanted sweets. We plopped down on the blankets. Since I knew dinner would be soon, I didn't pout too much about the apple. Hannah was telling me about making sure she mentally mapped the cave at the other falls while we ate. Everett and Declan were telling Sadie and Alissa about what we had done while we were gone. Neither looked overly upset that they had missed out. Apparently Alissa didn't know what she had missed, not seeing Declan in swim trunks. With the exception of Sadie's revelation, my first camping trip had several great highlights.

CHAPTER
twenty-one

Soul meets soul on lovers' lips.
    ~Percy Bysshe Shelley

Dinner was fun. We made hot dogs over the fire, then we enjoyed roasted marshmallows. I'd never had campfire food quite like this, and I was hooked. We were all messy and having fun getting the sticky pieces off the stick. The view of the stars was unobstructed out here in the valley. I wanted to lay out by the fire and watch as time passed, but Alissa suggested telling ghost stories. I didn't really have any that weren't based on something true and figured they might be too scary. I listened as the others each took a turn telling a story they had heard growing up. It was fun to watch as the group jumped at whatever part of the story that was supposed to get them. I zoned out by the time Everett got around to telling his story. I was visualizing how tomorrow could go. The more I was prepared, the better I could react.

I didn't know what time the earthquake was going to happen, or if there would be any tremors before the main one. I just knew that as soon as it started, I needed to get Gray and the group to safety, hidden away from Meph. He must not have known I was out here, or Declan might have made some deal with him because so far he hadn't made any appearances. I needed to set up a system between myself and Hannah throughout the night to make sure nothing happened while we were asleep. If he started to get desperate, he might change his game plan.

"Hannah." I leaned over towards where she and Gray were sitting. "I need to go to the bathroom. Walk with me?" With Gray in close proximity, it was the best excuse I would have to get her away from him.

"Sure. I need to go, too."

We quietly excused ourselves and headed to the wooded area.

"I was thinking about tomorrow. Meph hasn't bothered us today, but that doesn't mean he might not try something tonight. We should take shifts staying awake to make sure he doesn't try to pull something tonight and come for Gray."

"What if he comes during my shift?" she asked timidly.

"You yell. Loudly. I will wake up and come help."

"It's okay. I'll take the first shift."

"I'll lay out with you if you want. I'll be content watching the stars for a while anyways. They look so different from Earth."

"Thanks, but you need more sleep than I do. Besides, I'm not really sleepy right now. I think I have too much sugar coursing through my body."

"Me too."

Back at the camp, I made a show of yawning and stretching before saying good night. Inside my tent, I crawled in my sleeping bag. I was pretty sure it was going to be a fruitless attempt, but I had to try. I needed to be on top of my game tomorrow. Hannah had agreed to wake me in a few hours to give her a break. It only seemed like minutes had passed when I heard the tent being unzipped.

"I'm up."

"Shh, Angel. Scoot over."

"Declan! What on Earth are you doing?"

"I wanted to see how you're doing. I asked Hannah if she needed a break yet; she said she was okay. Scoot over. It's cold out here."

"Go away! Get your own sleeping bag!" I felt him push me effortlessly over to the side and slip in behind me.

"Alissa's in my tent. I really don't want to go back there. She crawled in a little while ago complaining she was scared. Once she fell asleep, I slipped out. I need sleep too, you know."

"Fine." I rolled away from him.

He wrapped his arm around my waist and pulled me close to him. He was warm. I could feel myself drifting back to sleep. "Bay, tomorrow is going to change everything. I just really want this one night beside you. I want to pretend that tomorrow isn't going to happen. I need you to tell me what you're supposed to remember."

"Since the beginning." I groggily responded.

"Yes, Angel," he whispered. I felt him scribble something into my hand, but I had already fallen asleep before I could decipher it.

"Bayla." I heard Hannah somewhere in my foggy haze. "Bay. It's your turn."

I was careful not to wake Declan as I slipped out of the tent. Hannah winked at me, then headed to Gray's tent. I plopped down on the blanket Hannah left out, and stoked the fire. She had placed a full bottle of water out for me and some cookies. She was probably trying to make sure I wouldn't fall back asleep. It was peaceful out. I laid down on my back, wrapped in the blanket and watched as several falling stars crossed the sky. I'd read somewhere that humans made wishes on these. They were supposed to be a sign of good luck. I wasn't one to believe in luck, but at that moment, I pretended I did. I could use any help I could get tomorrow.

"Not asleep, are you?" Sadie asked.

"No, just watching the stars."

Sadie sat down beside me close to the fire. "The stars are definitely more beautiful this side of Heaven, but I miss it up there sometimes."

"Why are you awake?" I chose to ignore her reference to Heaven.

"I thought you might need company. Besides, I can't sleep. I'm nervous about tomorrow, and I have been upset since I found out about Haddy."

"Don't say his name to me."

She nodded, and sadness emanated from her. "Bayla, I know you hate me, but I can help tomorrow."

"How do I know you're not still working for Meph and that this isn't all some ploy you two put together?"

"You don't. You just have to trust me. Nathaniel trusted me. Father Paul trusted me, but warned me not to say anything to you. I had no intentions of telling you who I was or who Nathaniel was, but when Declan found out who I was working for and what I had done to Hadraniel, he made me tell you. He threatened to imprison me in Hell if I didn't, and that's worse than the thought of being erased. That boy loves you."

"Declan does not love me. He's a demon. I'm his competition in this mission. He's using his demon ways to keep me close. Haven't your heard the human saying 'Keep your friends close, and your enemies closer'? The same is happening between us."

Sadie snorted. "You keep telling yourself that, Bay."

"So you were a Delivery Angel before you fell? My roommate, Aniston, is a Delivery Angel." At the mention of Aniston, her eyes lit up. "She's the one that Haddy was going to ask to be paired with...until you erased him." I could see that I had hit her hard with that, and it wasn't really fair of me. If she was being honest, she probably felt horrible about the deed. "I'm sorry. That wasn't kind of me. I'm angry, but I don't have to be mean."

"Tell me about Aniston."

"She's bubbly. When I was home, I could barely tolerate her, but now I miss her. I would give anything for her to come bouncing into my room telling me about the sweet baby cheeks she kissed before delivering them safely. She's the one that delivered Gray. If I make it home, she'll be surprised at the hug she'll get from me."

"So you, Aniston, and Hadraniel were all the same age group?"

"Yeah. Do you miss Heaven?"

"Yes. I made the wrong choice. I have to live with those consequences. I've met other Fallens that are like me. We are just living and dealing with our mistakes. Unlike the Rogues, we don't try to be evil. They wanted to join forces with Lucifer. The rest of us just wanted freedom of choice. It's not all it's cracked up to be, let me assure you. Do you trust me enough to sleep some more while I stand watch?"

"Not really."

"Didn't figure as much. You don't mind if I stay out here with you, do you?"

"Nah. It's fine."

I passed her the box of cookies. If she was going to stay up too, she was going to need the sugar. Sometime during the night, I decided I would wake the others up right before sunrise to climb back up the hill. I thought watching the sun rise one last time on their town would help them later when it was gone. I went to Gray and Hannah's tent first, then Everett's, then to mine to get Declan, saving Alissa for last. They all agreed that watching the sun rise on the town would be fun. Alissa was even up and ready to go with the rest of us with little arguing. Declan seemed a little odd. I wasn't sure if it was because of last night or if it was because he woke up alone. Either way, I didn't have time to worry about that.

The hike up wasn't as torturous because we didn't have all the gear with us this time. We still had a few minutes to rest and catch our breaths before the sun came up. The sky changed from dark blue to the light blues, purples, oranges and pinks that I'd come to know as Kentucky sunrises. It truly was a blessing to get to witness. The glass from the windows in towns were sparkling and making a great memory for the group. I looked over to Hannah, and with tears in her eyes, she mouthed 'thank you' to me. She knew why I had made this suggestion. I was glad I got to witness it too. It was a spectacular view. We lingered at the top for a few extra minutes before Gray decided it was time for breakfast. He was met with a chorus of agreement about needing food. I'd brought a portable coffee maker with us, just in case we had time to enjoy one final cup before the events of the day happened.

Declan held me back from the group, as the others headed back down the hill. His eyes were full of emotions this morning. He seemed to be struggling to find the words to convey whatever was on his mind. The gray of his eyes almost seemed to change shades with his emotions. They were darker right now, but when he laughed, they almost seemed to be silver. There was nothing more I could want than the opportunity to stare into his eyes for all time, learning all the different shades of emotions without any concerns for the world, but we had things to do.

"You didn't answer me last night."

"I said, "since the beginning.'"

"No, about the other thing."

"What other thing?"

He looked at me like I had two heads. "I wrote I loved you in the palm of your hand."

"I felt you scribbling, but I thought it was nothing, so I just fell asleep." Knots were building in my stomach.

"Okay. Well do you?"

"Declan." I whined a little. He was really wanting me to profess my love to him when I might have to kill him later? "Why now? Why are you asking me this now?"

"I want you to know, so that whatever happens, you have that to hold on to at least. If you feel the same way, I would like to hear it today before it's too late." There was a hint of despair in his voice.

Tears of anger and fear escaped the corners of my eyes. This man was not going to make anything easy for me. I'd lost Haddy, and if things didn't work out today, I was losing Father Paul and Aniston, and yet he wanted me to tell him I loved him even though I was going to lose him, regardless of today's outcome. It wasn't fair. "Yes!" I screamed at him. "Not like it does either of us any good to know. One of us is going to lose, and no matter which of us it is, we both do by telling each other 'I love you.' This is the worst possible time in the world to do this to me, Declan - "

Before I could finish my thought, he pulled me in for a kiss. It was different than the first two. This one felt like we were both in search of something to help us breathe, to help us survive. I wrapped my arms around his neck and kissed him back. We probably would have stayed that way forever if the group didn't start whistling and clapping. I didn't even realize they were still in sight of us. I quickly pulled away, blushing. Declan, being Declan, bowed. Causing more whistles and cat calls. Alissa was the only one who didn't look happy. A part of me wanted to gloat, but I couldn't. Everything for her was about to change, and now the hope of being with Declan was just taken away from her too. The walk down was full of jokes in the direction of Declan more than me. They could see I was a little more embarrassed about the audience while Declan pretended to have planned the whole thing. Hannah dropped back to walk beside me.

"Is that even allowed?" Hannah asked, her eyes widened in surprise.

"I don't even know anymore what's allowed. I've broken so many rules this mission." I shook my head. "I think at this point, it's game on, so I'm done with the rules. I need to get my head in the game." She simply nodded and walked with me in silence the remainder of the way. Just as we got to the bottom, the first little rumbling tremor occurred. It wasn't enough to be too worrisome, but it was enough to be felt.

"Sadie, what's your dad's testing show? Are we safe here? That was a little strong," Gray asked evenly. He didn't seem to be panicked, but I could tell he would end the trip if he thought it was unsafe to remain here.

"Everything he has researched has shown that we are fine. Just the plates adjusting themselves some, nothing major." She did nonchalant well. If I hadn't been aware of the truth, I would have believed her.

"Then let's get breakfast."

CHAPTER
twenty-two

Or have they ceased to care at all for if I fall or stand.
~Cathi Desurne

At camp, our tents looked like they had been ransacked. I know the quake wasn't strong enough to have done it. Meph must have been here searching for something. He obviously could see that we were all gone, so it had to be an object he was on the hunt for, not a person. Declan mumbled something about a deer or raccoons, and everyone seemed to buy it. He had been talking about animals all weekend so he would know. I looked sideways at him. He seemed to know what Meph may have wanted, because he headed straight for his tent. He emerged several moments later looking content that everything that he needed was still there. I took a walk over to the tree where Hannah and I had hidden the sword and made sure it was still there. Thankfully, it was. If nothing was missing, maybe it really was just an animal. Or it could be Meph trying to mess with my head.

My nerves were on edge the whole morning. Anticipation was starting to get the best of me, so I suggested a walk to the falls. The ones where we fished at yesterday, not where we'd swam. I needed to do something, anything, besides sitting around waiting. We decided that if it was deep enough, we could swim in this pool, too. Everyone was ready after taking time to put their swimsuits on and grabbing towels. Alissa and Sadie joined us as well. I think finding the camp as we had this morning made them uneasy. I double-checked that I had my small sword on me before heading towards the water. Declan kept his distance from me this time. In case Meph was watching, he didn't want to be seen being too friendly with me.

The water was just as cold, and just as invigorating for me today as it had been yesterday. Sadie and Alissa laid their towels out and dipped their feet in, but stayed on the bank. Hannah joined in with us to swim. She was using her time wisely to enjoy it as much as possible. I figured she was like this always, though. She seemed to be full of life, and ready for any kind of adventure. From the stories she'd told when we were at her house, she got this from her parents. Most of her childhood had been spent taking trips to new places.

Declan started a splash war between the guys, and Hannah and I quickly joined in, teaming up to defeat them. The late morning passed without another tremor, but just as we were getting out, a second, larger one occurred. I had a feeling the next one would be the big one, and it wasn't a good idea to be in the water, or out in the open for that matter. If we were in the trees, we could avoid being easy targets for Meph. Gray seemed to begin second guessing Sadie.

"Usually, there's two or three tremors like that if plates are moving." Declan had authority in his voice. His reputation for being a walking encyclopedia was going to be useful today if we were going to keep everyone in this valley. "Just in case though, let's go to the meadow. Open spaces like that are the safest places to be."

I knew the safest place to be was the cave, but without any timeframe of when the next one was going to happen, I couldn't find reason enough to push everyone in there at the moment. I needed to come up with something, and quickly, to get them in there before it happened, all the while keeping Meph from seeing where we went. All of the previous plans I'd made weren't going to work. As everyone seemed to be on edge, I did the only thing I could come up with.

"I know where there's a cave. We could pack our lunches, go exploring and have a picnic there. Best part is, if there is another tremor, we'll be safe in there."

"I'm game for exploring a cave," Hannah chimed in. I shot her a grateful look for seconding my suggestion.

No one else had a better suggestion. We gathered blankets, food and water before packing up our bags. I convinced them to bring our packs in case we wanted to hang out for a while and do further exploring, and everything seemed to be falling into place. Right before heading out of the trees, everything went silent. The birds stopped mid song. Meph was close. For a second I panicked but saw Sadie indicate we needed to keep going. I knew she was right. There wasn't anything left to do now but go. I steadied myself, moved closer to Gray and headed out. We were halfway to the falls when the ground began to rumble again.

I saw movement out of the corner of my eye. I turned just in time to see Meph running towards Gray. Sadie pushed him forward and yelled, "Run!"

"Hannah, go! Take the group. You're know where you're going. Go!" I yelled as I was pulling my smaller sword out of my boots.

It took her a minute to comprehend what was happening, but once I yelled go the second time she didn't need another word. She grabbed Alissa, pulling her into a full-on run while telling Everett and Gray to follow her quickly. Sadie stayed closed to where I was, but when I looked around, I couldn't find Declan anywhere. It was time. We were now enemies. Words shared earlier no longer had meaning. In the end, one of us would be the victor, and the other gone. Sadie suggested we put our backs to each other. I was facing the group. It was hard to watch them stumbling, as they tried to make their way to the cave. The ground was rippling, and crumbling all around them. More than once, Hannah had to pull Alissa up, and Everett and Gray helped them jump over places the ground had separated. Fear struck in me, as I realized the water was sloshing up out of the edges of the pool, which would make getting into the cave a challenge.

I turned after noticing a movement in the corner of my eye, and saw Meph heading in the direction the group had gone. I told Sadie to look for Declan. I ran into the woods and grabbed the larger sword. I needed to have a bigger weapon if I was going to defeat Meph. At a full run, I caught up to him just as he reached the water's edge. I tackled him. The group was out of sight already, and I hoped they had reached the cave before he'd been able to see where they went. We were wrestling, but with the ground moving as much as it was, it was hard to do much. The quake's intensity was growing. The falls increased in power, and large rocks were rolling down the hills. Another shake caused me to topple backwards away from Meph, allowing me to time to push up onto my feet. I picked up my sword and swung at him. He rolled out of the way and was back on his feet before I had a chance to swing at him again. He was circling, but I made sure to have him in front of me at all times. Meph was a dirty fighter, and he wouldn't be following any rules.

"Tell me, Angel," he snarled, the word sounding like it left a foul taste in his mouth. "How do you plan to keep Gray alive when I just saw Declan enter the little cave with your friends? Don't look so shocked. I know all things. I knew there was a cave, and I knew you would use it to your advantage. Good thing for me, Sadie and Declan were able to trick you enough that you would trust them. So while you're out here worrying about me, they're on their way to do my deed for me."

"I don't believe you."

"You don't have to believe me for it to be true."

I made an advance to head towards the falls, but he wasn't going to allow it. "Ah-ah. No ma'am, you are not going to get in there. It's me and you, Angel."

"You can try to keep me out, but I doubt you'll have much luck." With another large movement of the earth, trees began to fall. Each tree falling caused the earth to shake even more and made maneuvering more treacherous. The water had slowed to barely a trickle. I glanced towards the opening quickly, but Hannah must have had them in the back part of the cave.

"I don't have to try for long. Even as we speak, Declan and Sadie should be taking care of your friends."

I swung full force at him. He dodged but not fast enough, and I nicked his arm. He bellowed in pain and covered the spot with his hand. Blood was seeping through his sleeve. The pain enraged him, and he made his move to attack. I needed to kill him quickly. I was good at changing my pattern thanks to the training with Hannah. Just as he was about to grab my midsection, I stepped to the side and knocked him across his back with the broad side of the sword sending him lunging forward. I wasn't quick enough to jab him before he was out of the way. Just then, the water came flowing quickly back into the valley. The main quake was happening, and the river had reversed. The town would be flooding soon, and I still wasn't sure about the valley. Meph pulled a knife from his boot, and he made another lunge toward me. A rumble caused the ground beneath me to crumble. I couldn't move quickly enough, and he slashed my right arm, deep and close to my shoulder. It burned and caused me to drop the sword. I hadn't thought to practice with my left hand, but I was going to have to learn fast.

"Give it up Angel. You'll never be able to defeat me!"

"I don't have to defeat you, just distract you long enough for this to be over." I jumped to where the sword landed and lifted it with my left arm. It felt awkward and heavy. Instead of advancing this time, I backed away. If I could get him closer to the wooded area, I could use the trees to my advantage.

"BAYLA!" I turned to see Sadie limping towards me from the cave.

She had something in her hand. My other sword. Unfortunately, just with that split second of time, it was all Meph needed. He was on me before I could lift my sword knocking me to the ground, and we were rolling towards the trees. I was kicking and scratching with everything I had. The breath was knocked out of me when I landed against a tree with Meph on top. Sadie was hitting him but didn't seem to be trying to actually kill him. He swatted at her, sending her backwards. This was all I needed to make a move. I gave a quick jab to his abdomen and rolled out from underneath him. Sadie helped me up, and we took off towards the woods.

We ran a ways before I felt it was safe enough to stop, and catch our breaths. One of my ribs must have been cracked when I hit the tree because breathing was extremely painful. "Sadie, what in Grace would make you yell my name?"

"I was trying to find you, and I didn't see Meph at first. Declan is inside fighting off some other demon that Meph had placed in there. Just as I was running out to help you, Gray was knocked out."

"Go help Declan. I don't need your help. I need Gray to stay alive."

"Declan sent me to bring this sword for you. He said this is the one you needed."

"I have it, now go. See if you can help. NOW!" She jumped at my voice but took off. She was going the long way in hopes of avoiding Meph. I, on the other hand, had no intentions of running. I was waiting. He would find me, especially if he had another demon in the caves. He would want me. I wasn't going to run.

"You disappoint me, Bayla." I had to give it to him, he was fast. "I was expecting a chase." He was leaning against a tree holding his side.

I held up the new sword in my left hand. "Sorry. I'm not one for running. Besides, I knew you would find me."

"Why here, though? Not wanting an audience for the end?"

"According to you, there won't be an audience. You said Declan was doing your dirty work. Too afraid to do it yourself, Meph? Been out of the game too long?" I could tell I had struck a chord.

A blaze of hatred filled his eyes. "It's not going to work. My job is here with you, not in the cave."

As he spoke, I was slowly moving backwards out of the woods. If he was as injured as he acted, I had a chance of getting to the cave without him. I could help Declan and Sadie. Meph was not the mission. Gray was. I took another step. The next step was on a branch, and I stumbled but was able to quickly regain my balance, just not quick enough. Meph must have put two and two together. He was moving towards the trees at a faster pace than he should have been if he was hurt.

I turned and took off. I needed to get to the cave. I needed to check on the group. As I exited the tree line, I glanced to my left and saw Meph. He was ahead of me but not by much. The ground was getting muddy from the increased water. I was slipping in the mud, struggling to catch up. I heard a loud crack and noticed a tree coming down behind me. I jumped to the left and kept running. I was still running, keeping an eye on Meph who peculiarly had stopped, and was taking a special interest in watching me. He wasn't advancing towards the cave, and in my confusion, I faltered. His smile was the last thing I saw before everything went dark.

I surfaced to the feeling of being lifted. My wings seemed to be outstretched, and it felt good, less cramped. My consciousness seemed to go in and out, and I felt as if I was being carried. My body was limp, and my head felt heavy. I tried to open my eyes, but I couldn't. Something somewhere seemed to be urging me to glance up, and when I did I realized I was in someone's arms. I just couldn't make out their face. Finally, my eyes cleared enough, and I made eye contact with Meph. He was looking solemn. His pace was one of purpose. I was fading again, though, and just before I passed out again I heard my name being screamed in the distance. It was a painful sound, full of heartache. I took a deep breath and let go.

CHAPTER
twenty-three

Sometimes it takes a good fall to really know where you stand
~Hayley Williams

Hannah

We made it to the cave with relative ease. No one asked why we were running, or hiding for that matter, until Sadie and Declan showed up. As Declan tried to explain something to me, I noticed Sadie giving Gray a menacing glare.

"Is there something wrong, Sadie?" My mentioning her name made Declan turn his attention to her.

"Just a little disappointed that it's going to be this easy."

Just then she grabbed a sword that was propped against the wall and advanced towards Gray. Right before she struck him, Declan was able to block her. Her sword gashed his arm but he managed to knock her back. In the process, he knocked Gray back too. When Gray fell, he hit his head hard against the wall and lost consciousness.

"What are you doing?" Declan asked, taken aback at the sudden change of actions from Sadie.

"Completing my mission. It was too easy getting you and that Angel to believe me. I've been working with Meph this whole time. I lied about Haddy too. I always knew it was him." She was back on her feet, looking like a nervous rat trying to find her way past Declan to Gray.

He rushed towards her. His swordsmanship was more advanced than hers, and before long, she was out of the cave and through the falls. He stood on our side of the falls for a while in case she decided to try to enter again. When he felt it was safe, he made his way over to where Everett and I were tending to Gray. He had a bump on his head, but his breathing seemed steady. Declan was helping us prop Gray up against the wall when we heard Sadie yell Bayla's name. We looked at each other and quickly made our way towards the falls. We both sneaked out on opposite sides. Sadie was running towards Bayla, sword in hand. Declan started in their direction when Sadie did something that surprised us both. She seemed to be helping Bayla escape Meph. She helped Bayla stand, then they disappeared into the woods. Declan scanned the tree line, unsure if he should follow her or stay here with us. It was only a few seconds later when Sadie came flying back out of the trees, heading in our direction.

We quickly got back into the cave and made our way towards Everett, Alissa, and Gray. Declan had his sword in hand and was waiting for Sadie. Her eyes were mad and she didn't even look like herself anymore. She was making a beeline for Gray. She moved in one direction and then feinted, turned and went in another. She made it past Declan and was close to Gray when Declan struck her from behind. She turned into a rubble of stone and just was decimated. He explained later that she wasn't just killed, but had been erased. Angels and Demons cannot technically die. He told me to watch the group and handed me his sword. We were down to one, since Sadie had given Bayla the one Declan had hidden yesterday.

"I need you stay here. Bayla may need me. She looked hurt after that tumble with Meph, and who knows what Sadie did to her once they were in the trees. As far as Bayla knew, Sadie was on our side." He shook his head angrily. "I cannot understand why she didn't register to me as Rogue."

"Declan, you can't blame yourself for that. She had all of us fooled into thinking she was our friend this whole time."

At the front of the cave the water, that had been flowing so hard we could barely get out just moments before, had nearly stopped. We were able to see the valley without leaving the cave. We could see trees falling everywhere, signaling that the earthquake was still going. We couldn't really feel anything inside the cave. Bayla had mentioned that we probably wouldn't. Declan was finishing his instructions on how to use the sword against Meph or any other demon when we saw movement. Meph was running from the tree line. Moments later, just a few yards south of him, Bayla exited the trees too. They seemed to be moving towards us. The ground had become muddy from the flood of water. Everything seemed to move in slow motion. We watched as the tree behind Bayla began to fall. We saw Bayla slip and yelled for her to get up yet knowing she couldn't hear us. We watched in horror as she turned to see the tree coming down. She jumped to the side, but it wasn't enough. We saw as a limb hit her and knocked her down. Declan jumped out on the ledge just as Meph picked up Bayla's body. She looked broken and limp. We couldn't tell if she was awake or not. She didn't seem to be moving at all. Declan was frozen at first at the sight of Bayla being carried away, and then he went berserk. It took everything that Everett, Alissa and I had to hold Declan back. Declan was ready to go after her, but I knew we couldn't let him go. Meph was too far away. Declan finally calmed down enough for us to release him when Meph was out of sight. He punched the wall of the cave before sliding down to the ground, sobbing. I wanted to join him. Bayla had saved us, and we hadn't done anything to save her.

"She made me promise to keep everyone in the cave," I said just barely above a whisper. "I had to swear to her that you and Gray would be safe."

Declan's sobs were slowing when Had appeared suddenly, a man I didn't know with him. Declan quickly stood at the sight of him. It took him a moment to gather his composure. He seemed to blanch at the sight of Had, but quickly recovered and went and gave him a forceful hug.

"Where's Bayla?" Had scanned the group after stepping back from Declan.

"She...she was taken." Declan struggled to speak the words out loud.

"Taken? Where? By who?" Had's panic was noticeable.

"Meph. He just carried her away. I just stood there and watch..." Declan's voice cracked again.

"And you didn't try to stop him?" Had yelled.

"We held him back. Bayla made me promise." I said as the tears I had been fighting escaped as a sob.

"You couldn't stop three human teenagers from holding you back? You are an angel Declan, for Heaven's sake! You could've gotten free. You should have saved her. You have no idea what they will do to her. What is wrong with you?" Had was being held back by Father Paul.

"I'm sorry." Declan repeated over and over between sobs.

"Everyone, let's go to the top of the hill, please. Everett, Alissa, and Gray when he's awake, there are some things I need to tell everyone. The earthquake is over, so it's safe to head back up." He made it sound like a request, but his actions led me to believe it was more of a command. His face was tight, like he was trying to hold back his emotions.

Everett helped Father Paul get Gray up and moving. He was still somewhat groggy, but with their assistance, he could walk. Bayla was successful in her mission, even if she wasn't here with us. She had saved Gray from the earthquake, and from Sadie.

The climb up seemed almost foreign due to the change in the landscape. I hadn't had time to prepare everyone for what they were going to see. We climbed in silence, and as we neared the top, I could see why the falls had slowed so much. The side of the hill that had been close to Bayla's cottage was now gone. Even knowing what to expect, I was in shock. The town I had grew up in, my home, everything, was now underwater completely. Even the top of the church steeple was no longer visible. I sat down. Alissa was sobbing, Gray cursed, then quickly apologized to Father Paul. Everett seemed to be in shock.

"What do we do now?" I asked Father Paul.

"Well, I'm sure you should probably head up to wherever your parents are, Hannah. From there, they can help you make plans for the best course of action."

"But who's going to keep Gray safe? Won't Meph or some other demon come back to complete their part? It can't just be completely safe now that the earthquake is over. Gray is still alive, and whatever made him important to history is still depending upon his surviving past this."

"Don't worry about Gray. Take care of yourself. We will make sure you have a Blue with you. I'm not sure who will be assigned to you as a Watcher, but we will make sure Gray is safe as well as his children and children's children. He is still vital to history. For now, go to your parents. Lucifer has something more important than Gray." Father Paul's words helped calm me.

A woman seemed to appear out of nowhere next to Father Paul. She looked upset and sad, but kind. "Father Paul."

"Dabria," he replied, he face solemn.

"Does my being tasked to collect the souls of those lost here mean what I think it means?"

Father Paul nodded solemnly. Dabria frowned, patted Father Paul on his back in sympathy, but didn't stay around long. She went to Declan and thanked him for trying his best. He shook her hand, continuously apologizing for failing. He looked broken. I was afraid he might not ever be whole again. Gray came and sat on the ground beside me and wrapped his arms around me, pulling me in close.

"We have a lot to discuss, I suppose." I said to him.

He nodded but didn't seem in any rush to hear what I had to say. I could feel the shock starting to wear off and reality hitting me. My body was trembling. I had just watched Gray almost get killed and saw Bayla carried away by her enemy.

"Hannah, Declan, can you please come over here?" Father Paul called us over, sending Had to fill in the others on the basics of everything that happened today. "I need to tell you a few things before you take the group to Hannah's parents in Ohio. First, Hannah, thank you for being of assistance to Bayla. She broke rules talking to you, but you did your best and were of great assistance. We were not aware that Sadie was in leagues with Mephistopheles until after speaking with Nathaniel. He stayed here longer than he had originally planned because of her presence. She fed Nathaniel the same tales she was telling you," he pointed to Declan, "and Bayla. Sadie was already Rogue before she met Mephistopheles, but enjoyed the extra power she got from being under his wings, so to speak. We also recently found out, after talking to a few other Fallens, that Mephistopheles was the leader of the Rogues. Those that were wreaking havoc without his permission were put onto a list for you to track down, Declan. However, Lucifer allowed those under Mephistopheles' command to remain under the radar. That's why Sadie didn't set off any alarms for you."

"Wait, who's Nathaniel?" I was confused.

"Nathaniel was Oliver. He was sent to be Gray's Watcher as he grew up. We were able to alter the memories of those around here to believe he had always been a part of the family, as not to raise any suspicions. We were afraid to let Gray be here alone."

"Oliver wasn't real?" The thought was heartbreaking. I hoped we wouldn't have to tell Gray.

"Oliver was very much real. Everything that happened with him, all of your memories, are very real. He just wasn't Gray's actual brother. He didn't 'die' either. He simply completed his mission and left. However, in your reality, he couldn't just leave, so he had to create the story of being sick. His mission was to keep Gray safe. Gray was on the wrong path. Nathaniel made the decision with one of the Elders as to how to leave and ensure that Gray would change for the better."

"Can we not tell Gray all of this?"

Father Paul nodded his agreement. "It would do no good."

"Why didn't Sadie try to kill Gray before today if she was really working with Meph this whole time?" Declan didn't seem to understand any more than I had.

"Well, because he had commanded her to wait until he could have a chance to take Bayla. There's a lot about Bayla you don't know, things Bayla herself does not know. Mephistopheles wanted her, and found his opportunity today."

"So what makes Gray so special?"

Father Paul smiled. "You're quite the inquisitive one aren't you, Miss Hannah?" There was kindness in the reprimand though. "To answer your question, Gray will have an important role in years to come and needed to be kept alive. It was in Mephistopheles' best interest to have killed him long before Bayla got here, but that's not how he works. From what we've pieced together, he asked Lucifer to assign Declan to this in order to allow himself to stay out of our sights for as long as possible."

"Meph wanted Bayla?" Declan asked through clenched teeth. "If he hurts her, I'll kill him."

"Declan, I can't tell you if she's been erased, but I can say that, for the purpose Mephistopheles needs her, she must be alive. He will do everything in his power to keep her that way."

"Why are we not on a mission to rescue her, then?" At some point, Hadraniel had joined us.

Father Paul sighed in exacerbation. "Elder Michael already told you, Hadraniel. There are some things that must be worked out."

"I know what Elder Michael said, but what I don't understand is why a rescue mission isn't part of the answer to this situation."

"That is not how it is written."

"Speaking of being written, how is it that you survived?" Declan turned towards Had.

"Sadie didn't have the right ammo for the weapon she used. When she shot me, it was a direct hit. But thankfully, it was only very painful. I hated that we couldn't tell Bay I was okay. Now, she may never know." He seemed almost as broken as Declan.

"She loved you. I don't know if she told you, but you could tell from the way she was after you were gone. She was devastated." Declan patted him on the shoulder. His words weren't much, but they did seem to help Haddy somewhat.

"She loved you too." Had reassured Declan, to which he responded with a sad smile.

"I know."

He didn't share with Father Paul or Had the profession of love that occurred between the two yesterday in front of the rest of the group. I wasn't going to share either. I'm sure he had his own reasons for not wanting them to know.

"Hannah, if you go back into the valley, cross to the other falls and climb up that side of the hill, there will be a rescue team waiting for you all. We were able to get word out that there were teenagers here camping. They will take you all to a shelter before allowing you to travel to Ohio. You may collect the things that you brought from your home before heading that way. You all have until tomorrow morning to meet them there."

"Why until tomorrow?"

"I figured you might need some time to process everything. Once you are rescued, everything will happen quickly."

"How will we know who the Watcher is, and that they're not a Rogue or Demon?"

"I will bring the Watcher to you. I promise I will bring someone great. We have to honor Bayla by making sure her sacrifices were not in vain."

"Don't talk about her like she's dead." My words caught in my throat.

"I'm not, but until we can find out her status and come up with a way to rescue her, we need to do everything we can to make sure she didn't do all this for nothing. That's all I meant."

"It's alright, Had." Gray came up beside us. He wrapped his arms around me from behind. I felt safe and warm. His arms were helping hold my pieces together. I glanced over and noticed Everett was holding Alissa. She seemed content with being in his arms. Other than my parents, we only had each other now.

"If y'all do end up trying to rescue Bayla, you better come find us."

"Yeah!" Everett spoke up. "It's only fair we get to help save her. She's done so much for us. She could have left us to die and only saved Gray and Hannah."

Alissa nodded in agreement.

"That's not how things are done." Father Paul spoke again leaving little room to argue.

Everett and Gray made eye contact and then looked at Declan who gave a slight nod. Whether he was on the good side or bad side, he was going to make sure we got to help if and when the time came. He wouldn't let us not be there for Bayla. She was our friend now.

"Father Paul, can I finish out this mission by accompanying the group to the rescue sight before returning?" Haddy sounded very much like a soldier.

"I want to go with them too." Declan said.

I wasn't sure why Declan was asking for permission from Father Paul.

"You may both join them. Keep them safe until you see the team, then immediately return home. We need to complete a mission review with the Elders upon your return."

"Yes sir," they said in unison.

"Father Paul, do you have Bayla's things?"

"Yes. Why?"

"She wrote notes. I wasn't supposed to mention anything unless…" I couldn't bring myself to finish the words. "There's one for you, Had, and for someone named Aniston. She wanted me to tell you to make sure they got delivered."

He nodded and was gone. We gathered what we had salvaged prior to heading to the caves. I was quick about explaining my need to get the tub that was hidden at the old falls before making our way to the other side. No one seemed too upset that I had known and was able to save a few things. At the last minute, I had made sure to grab at least one picture that included each of their families so that they had a keepsake. The walk down was strange. I hadn't been here without Bayla. I didn't know how to be here without her. She had become such a big part of our group these last few weeks. The mood among us all was solemn.

"Why didn't she leave me a note?" Declan asked. He had made his way up to the front where Gray and I were leading the group.

"She did. I just wasn't supposed to give it to you unless I knew for sure what side you were on."

"And are you? Sure, I mean?"

"Not really."

"I helped save Gray instead of letting Sadie kill him. Father Paul just told you I was returning to Heaven. What more proof do you need?" He seemed more hurt than angry.

"I want to know why she thought you were her enemy. Why did Lucifer and Meph think you were on their side?"

He words were almost monotone, like he was numb. "I technically belong to their side. It's a long story. I'm not a demon or a Fallen. I have my own mission. Just as Bayla doesn't know everything about herself, she doesn't know everything about how this whole mess even got started." He made a circle with his hands, as if to encompass this situation.

"So explain it to me."

"I can't, at least not now. You just have to trust me. Do you?"

I stopped walking. I stared at him for a minute. He genuinely looked like his whole world had been turned upside down. I remember what Bayla had said in the woods to him when we were training. "Unconditionally."

Falling in love was never in my plan. Until one day I just realized that I love this person too much.

~*Unknown*

Declan

The trek to the other side of the hills wasn't as treacherous, but it seemed worse than all the others combined. Collectively the group was tired. Physically and emotionally. Hadraniel tried to explain how the Elders were planning on handling the situation and rescue of Bayla. I knew more than Hadraniel. They were not going to try to rescue her. What's done was done, and the beginning of the end was playing out as it was supposed to. I tried to participate in conversations with the group but I was lost. I felt like everything inside of me was dead or dying. Just this morning I was kissing Bayla. I told her I loved her, and after a small battle the fiery response that she loved me too sent me soaring. I felt like I could've taken flight. And now, now she was gone. The letter I was carrying felt like it was the heaviest thing in the whole of the universe, and yet it was small. It was light, so light there was no effort at all to hold it. I waited until the group was meeting the rescue team to open it. I took a deep breath, and read the final thoughts of Bayla.

Dear Declan,

If you're reading this, that means one of two things. Either you won, or I have been erased. Either way, I'm gone. This mission has been unlike any other with which I have been tasked. It's been the toughest one for me personally, even if it's not necessarily been the hardest professionally. When I first found out that I had to allow some demon the opportunity to work close to us, I was angry. Why would I want to allow some demon from the opposing team in on my secrets, to give some stranger the chance to ruin my perfect record? Then you walked in the café that first night, and everything went sideways on me. It was hard for me to not stare at you. You were like water to someone who was dying of thirst. I couldn't drink in the sight of you enough to ever be fulfilled. This made me angrier than you could imagine. I had never had any emotions or attachments to anyone. Now, not only had I started to develop sisterly feelings towards Haddy, but you came along and just ripped my heart wide open. That day I went with Gray to see the valley for the first time was due to having to escape from you, and this new reality I was given. For some reason, I was tasked to make sure I saved you as well as Gray. Father Paul led me to believe that you were a Fallen, and I was given this huge mission to work on redeeming you. As we worked together, and I got to know you more, I just couldn't see you as a Fallen or a demon for that matter. I still don't know what you are other than my savior. Even if you're the one who ends up having to erase me, you saved me from the loneliness I had assigned to myself. I saw how Dabria was after dealing with Noah, and I vowed never to let my job get to me like that. I cut myself off from friends and feelings, not just for the humans I had to work with, but with everyone else except Father Paul. You and Had showed me that it was okay to feel human. I didn't plan on writing this letter. However, as I sit out in the dark, watching your shadow sleeping in my tent, I can't leave you with nothing. I think I may love you. It's not fair for me to say it though. How can I let myself love you when at the end of this, one of us is going to be hurt? But I do love you, Declan. I do. With every single cell inside of me, I love you. I ache when I think about how this is going to end. If I survive and go back to Heaven without you, just know you are in me. Forever. Those kisses were enough to last for my whole life. Fire has been ignited in me for my eternity. I want the in-betweens you spoke of, I want them with you, but I know it's not possible. I will live a lifetime of in-betweens in your name. I hope though, if you're reading this because I've been erased that you will follow my lead and live a lifetime of in-betweens for me. Please, promise me that. As I lay here watching the stars, I feel content. The stars from this side of Heaven are so beautiful. They are my favorite thing about this place. If ever you are missing me, look to them. And if you see one Falling, it's me.

I love you.

Goodbye,

Bay

Made in the USA
Charleston, SC
20 April 2016